BRUTAL BEAUTY

BRUTAL SAVAGES
BOOK 4

SAMANTHA BARRETT

For my Tia,
This one is for you babe,
I am so proud of the amazingly talented young woman you have
become.
The sky is the limit for you my girl,
I love you, Kid.

ONE

CALIFORNIA

I begin to stir and slowly blink my eyes open; I slam them shut when the sunlight penetrates my hazy gaze. I groan, I am never drinking again as I pull the covers up over my head and roll over, my eyes snap open when I feel something—no someone next to me.

I grit my teeth staring at him, long black lashes, scruffy blond hair, and a perfect nose. His lips have that cupid bow, full and pouty. I can't see the color of his eyes, thanks to him still sleeping, I discreetly lift the covers and peer down at myself and cringe, I'm completely naked! peering over to his side cautiously aware of awakening him, I stifle my gasp.

Lord have mercy on my vagina!

I clench my thighs together and feel the dull ache, that man's huge ass baby arm cock was inside my delicate pussy. I mentally facepalm myself for not being able to even recall a single thing about last night, I can smell the whiskey wafting from my pores, my breath tastes like ass. There is only one option right now, I slowly and quietly slip out of bed and stare down at him. Poor guy, he probably thought he rocked my fucking world last night. Oh well, stage one of my plan is in motion, and I will not let guilt eat at me about it!

I tip toe across the room to retrieve my bra, quickly clasping it on I spot my crumpled dress in the corner silently sighing in relief. I slip the red silk dress on and cringe when the stale scent of cigarettes, liquor and weed hit me, I spin around trying to find my panties, but he stirs causing me to still. I wait with bated breath until his breathing evens out, leaving my panties as a thank you gift, I hightail it the fuck out of here!

There is no way I am going to do the awkward morning after talk today, I creep down the hallway and spot my clutch on the arm of his black couch. Heading for the front door, I look down to see my black Louboutin's at the entrance, and I thank God I didn't lose those in my drunken haze. I would never forgive myself for losing my babies, I decide to carry them to avoid the sound of them clicking against the marble floors and waking my sexy stranger.

I unlatch the door and turn the handle as quietly as I can and when the gap is big enough, I slip through it and close it soundlessly behind me, I furrow my brow when I notice that we are in a hotel, the lifts are to my left and the stairs are at the end of the hall. I am not walking down however many flights of stairs–noise from inside the suite I just ran from makes the decision for me, bye bye lifts, hello stairwell. I shove the door open with enough force that a loud bang sounds out when it hits the wall, I rush down the stairs well, as lady like as I can, given the fact that this skintight dress is showing all the boys and *girls* my goodies.

I break through the door into the lobby and screech to a halt when curious stares swing my way, I regain my composure and straighten myself, whilst trying to even out my breathing. Holding my head high, I walk toward the exit and ignore all the heated stares, obviously judging me and their curiosity getting the best of them. I feel directed at me, I can scent their curiosity and judgment. I push the revolving door that will lead me to my freedom but freeze when a hand lands just above mine, I fight the urge to growl in front of all these norms and spin around. I stumble back a step-in shock; his arms whip out and grip my waist to steady me. My mouth hangs open as his hazel eyes bore into me, I run my gaze down his body with internal groans, gray sweats, and a rumpled plain white shirt, a man who is not on a movie set shouldn't look this good rocking that attire.

"Not gonna say goodbye?" The gruff tone of his voice sends a shiver down my spine, smiling as his perfect white teeth blind me for a second.

"I-Uh." I clear my throat and pull out of his hold, his brow furrows at the distance I have put between us. "I have things to do, and you seemed–."

"Asleep? Fucked into a coma? Sated? All of the above?" I balk at his crassness, I dart my gaze around and thank my lucky stars that no one is close enough to hear our conversation, their curious stares still lingering. Deciding I have to get the hell out of here before Hunter figures out that I snuck out last night, I go for cold indifference hoping he gets the hint.

"You're sexy and have a dick that rivals the Greek gods but, I also don't do commitment. I'm just out for a good time and enjoy life, sorry if that wasn't made clear last night." He smirks and closes the small space between us, he's that fucking tall I have to crane my neck back to see his face. He smirks and leans down so his lips brush against the shell of my ear.

"I never said anything about commitment, would I fuck you again? Hell fucking yeah, because your pussy is divine." I gasp and stare up at him in shock when he pulls back, I am woman enough to admit that his close proximity and dirty words have a flutter beginning in my belly and has my pussy clenching on nothing but air. "You can go now kitten." I open my mouth to... argue? Cry? Shout? I don't know what the hell I plan to do, but when he spins around and stalks off toward the lifts, the decision is made for me. I think I just got beat at my own damn game, and it stings like a bitch!

I groan as the cab pulls up in front of the small apartment that I currently reside, with my unwelcome houseguest, his sleek black Mercedes is parked there gleaming in the early morning sunlight. Who the hell owns a car in New York-freaking-city? I flick some cash to the cab driver and climb out, I take a breath and cringe. The air out here is like sniffing stagnant sewer water, there is no freshness, and it is never quiet–hence why I love it. Thanks to never having any peace, I don't get a chance to think about...her or *him*. I rake a hand through my long brown hair trying to untangle the oily mess, especially the back where it portrays sex hair.

I shove my key in the lock preparing to climb the stairs, I pause outside my apartment lightly pressing my ear against the door listening intently, I send up a silent prayer of thanks that Hunter is still sleeping, I quietly push the key into the lock and turn it, I nudge the door open slowly and tip toe inside closing it quietly behind myself. I rest my forehead against the cool metal and sigh, home free–.

"Look what the *pussy* cat dragged in." I flinch at the coldness in his tone, taking a minute to compose myself while putting on my game face, I turn to meet his scornful look. Hunter stands in the open living room with his arms crossed over his chest and a nasty glare pointed at me, his black hair is a mess, as if he's been tugging at the strands. His blue eyes shine with contempt and accusation, which instantly pisses me off.

"Don't you dare stand there and judge me!"

"Why the fuck not? You are mated to *my* brother and yet I can smell another male's scent clinging to you, classy California, real fucking classy."

"Who the fuck are you to judge me? Why are you even fucking here Hunter?" He grinds his teeth so hard I fear he may need dentures if he doesn't stop. I drop my purse on the counter as I storm past him and head to my room, effectively slamming the door to drive my point home that I am fucked off. Throwing my shoes on the bed and face planting beside them, I groan into the mattress when my door bangs open.

I'm gonna kill him!

Our mate would not be pleased.

I slam the link between Kora and I closed, my wolf and I have not been on the same page for months now. I can't forgive her for mating with Cassius Wilder, alpha to all wolves. Some would think that being mated to a wolf with such high standing among the shifters would be an honor, but I loathe it, unfortunately he isn't the one I want.

"You are a spoilt little shit and have never had to work for a fucking thing in your life, daddy made sure of that–." At the mention of my father, I leap off the bed onto my feet within a second and in Hunter's face, crowding him.

"Shut the fuck up! You know nothing about me or my life–."

"What's there not to know? Your brothers still wipe your ass for you–."

"Don't project your guilt onto me because you couldn't save your own brother!" As soon as the vile words have fled my mouth, I regret them instantly. Hunter's face morphs into one of pure and utter contempt, his hands clench and unclench at his sides. I release a ragged breath and reach up to place my hand on his chest, but he flinches back as if I burnt him. "Hunter, I didn't–." When his gaze collides with mine, I snap my mouth closed.

"Yeah, you did, you meant every word you said, and rest assured you self-righteous brat, they hit their mark."

TWO

CALIFORNIA

After showering and making sure to scrub the lingering scent of Whiskey and weed from my pores, I change into some sweats and a lose shirt. I am appalled at myself for allowing those harsh words to escape my mouth. I may be angry and bitter over the bond I now share with Cassius and the loss of...*her*, but that doesn't give me the right to hurt Hunter like I did.

Words have a lasting effect and I know that better than anyone. I decide to woman up and go in search of the youngest Wilder brother, I find him in the kitchen stirring something on the stove, his hair is flopped forward onto his forehead. He stands there in a pair of low-slung jeans and a shirt stuffed in his back pocket, I stand on the other side of the counter and wait for him to look up. After a minute when he still refuses to acknowledge me, I huff and break the tension filled silence.

"I'm sorry okay—." His angry gaze saps to me, his blue eyes shine with malice as a growl tumbles from his full lips.

"You're not fucking sorry Callie!" I flinch at his cold harsh tone; I know I deserve his wrath after what I said so I steel myself for his assault. "All you do is run around crying and feeling sorry for yourself. You are not the only fucking person who lost someone they loved!" He roars, his eyes flicker to the green of his wolf. He yanks the pot from the stove and drops it into the sink as he turns to flee. I feel like absolute shit, I have to fix this, the muscles in his back start to tense, and I get the feeling are I know he needs to shift.

"You're right!" He pauses but doesn't turn to face me. "Ever since Sk..." I take a deep breath and will my tears to remain inside of me, the mere thought of her has me wanting to crumble and weep for days. "Ever since Sky died, I have been in a spiral and I don't know how to get out of this blackness. It consumes me Hunter, as selfish as this sounds, I want everyone to feel what I do! I see my brothers and everyone else happy and content, but I don't understand how–."

"They could be happy when your whole world has stopped?" His whispered words hit me like a strong gust of wind. He gets it.

"Yeah." I breathe the word barely above a whisper, he turns to face me slowly. The anguish and pain in his eyes flays me open inside. "I had no right to say what I did, I was a grade A bitch and I'm so sorry Hunter. I didn't really know your brother, he seemed like a wicked guy and even I could tell he loved you, Belle and...Cass." Saying his name has my wolf stirring inside me, I slam my eyes closed and try to fight the urge to run to him like Kora wants so badly. She has been miserable since I fled to New York months ago, she wants to be with Cass, she thinks he can make me feel whole again. We aren't like Cairo; I feel the bond the same as she does but I can't give into it. I won't give into it. Sky meant so much more than anyone will ever understand, I will not tarnish our love by running back to him because he can erase the pain I feel. The pain is a constant reminder that everything we went through was real–it meant something!

"Blake was the best of us, he was kind, loving, loyal and above all else, he was a fucking hero." I move toward him and stop when there is a foot of space between us and stare up at him, Hunter looks like he has aged 20 years in a span of four months. He doesn't have the same carefree look in his eyes anymore, laugh lines don't mar his face any longer. I really have been such a spiteful bitch; that changes now, and I know I can't keep hiding out here. Jess is due to give birth to my niece in 5 weeks and I should be there.

"Help me find *her*." If he is taken back by my request, he doesn't show it, knowing fore well who I'm referring to as *her*.

"What do you plan to do *when* we find her?" A whoosh of air escapes me and I deflate a bit, I shrug my shoulders and decide that I need to be honest. I have put Hunter through hell since the moment he sat next to me on the plane. In all honesty, I constantly push him away because he reminds me of Cassius. I know he sends Cass updates about me, and I shouldn't give a shit, but the truth is...I do, and I hate myself for it.

"I don't know, I guess I just need some form of peace knowing that she can be laid to rest back home with her family." He reaches out and places a comforting hand on my shoulder.

"Do you know where she is?"

"I have someone working on finding us a way in."

"Ah, yeah, your infamous P.I that gave you the tip to come here." I cringe internally, it sounds so pathetic when he says it like that, but Kayla made it clear I can't tell anyone about her or she wouldn't help. I can't take that risk, so for now Hunter has to stay in the dark.

"Yes, she should have news for us in a couple days."

"How about, I order us some pizzas so we can Netflix and chill for the night. You know, like friends and not frenemies?" I chuckle and nod my head.

"That sounds really good, I have the hangover from hell and could use some good old carbs."

"You must of drank a shit load considering being a shifter means–." He raises his hands in the air then mimics zipping his lips shut when I glare at him.

"Good choice Wilder, good choice." He chuckles and flips me off as he heads to his room to collect his phone.

Hunter and I decided that comedy movies will be our go to for tonight, neither of us want to dwell in our brokenness. We chose Adam Sandler as he was more fitting for a good laugh, turns out Hunt and I do have a lot in common. The shrill ring of his phone shatters our blissful moment, our proximity is close enough for me to see the caller I.D, he looks to me with panic in his eyes, I begin to feel uneasy.

"Shit, Callie I forgot about him–." I wave off his concern.

"Just answer it, it's fine Hunter, he's your brother." He shakes his head and runs a hand through his hair letting the phone call ring out before it starts again, he never does that. "Hunter?" I'm beginning to worry something has happened back home.

"Look, I was angry this morning and then–." He's cut off at the sound of someone pounding against the door. His eyes widen in overpowering fright, I catch the scent of the person on the other side of the door, everything inside me stills as I stare at him.

"What did you do?" I whisper in shock. He tries to reach for me, but I scramble off the couch putting distance between us, he looks hurt, but right now I don't give a fuck.

Hunter sold me out!

"I didn't know he would come; I swear." I throw my hands in the air and growl.

"What the fuck did you think that overbearing asshole would do, twiddle his thumbs and wait? He has been biding his time waiting for a fucking excuse and you just gave him one!" The pounding at the door intensifies but neither of us are willing to acknowledge it more than we already have.

"I'm sorry–."

"Your fucking sorry? Spare me the bullshit Hunter, I fucking opened up to you this morning, I haven't told anyone that shit, and you stab me in the back!" He pales, Kora is thrashing against my ribs to break free, she can suck a fat dick, she isn't coming out to play because this is all her fault.

He wants me.

Fuck off Kora, if you weren't such a hussy we wouldn't be in this mess.

He's, our mate!

No, he isn't.

I slam the link closed and focus back on Hunter, he opens his mouth but snaps it closed when the front door shatters, we both spin toward the noise. The door is hanging on by one hinge, the culprit stands there staring at me, panting with an angry glint in his eyes. His gaze runs up and down my body analyzing everything about me, I do the same. I would be lying to myself if I said he was ugly, far fucking from it actually. He's wearing black jeans which cover his mammoth thighs. Cassius Wilder is thick in all the right places, he rocks a black and white OG Able shirt, I walk ever so calmly until I'm standing in front of him, Kora is whining inside of me, his forest green eyes spare me, his tongue darts out to moisten his full lips, I shiver as a memory of what his tongue can do to me. His black hair is hidden beneath his purple LA Lakers snap back; black stubble coats his face, rocking that ruggish bad boy look.

"You just broke our fucking door, dick." Cass doesn't break our stare off; I can see from the tight pull of his eyes that his wolf doesn't like the challenge in my gaze and wants me to submit. Cass being the bastard that he is, would never let his wolf out to fight me, he knows I would enjoy inflicting as much pain on him as I could. A growl tumbles from him but I ignore it and scoff as I head toward my room, I'm over him and his trying to show off his big dick energy. I release a growl when the bastard darts in front of me to block my path. "Cass, let her go brother."

"I don't need your help, traitor." I spit, Cass cocks a brow as he stares down at me.

"So, you can speak."

"Of course, I can, I just choose not to speak to your dumb-ass, now fucking move." He stands tall stuffing his hands in his pockets causing his shirt to tighten around his arms. He widens his stance and fuck me, those jeans hug him in all the right places.

"Say please, baby." Son of a bitch! Two can play this game, *baby*. I relax and allow my body to loosen as I close the space between us, I hear Hunter groan behind me, he's spent enough time with me lately to know I'm up to something. When my chest brushes up against his, a small hiss escapes him, I fight the smirk that wants to break free, I place both my hands flat against his chest, he grips my waist, and for a second, memories of that lustful night start flooding my head, quickly shaking it off I feel his fingers dig into my hips, and I allow the moan to tumble from my lips, the docile bastard eats it up.

"Cass–." I don't take my eyes off Cass as I cut Hunter off.

"Shh Hunter, the adults are working things out, be a good boy and go play." Cass smirks and leans down, just before his lips reach mine, I turn my head to the side exposing my neck. He starts licking from the base of my neck to my ear, without faking the shiver that travels down my spine. My breaths are coming in short rapid pants, I have to end this now, or I'll give into my wolf and allow her to ride Cassius like she wants. I run my hands up his arms and rest them on his shoulders, he hums his approval, tilting his head back moving in for a kiss, just as his lips ghost over mine I lift my knee and slam it into his dick. The fucker wails and drops to the ground like the sack of shit he is, Hunter's laughter echoes through the apartment as I glare down at his bitch of a brother cupping his jewels.

"You're fucking going to regret that." I roll my eyes as I step over him and head to my room. "California!" I peer over my shoulder at him, making sure to keep a solemn look on my face.

"Hmm?"

"Pack your shit, we leave in the morning." Motherfucker! I take a calming breath and count to three in my head before I lose my shit and stomp on his dick while he lays there.

"Of course, *baby*, I'll meet you there first thing in the morning, promise I won't miss our flight." I wink and turn but his voice has me pausing again.

"I'll fucking handcuff your sexy ass to me if I have to, don't test me." I spin around and glare at the fucker as he climbs to his feet, he is going to regret coming here.

"Of course, I'll go pack now, pinky swear babe." I blow him a kiss and ignore the stupefied look on his face as I slam my bedroom door.

Operation get Callie laid to fuck Cass off, begins in T minus three hours.

THREE

CALIFORNIA

I can hear them bickering from the confines of my room, I tune out their shit and give myself another once over in the mirror. The gold Gucci dress I opted for is short enough that if I bend over my pussy will be on show-just the way I like it. It's a halter neck dress and the back is completely open, the length stops just above ass. The front drops down to my belly button and has a very thin string across my chest, where it is impossible for the naked eye to see, it protects my girls from popping out.

I'm wearing the straight hair look tonight, leaving it out, so it tumbles down to my waist. My makeup is thick, heavy winged eye liner matching a nude eyeshadow that enhances my green eyes. My contouring is on point tonight, I dab some cherry gloss on my lips and call it perfect. I slip into my six-inch custom-made heels that Cole brought me for our birthday two years ago, they are very sparkly and a perfect match for this dress. I thought the silver of the heels against this gold master-piece won't work, but it does. I snag my gold clutch off the end of my bed and head for the door, ready to watch Cass fall from his self-proclaimed throne.

All conversation stops as I enter the living room, Hunter looks me up and down, then drops into the recliner near the window that overlooks the park below shaking his head and muttering that I have a death wish. Cassius on the other hand... he looks like he is about to strangle the shit out of me. His eyes are wide, and his fists are clenched at his side, a vein is popping out the side of his neck, his body is taught with tension. I wink and flick my hair over my shoulder as I head for the front door, might I add is still broken. I grip the handle and peer back at him over my shoulder and speak.

"You broke it, you fix it asshole." I yank the bloody thing open and thank my parents for being wolves, if I was a human there is no way I would have been able to open that with their pathetic strength. I take one step and I'm yanked back by my elbow, if I wasn't a fucking pro at wearing six-inch heels I would have slipped and fallen on my ass. I try to yank my arm free, but he tightens his hold and growls right in my face.

"Where the fuck do you think you're going?"

"Well, out of course darling. Don't wait up though, I don't plan on coming home tonight if you know what I mean?" Just to piss him off more, I lean forward and place a quick chaste kiss on his lips, the move stuns him enough and he drops his hold, leaving me a quick exit. I have about three seconds before he snaps out of it and comes after me, so I don't fuck around, I race down the stairs and I'm busting out the door running, I stop at the curb and flag down a cab coming my way, when I hear the door slam open I turn to see him storming toward me.

Shit!

I decide to meet the cab halfway, he quickens his pace as I start to run. I yank the back door open and dive onto the seat with my legs spread eagle and my pussy on display screaming at the driver to floor it. Cass comes barreling toward us and smacks his hand against the side of the cab as we pass him, I turn and wave to him out the back window before settling into my seat and telling the driver to take me to the same club I was at last night. I'm hoping to see a blond-haired green-eyed man again and hopefully this time, I'll remember him fucking my brains out.

We need to shift. I scoff at Kora's lame ass attempt.

Right, so you can go running back to that asshole. I'll pass.

It's been weeks!

Every time I let you shift; all you do is howl and try to find him. I don't want him, Kora!

You lie! I feel what you feel, and the mate bond is complete, all you are doing is hurting us both.

He fucking tricked me!

You knew who he was the moment you allowed him into our bed.

He marked me when he shouldn't have.

We belong to him. Her words send a pang of sadness through me.

No, I belonged to someone once and she left me. I belong to no man Kora.

Then you weaken us by your stupidity. You didn't escape him, he allowed you to leave tonight, so maybe think about that.

This time, she is the one to slam the link closed between us. I reach up and try to rub away the ache in my chest, Kora does have a point. I hate to admit it, but it did seem like he wasn't exactly trying *hard* to stop me.

I sit at the bar sipping my dirty Martini acting like I'm not searching for my mystery man; it's been an hour and I'm not even buzzed yet. Meanwhile three guys and one girl have hit on me, it's not that they weren't attractive it's the fact that they reeked of desperation and that is such a turn off. Clubbing was never my thing before, now it's the only place I can get out of my own head and not feel like I'm drowning. The music is so loud, my senses are overwhelmed by all the smells and the flashing lights distract me.

I know I'm finding solace in the wrong places, but I have no idea how to cope with this crushing grief inside me. Half of me feels dead inside at the loss of her but the other half longs for the mate I rejected, and I hate that part. Being near Cass makes me feel like I'm tarnishing what her and I had, when she was taken captive, I gave in to Kora's desire for him, unfortunately that stupid decision changed everything. A one-night stand turned into a forever thing, it's not as if I've been slutting around town or anything like that. I have only slept with one other person since Cass, well at least the ache between my legs this morning told me I had.

Did I sleep with him?

"You lost or looking for me?" I slowly turn to my left and smirk as my dusty blond mystery man stands there with a cocky gleam in his eyes.

"Who said I was lost?" He smiles rolling his bottom lip between his teeth as he gives me a once over. A tingle of awareness zaps down my spine and I scan the crowded club searching for him, there is only one person that can cause that feeling. I may not be able to see him but I sure as shit know he's lurking around here somewhere, watching.

"Looking for someone?" I focus back on mystery man and shake my head.

"I'm Callie."

"I know." *Shit*, so he knows my name and I have no idea what his is.

"You have me at a disadvantage then, I don't recall your name." He leans down until his lips brush the shell of my ear.

"I never gave it." I balk at him when he pulls back and smirks down at me.

"Do you plan on telling me?" He presses forward until I am forced to lean my back against the bar, he pushes his way between my legs causing my dress to ride up further. If he pushes in any closer or if I shift slightly my dress will be around my waist and my thong will be on display for all to see. I ignore my wardrobe malfunction and stare up at him with a look of indifference when he places his arms either side of me caging me in. He leans down until our noses are nearly touching, he opens his mouth as a surge of heat courses through me and the tingles begin to take over my body.

Shit, he's close–good.

Before I get a chance to focus back on my guy, he is yanked away and I slam my legs closed, I climb to my feet as gracefully as I can. Cass and Mr. I-won't-give-my-name stand chest to chest in a stare off, I wedge my way between them pushing each of them back a step before pinning Cassius with a heated glare.

"The fuck you looking at me like that for?"

"Because you're acting like a jealous fucking boyfriend." I swing my gaze to the other guy and smile sweetly as I purr out. "He isn't my boyfriend by the way."

"Good to know." His indifferent reply has Cass vibrating with rage, I can feel his chest rumbling under the palm of my hand. Of all the times for my brain to spiral, it chooses this moment.

I wonder what it would be like to be penetrated at the same time by both of these men?

"We're leaving, now!" I shake my head and scowl at Cass

gripping my wrist and pulling me at the same time, I pull free of his hold and glare at the fucking beefy bastard.

"Seems the lady would rather be here with me, promise not to destroy her too badly." I groan, this is going to end badly thanks to Mr. no names comment. Sure enough, Cass swings and I duck out of the way before I get caught in the crossfire. I watch as the two of them trade blow for blow, I can see Cass is pulling his punches not wanting to kill the human. They both tumble to the ground with Cass on top and landing hit after hit, shouting at them to stop is a waste of time, I search for a security guard but to no avail, I stumble forward a step when someone knocks me. I look up to see Hunter, I sigh in relief when he rips Cass off the human and shoves him back until he is flush against the bar beside me. I break away and attempt to help my mystery guy but his ferocious growl that calls to my wolf has me stopping in my tracks.

"Touch him and I'll break every fucking bone in his body while you watch, California." The threat in his voice is real, Kora begs me to heed his warning and check on our mate, but I ignore her. I just stand here and war with myself in the middle of this packed club, I look around and that's when I notice bystanders have their phones out recording. Are they fucking serious? No one wanted to help break this shit up, they would rather stand there and record the fight. Humans are fucking thick; their peanut size brains have no idea that Cass could have just killed this man with his bare hands. A woman comes forward and offers the man a hand, which he takes. Her back is to me, she looks familiar, when she turns to face me, my eyes widen, and my mouth drops open.

"Kayla?" She smirks and shrugs, she leans up to whisper something in my guy's ear which has him nodding.

"Follow us, we need to talk." I'm stunned silent for a moment as I watch her and my guy stalk away, I snap myself out of it and chase after them. I can feel the two hellhounds hot on my heels but ignore them as I follow Kayla up a flight of stairs and down a long dimly lit corridor, we all come to a stop at a door where no-name punches in a code on the lock. He pushes it open and strides in with Kayla following, I peer over my shoulder at Hunter, he seems reluctant to follow but Cass being the information whore that he is pushes past both of us uninvited of course. Not one to be left behind I go next; I scrunch my face in confusion as I look around. A huge window that stretches from one end of the room to the other overlooking the club, very cliché if you ask me. A couple of bookshelves line the back wall, some oil paintings adorn the walls, black leather couches scattered around a...seriously a fireplace? The walls are painted dark green and the color actually works with the lighting in here. An oomph escapes me when a ball of material smacks me in the face, I glare at Cassius.

"Put it on." He grits out.

"Why?" He snarls, I ignore the others in the room even though I can feel their eyes on us.

"Because I fucking said, don't push me California." Oh, but now I have to since he said that.

"Sweetheart, I'm proud to show what my mama gave me."

"Callie..." The warning in his tone is clear.

"Cassius..." I sass back.

"Jesus Christ, sit the fuck down the pair of you. Callie put your pussy away so you can stop distracting the three hot blooded males in the room." I pull my stare from Cass to eye Kayla, the stern look in her eyes tell me if I don't do as she asks, I won't get any answers from her. I reluctantly pull the hoodie on, a growl comes from Cass, and I ignore him, I pop my head through the hole and stumble back a step when I see Cass directly in front of me. His jumper is so big that it stops at my knees and the sleeves hang over my hands.

"Don't fucking lift your arms again."

"Huh?" Cass glares down at me.

"That dress is too fucking short." *Oh.* I lean up on my tip toes and fake whisper.

"Would it help if I told you that he's already seen it?" The only warning, I have is him growling, and then his hand is around my throat and we're gliding through the room until my back smashes against the wall. I hear a commotion behind Cass, but he refuses to break eye contact. My wolf is preening at the way her mate is handling us and asserting his ownership.

"You wanna go around fucking everything that moves?"

"Go fuck yourself asshole, I'm no slut."

"Bitch please, if dicks could fly your mouth would be an airport." I growl in frustration at Kayla's petty as fuck remark. Cass drops his hold on me and spins around to face the others, I step out from behind him noticing my mystery man is behind a desk, Hunter and Kayla both stand in front of it with their gazes fixed on us.

"I get to fuck with her, not you, so stay the fuck out of this." I throw my hands in the air, first he berates me and then sticks up for me, he is such a cluster fuck. I storm away from him and drop down into one of the seats in front of the desk, Kayla takes the one next to me. I feel Cass behind me not paying him any mind as I watch the dusty blond god lower himself into his seat resting his forearms on the desk. Silence encases the room, as I sit here and really look at him, I begin to think he looks familiar somehow.

Where would I know him from?

"So, clearly you have all met Tristan." *Tristan,* so that's his name. The man himself smiles wickedly at me and I can't help but return his gesture. I hear Hunter groaning from the other side of Kayla but ignore him.

"He met my fist if that's what you mean." Tristan scoffs at Cass's remark.

"I saw that Cassius but let me assure you that Tristan allowed you to have the upper hand down there." Now I'm confused.

"I don't fucking think so." Cass snaps.

"Oh, believe me, Kayla is right. I could have ended it if I wanted to."

"Oh, and how would you have done that you little wimp?" Cass needs to shut the fuck up.

"I guess I should formally introduce myself." I feel like something big is about to happen with this introduction, he stands and extends his hand to Cass over his desk. "My name is Tristan Cage, and I am high warlock to the Cage Coven."

Oh Jesus Christ!

Tears well in my eyes as I stare up at the bastard, he knew who I was when we slept together. Being near Cass made me feel like I dishonored her memory, but I just shit all over her by sleeping with her *brother*.

FOUR
CALIFORNIA

Their voices echo around me but nothing is registering, my chest is caving in and I'm struggling to breathe. In my attempt to push Cassius away and escape this never-ending pain inside me, I did the unthinkable. I lean forward and cover my face with my hands, in the hopes of blocking everything out, what the fuck have I done? A distraction comes in the form of Cass's scent, lingering from the sleeves of his hoodie, and as much as I hate to admit it, its quite calming and comforting, I choose to ignore that fact and focus on the distraction it gives me.

"Callie?" I don't bother to answer Kayla, she may be helping me but her and I have never been friends and probably never will be. She made Jess and Creed's life a living hell when Jess first got to Rosewood. "Callie, I need you to hear this—."

"She doesn't need to do shit!" I cringe, even after I just admitted to him that I slept with another man, Cass still defends me. I don't deserve his help, I fucked up and slept with the person I swore I would kill when I found them. Tristan Cage stole the body of the woman I loved, and I dropped my panties for him like a wanton hussy last night.

"Yeah, she does, Tristan has offered access to his coven to visit Sky." That catches my attention, Cass inhales a sharp intake of air as I drop my hands and look up to find Tristan's gaze already on me.

"Is she telling the truth?" I ignore Kayla's scoff as I focus on Tristan scanning his eyes for lies.

"Yes, and for the record Callie. I had no idea who you were last night, I only found out this morning after you left, if I had known–."

"let's move on before my brother Hulks out again, yeah?" I roll my eyes, Hunter is right though, this conversation doesn't have to take place with Cass present.

"When can I see her?" I say barely above a whisper, for the first time tonight Tristan's features soften, and his eyes take on a sad look.

"Tomorrow, I will send a car to collect you–."

"She isn't going on her own!" Tristan snaps his gaze to Cass.

"Very well, I will send a car to collect the four of you first thing in the morning. But Callie?"

"Yeah?"

"My sister will remain with me."

I'm lead through the club by Cass with my hand in his, the music doesn't even register, the people that smack against us or the sickening scent doesn't even compare to the turmoil thrumming inside. Someone bumps into me, and I stumble, I would have fallen if Cass wasn't quick enough to catch me, he peers down and whatever he sees on my face has him sighing, he lifts me into his arms and I wrap myself around him burying my face in the side of his neck, finally letting the tears fall, his hands cover my ass which I'm thankful for.

I don't register that we have stopped moving until he speaks. "We're at the car." I shake my head. "Hunt, you drive, and I'll sit in the back with her."

"Yeah, okay." Hunter sounds dejected and a bit out of it, but I don't care.

"I call shotgun." I tighten my hold on Cass at the sound of Kayla's voice.

"You two get in, we'll just be a sec." When the sound of the doors closing rings out in the still night Cass relaxes slightly. "Want me to put you down?" I shake my head. "Okay." He maneuvers us strategically into the backseat, the ride home is silent, and I still can't stop the tears that are leaking from my eyes.

I have no right to cling to Cassius like I am, but right now after who I slept with and the fact that Sky is within my reach has everything crashing down around me. Guilt gnawing at me and without trying to push it down, I allow it to consume me in my bid to self-sabotage all I have done is make myself look like a fool and hurt so many people, including the one person who is comforting me now. The car comes to a stop, and I tighten my hold on him, not wanting to burst the bubble I am currently in; he opens the door and manages to stand whilst never letting me go. We climb the stairs or should I say he climbs the stairs to our apartment, the broken door is shoved open, Cassius well aware that he has to repair it, ASAP. Cass moves us inside, but I still refuse to lift my head or even open my eyes, he keeps moving until the familiar scent of my bedroom overwhelms me, he kicks the door shut and drops down on the edge of my bed.

"You can come out of hiding now." I shake my head electing a chuckle from him. "You gonna hide in there all night?" I nod which causes him to laugh. "Want to talk about it?"

"Why are you being nice to me?" I mumble as my lips brush against his neck sending a jolt down his body. He moves one of his hands from my ass to grip the back of my neck and squeezes until it becomes apparent, he wants me to come out of hiding. I sluggishly pull away from my hiding spot and slowly open my eyes, a timid smile graces his face causing the guilt inside me to rear its ugly head.

"Because we all make mistakes Callie, it's how we over-come them that matters."

"I slept with someone else and yet here you are comforting me, I will be seeing the woman that was everything to me tomorrow and you still want to be near me, why?" He blows out a loud exhale and I stare at him; I have done nothing but push him away and treat him like shit for months. I have purposely gone out of my way to cause him pain and he still sits here looking at me like I hung the fucking moon for him! I feel his chest rumble and when he slams his eyes closed, I know he is wrestling with his wolf for control, he doesn't want to admit it, but his wolf hates that I had sex with another.

"The thing is, I don't think you feel bad about hurting me or sleeping with someone else." I reel back in shock at his blunt-ness, I scramble off his lap and glare at the asshole as he slowly climbs to his feet. This right here, the anger and hatred that vibrates between us is familiar and safe for me, him being kind and loving isn't something I can handle right now.

"What the hell is that supposed to mean?" His eyes narrow to slits.

"You're only cut up about it because you just found out you fucked Sky's brother, if it was anyone else your smug ass wouldn't give a shit."

"Fuck you Cassius." I seethe.

"Not tonight thanks, lord only knows who else has come in that pussy since I did." My jaw drops, I quickly snap it shut and huff out my annoyance, I yank his jumper off and chuck at him. Then just to be a bitch and wipe that disgusted look off his face, I reach behind the back of my neck to undo the strings of my dress and relish at the sight of his wide eyes when the garment falls to the floor, standing here in nothing but a thong. His gaze runs down the length of my body and Kora preens inside me at the heated look in our mates' eyes as his gaze lingers on the apex of my thighs.

"Well, since nothing I have interests you, I think you should leave, so I can finger fuck myself into a coma and sleep like a baby." His gaze snaps to mine and I can see the war raging inside him, his wolf wants to stay and claim me, but the man refuses to give in, good, I wouldn't fuck him if he was the last penis to ride on Earth. I had no idea I was attracted to men until I met him, I've only ever been with girls my whole life. I was elated when I found out my mate was a female, I thought that fate finally got something right, what a joke right?

"You're playing a dangerous game here *Alma*, you can only poke a bear so much before it snaps and takes what it wants." I roll my eyes.

"Coming from the guy who just said my pussy is rank?"

"Oh baby, I said no thanks to fucking you *tonight*, but I never said I wouldn't fuck you tomorrow, or the next day or the day after that." Oh god, his words have me clenching my thighs together and of course he doesn't miss it, I can scent my own arousal and when the smug prick smirks at me, it's clear he can to. He can try and act like I don't affect him, but I can feel his need through the mate link. "Keep telling yourself that you don't want me, your mind says no but your body is begging for me to fuck it."

I've been lying here for two fucking hours and still can't sleep, failing that I decide to enhance my libido using my vibrator, dildo, even a satisfier pro and still I can't fucking come! All I can think about is Cassius-fucking-Wilder and his stupid promise to fuck me. Just the thought of him has heat gathering at my core and my pussy clenching on nothing but air. I roll over and punch my pillow before groaning, I have never been this sexually frustrated in my life! Giving up on sleep I make a decision to call the other person I've been avoiding for months, I cringe at the time being four in the morning but fuck it, I scroll for the number and hit dial. I contemplate whether to hang up or continue to hold, low and behold he answers.

"Callie, is everything okay?" I try to speak but no words come out. "I can hear you breathing." He sounds sad, and it eats at me because he is the only other person that has any kind of idea about the pain I am going through.

"Kayla found her." I finally say after a beat.

"I know Callie, that's why I tried to call you weeks ago." I jolt up in bed shocked to hear this.

"The fuck, Cairo?"

"Hang on." I hear him shuffling around and then a door open and close before he speaks again. "Sorry, I didn't want to wake Belle, she hasn't been sleeping much." Alarm bells go off inside me.

"Why is she okay? Is the baby okay?" A dejected sigh comes from his end.

"She's fine, she's just scared because she doesn't have long before baby gets here, and with the unknown power inside our child, it...scares us both." I hunch forward.

"I'm sorry."

"Don't be, Sky did this to give our child a chance at survival. I just wish we had of known sooner to give Belle that choice of being a shifter."

"I promise I will help you figure this all out."

"Why now Callie? You avoid me for months, blame me for Sky, and then suddenly you have a change of heart?" I flinch at the anger in his tone, but he's right.

"I did blame you Ro–."

"Did or *do*?" I sigh and run a hand through my hair.

"I *did*, I shouldn't have, but I felt like you could have stopped it all and saved her." A lump begins to form in my throat, tears start to gather in my eyes. I haven't talked about her this much since the day we buried her.

"Believe me California, if there was any remote chance of saving her, I would have given my own life so she could live." I clamp my hand over my mouth to muffle my sobs, mindful of waking the others. I feel Cairo's sensitivity as he remains silent, graciously giving me the chance to weep.

"I-I miss h-her so much." I hiccup out.

"I do too, I'm about to be a Father Callie, and my best friend isn't here to share it with me. Belle is my mate, but Sky will always be my human sides soul mate, I miss her every fucking day." I can hear the truth and anguish in his words and I feel like even more of a bitch for taking my anger out on him. Ro loves Belle more than anything, he loved Sky like a sister, it just took him a while to realize that.

"I'm so sorry I blamed you Cairo, I know you loved her just as much as I did."

"She always loved you Callie, from the very first-time she

saw you, we went to that party to claim Jess. Do you want to know what she told me when we left that night?" I sniffle.

"Y-yeah." He chuckles as if he is reliving that very moment again, and it brings a watery smile to my face.

"She was gonna make you fall in love with her, and no matter what it took or what magic had to be used to get you to notice her, she would do it." I laugh quietly.

"No magic was necessary, I noticed her exiting the woods." More tears flow down my cheeks at the first memory of seeing Skylar Cage, she took my goddamn breath away and I never managed to master the art of breathing without her again.

"She loved you so much Callie, which is why I know she wouldn't want you hurting like this." I growl but there is no force behind it.

"I can't stop it, every fucking second of the day feels like my chest is cracking open and my heart is being ripped out. Nothing I do eases the pain!" He stays silent for a minute before he tentatively asks.

"Is that why you've been enjoying or should I say living it up in the big city, and might I add sleeping with someone who isn't Cass?" I gasp. "You are living with my mates brother Callie, Hunter gossips more than fucking Cole so just assume that we know everything that has happened there." I growl, this time there is malice behind it. Kora doesn't like the idea of Hunter sharing our private business with anyone, since we don't have a pack anymore, Kora has become very...private.

"I'm gonna kill that dweeb!"

"Please don't, or at least wait until I can find some miracle cure to reattach my balls after Belle tears them from my groin." I snort laugh.

"Why the hell would she do that?"

"She blames me for you leaving and her brother having to be there with you." *Oh.*

"I didn't leave because of you." I whisper.

"I know why you left Callie, Sky was my best friend, so I believe I have the right to tell you this=."

"Don't. Ro."

"He isn't your enemy; he is a good guy and cares about you–."

"You have tried to kill him more times than I have!" He scoffs.

"We're talking about you not me! He's an overbearing ass because I'm fucking his sister and knocked her up, plus the fucker is using his newfound power to keep an eye on me–."

"Cairo!" I gasp and Ro goes silent at the sound of his mate's reprimand.

"Shit." I chuckle at his muttered curse. "Shut up Callie, babe, I was just–."

"Talking shit about my brother?" I can picture Ro cringing in my mind's eye and I'm loving the fact of hearing Belle tear the alpha bastard a new asshole.

"No, I was just trying to soften Callie toward him, you know like, help a brother out kind of thing?"

"You're so full of shit your eyes are turning brown!" I laugh which just earns me a growl from Cairo.

"Shut up Callie, this is all your fault!"

"Don't you dare blame her; I didn't hear her say anything bad about him!"

"Oh, blow me, she hates him and runs away and *I'm* the bad guy?"

"We'll talk about this later, now, put the phone on speaker so I can say hi." He grumbles but does as she asks. "Hey Callie."

"Hey Belle, how are you?" She laughs.

"Oh, you know, I have a watermelon pushing on my bladder and I pee five times an hour." I chuckle but there is no humor to it, I feel awkward talking to Belle. I've been a royal bitch to her brothers, and she still sits on the other end of the phone being nice to me. "Callie?" I sigh loudly.

"Yeah, Belle?"

"I know what's happening tomorrow." I tense.

"What? Did you have a vision?" She ignores Cairo as she continues.

"You will be okay; I've booked Ro and I on the first flight out–."

"Wait what?" Ro took the words right out of my mouth.

"Callie, I'm gonna let you go, but Ro and I will be there tomorrow–."

"Wait do you mean like meet us *there*?"

"Yes."

"How do you know where to go?"

"My gift is visions Callie.

"Right, okay."

FIVE
CASSIUS

Hunter and I sit in the back with Callie in the middle, Kayla rides shotgun with the driver who has only spoken once to let us know we will need overnight bags. Of course, I query this, in the midst of his speech he adds, New England will be our destination. Kayla seemed shocked by this as she said she saw Sky was here in New York. Callie has barely spoken at all this morning; I may have left her room last night but that doesn't mean I strayed too far.

She was really unsettled last night, and I couldn't help over hearing her phone call with my future brother-in-law. I called them this morning, but their phones are off, I only heard Callie's side of the conversation and it made my heart ache for her. I know she loved Sky, anyone with fucking eyes could see the chemistry they shared. I never meant to mark her that night, my purpose was to get drunk and disorientate Atticus so he wouldn't chase her down, but it backfired. We ended up in bed together, and honest to God, it was the best sex of my life. I haven't bedded anyone else since her, I clench my hands into fists at the thought of her and that dead man walking Tristan sleeping together.

She cut me off the morning after we slept together, told me to stay away from her and never touch her again, that's a lot easier said than done when you're a wolf. Atticus has no regrets for his behavior, our scent clings to every pore of her body, any shifter can scent me on her. Okay, the man half of me likes that idea as well. I shuffle in my seat, and she moves further away from me, if at all possible, if she shifts anymore, she will end up on my brothers fucking lap.

I'll kill him!

You're not touching my fucking brother!

I slam the link closed between me and my wolf, his remark hit too close to home. The loss of Blake still stings me daily, I know Hunter only agreed to follow Callie here, so he didn't have to return home and face his responsibilities. He has no desire to rule the pack that Blake was given, and I honestly can't blame him for that. The pair of us have even limited our contact with our father, guilty of blaming ourselves for the loss of Blake. There are no ill feelings from our dad toward us and he constantly reassures us that Blake wouldn't have wanted to go out any other way. He sacrificed his own life to protect our sister, and if I had one wish, I would beg for it to be me, instead of him, he had so much more to offer this world than I do, he would have also made a better chief alpha than I could ever be. The sound of Callie's phone ringing pulls me from my thoughts.

"Hello?"

"I hear Hurricane California went off last night." I can hear the laughter in Colton's voice, Callie on the other hand doesn't find her brother very funny at all, and growls a warning. "Oh, don't be such a grump, you know I'm teasing."

"What do you want, Cole?"

"Okay fine, before I get to it, I have one very important question."

"What is it?" She grits out.

"Did you rip Cassius's balls off, or did you just hurt him a little?" She tenses as I growl, Cole the little shit laughs.

"I'm gonna break your teeth, Reeves." I snap.

"Oh, and here I was thinking we were becoming friends Pooh bear." Callie's gaze swings to me and I glare at her in warning when she mouths *pooh bear*.

"*Pooh bear's* balls are still attached brother...for now." Cole's laughter is so loud through the phone I grind my teeth.

"How far away are you?"

"What?"

"California, what made you think Cairo wouldn't call us. He's Creed's best friend and Jess's brother, we're all here waiting for you to arrive." I see Callie's eyes begin to mist.

"Why?"

"Because you're my twin, and we would never let you do this on your own?" Her eyes meet mine, for a moment I see hesitancy in her gaze, but I also see the scared little girl inside who is seeking approval. I nod my head and watch as a calm settles over her, why she wants my permission is beyond me, but I won't balk at the chance of her coming to me for anything. I feel her relax through the mate link.

"Thank you, We're about two hours away."

"Perfect." I tune them out as they discuss plans of our arrival; I retreat inside my own mind and get lost in my thoughts.

She will choose us.

How can you be so sure?

She needed us last night Cassius, not the bastard who laid with her or Skylar—us.

We have to find a way to break down the walls she has built.

Seeing her again is the first step in that happening.
I think it will backfire.
Just be ready to comfort her.

I scoff internally, Atticus is out of his mind thinking she will choose us instead of her twin brother. Cole and Callie are close as fuck, I would hedge to say closer than Belle and me.

We pull over at some run-down diner that's forty minutes away from the place where Sky is being held. Callie is practically bouncing in her seat, anxious to greet her family. It grates on my fucking nerves, I'm her mate, in yet she detests the sight of me and seeks comfort from another. I grind my teeth together and push the door open to escape the confines of the car as soon as it stops, or I will risk the urge to wrap my hands around my mate's beautiful little neck. I catch their scent and turn to the left, in the corner with a full view of the entry points is a blacked-out Escalade. The front doors open as Creed and Cairo step out, focusing on the person exiting the vehicle we arrived in, they stand there; ridged and still when Kayla comes into view. Creed is in shock, considering he fucked Kayla and his wife is sitting in the backseat of the car, Cairo being the only one knowing the secret of Callies informant.

"Creed!" Callie squeals as she takes off toward her brother, The back doors open and I watch as Jess and Cole climb out, Jess's belly is huge, and she looks exhausted. How the hell she managed to hide that on the plane is beyond me, my smile widens when I see my sister climb out of the other door, I feel Hunter close beside me. Cairo offers his hand to Belle, and I give the asshole credit, much to my dismay he really does love and care for her. That's all I ever wanted, was for someone who truly sees how special she is, Belle deserves nothing but the best, hey, I'm not saying that Cairo is the best, but she seems to be the apple of his eye, so he can live another day–for now!

"Bells!" Hunter is off racing, with me hot on his heels, I falter in my steps at the sight of her bump, she is glowing and the aura that surrounds her is pure light. She wraps her tiny arms around Hunt, embracing him ever so tightly, I yank him back by his shirt and laugh off his growl. I stare down at my sister and smile, before wrapping her in my arms and inhaling her scent.

"I missed you big brother." Her softly spoken words melt me.

"I missed you too Belle. If you didn't live out in the middle of nowhere, we might see each other more often. You and Jess shouldn't be flying when you're both this far along." She scoffs and moves away from me, Cairo is quick to swing his arm around her shoulders pulling her to his side, I glower. I'm aware they're together and having a kid, but it still grates me when I see the fucker getting handsy with my baby sister. He smirks as if he knows where my mind has wondered and extends his hand to Hunter then me, I stare at it for a moment before accepting the shake.

"I make you chief alpha and you still stand there and look down your nose at me, rude." I laugh at the fucker; Cairo's laughter joins mine a moment later. I greet the others and we catch up a bit before Jess butts in.

"Why is Kayla keeping her distance?" Creed's hazel eyes widen as he rubs the back of his neck.

"Princess–."

"Oh, shut up Creedence, jealousy is the last thing on my mind. We're married and have kids for gods' sake, plus she saved my life, so she doesn't have to stay over there in fear of me."

"I don't think it's you she's avoiding." Belle mumbles, I turn to see a knowing look in her eyes, she's had a vision. Before we lose more time debating about Kayla, I cut in.

"We can deal with that issue later; we have to get moving and scope this place out. I only have a couple of days before leaving." I snap my gaze to Callie when I feel anguish through the bond, I would love to say that she is upset over me leaving so soon, but I'm not an idiot. She is probably upset over the fact of having to see Sky.

"Let's do this." My gaze stays on Callie as I answer Creed.

"Yeah, let's go."

The driver pulls up to a wrought iron gate with the letter C smack bang in the middle, he rolls his window down to punch in a code. Who the hell are these people to have a locked gate that opens by pin code? We drive down a gravel driveaway, hedges line either side of us, the lawns are manicured and pristine to perfection. Atticus preens inside me wanting to run and frolic around on the lush green grass, I push him back down not wanting to be distracted by his wants. Everyone is silent as we roll to a stop next to a huge ass fountain, the fucking thing is huge and over eight feet tall, in the middle sits a woman with a clay bucket on her head where the water spouts from, turning to the other side I see a huge ass mansion!

It looks more like a fucking castle, it even has the pointy top things on either end, wrap around porches from what I can see. When the driver puts the car in park, we all climb out and take in the view. The house is painted in a grayish color that actually looks tactful, windows are scattered everywhere, and I can even tell from out here that they would let in an immense amount of sunlight throughout the day. I make my way around the car to Hunter and Callie–the latter made sure to get out on my brother's side. I smirk when I see Creed observing the house, of course that bastard would be creaming himself over the structure.

Of course this fucker lives in a mansion with no neighbors in sight and has every one of these fools frothing at the mouth. It's just a fucking house, granted a nice one but who the fuck cares! The driver motions for us to follow him, I look around at the group and hold up my hand before marching over to Kayla, I grip her arm pulling her with me, making sure there's a good distance between us and the others, preventing them from overhearing. When I release her, she places her hands on her hips and glares up at me.

"I am not a fucking toy you can drag around Cassius; I am a fucking alpha–."

"Shut up Kayla, my status trumps yours." She narrows her eyes; I really don't know this woman and from the shit I have heard, she isn't exactly someone you can trust. She has been a spy for Belle's sperm donor and hasn't once asked for anything in return. She came out here to help Ro find Sky and has been feeding Callie information for what? None of us know if she is still working for Alex, that old bastard won't say a word on the matter either.

"What the hell do you want?"

"To figure out what fucking game you are playing." I growl. "I don't trust you!"

"And I don't give a fuck, I'm just here to help Callie and then I'll be gone."

"Why the fuck are you helping her? I know you don't like

her or any of the Reeves." A pained look flashes in her eyes before she masks it, if I wasn't paying such close attention to her, I would have missed it.

"Look, you don't have to trust me okay. I'm not here to cause any problems, I only want to help–."

"Why though, why the hell do you want to help us?" She grinds her teeth, and her eyes harden at the edges.

"I don't owe you an explanation, all you need to know is that I am on your side and have nothing to gain or lose from this." I hear the truth in her words, and her jaw is stiff as granite, letting me know that's all the information you're going to get. I decide to leave it for now, making sure that from now on I keep a close eye on Kayla until I can figure out her motives.

"Tell me this, do you know if that fucker Tristan has anything planned for Callie?" Her posture deflates slightly, and her eyes take on a sad hue.

"The only thing I know is that he won't give Sky back to her. I'll say this once Cass, I may have helped Alexander before, but I am not the mole in your band of misfits. If he tries anything, I will strive to help you all as best I can."

"Strangely enough, I believe you. If that's the way you feel why not pledge your loyalty to me and join the packs?" Her eyes sharpen as she stands taller and squares her shoulders.

"I will never live under the rule of another male as long as I live, my freedom means everything to me."

SIX

CALIFORNIA

I stand in the opulent entryway and marvel at the beauty, everything is decorated in hues of gray and gold. This house has character, you can tell from the walls and the staircase that the entire home is old and has just been renovated. I've never liked brand new houses; I have always found them bland and sterile but something like this I could see myself living in and making a home here.

The driver clears his throat and motions for us to follow him, we walk down a wide hallway that has old oil paintings lining the walls on each side. You can see how they change in age, the first few look like they were painted a hundred years ago but as you continue on you see the difference in each painting. I slow my steps marveling at each of them, an equal number of men and women. Clearly witches didn't discriminate against sex unlike us shifters, I gasp and stop mid step when my gaze lands on the second to last painting.

My breath stalls in my throat, tears begin to cloud my vision as I stare at the painting right in front of me. Muddy brown eyes that hold so many secrets stare back at me, blonde hair fans her face. She doesn't wear a dress like the women in the other paintings, she stands proudly in a plain shirt, dark wash jeans and her signature black combat boots, a blade sheathed on each hip. I reach out slowly and tentatively trace my index finger across her plump pink lips. I feel every one's eyes on me, I'm transfixed on the beauty in the painting, I would give anything to touch her again, smell her, kiss her and run my fingers through her beautiful hair.

"Master Tristan is waiting–." The driver is cut off when growls sound out around me.

"The pompous fuck can wait until she is ready." A warmth begins to spread inside me at Cassius's words, here he is mated to me and yet I stand before him mourning the loss of the woman I love more than anything in this world. I trace my finger down her body and smile, Skylar Cage was a woman who many feared, her name alone had grown ass men trembling at the thought of ever having to face her. I never knew that side of Sky, I only knew the woman who loved me like there was no tomorrow. Just one look from her could set my body alight and make me feel like I was the most breath stealing beauty she had ever laid eyes on.

"Fuck, I miss you so much that it hurts baby." I whisper, before the tears start to fall, I rip my gaze from the painting and turn toward the driver motioning for him to lead the way. I stiffen when I feel Cass creep up beside me and place a hand on my lower back. I grit my teeth in frustration at the fact his hand on my body can cause me to relax slightly and breathe easier.

"People will tell you she is in a better place, but the truth is there is no better place to be than in your arms, California. I didn't say it before, but I am saying it now, I am truly sorry for your loss." I turn and stare up at him in shock, I can hear the truth in each of his words and it baffles me. "You may think me a liar, but I would never have created this bond between us if Sky was still here, I am many things Callie, but I am not a homewrecker. I can see the love you have for her in your eyes, Sky was one lucky woman to have a goddess like you to love her daily." He drops his hand and steps back leaving me alone with my thoughts as we follow the driver, nothing around me registers, not the conversations or the décor. Cassius Wilder has stunned the hell out of me.

"Please, take a seat and Master Tristan will be with you shortly." I shake my head to clear my thoughts and focus back on my surroundings, it's now I notice we are in a large conservatory with old cane lounges and a small table in the middle that is littered with sweets and drinks. I look around this breath-taking room, it is encased with windows complimented with different size plants to give you the illusion of being outside. I never thought a mansion like this would have upcycling furniture, like the cane loungers for instance. Cole wastes no time in helping himself to the tiny cakes and finger sandwiches, Belle attempts to grab one but Cairo stops her.

"Seriously?" Belle snaps, clearly, she is exasperated with her mate's overbearing nature, I find it sweet.

"I'll try one first, just in case." Cairo is trying to remain calm and its comical.

"Why?"

"Because Beauty, Sky fled for a reason, and I wouldn't put it past these fuckers to try and off us." Belle pales and I flinch at the reminder of my girlfriend growing up alone until she found Cairo.

"If I wanted to kill you, I would have done it already." We all turn toward the other end of the room, Tristan stands in the threshold of the glass sliding doors in a pristine pinstriped suit, his scruffy blond hair is slicked back, his hazel eyes scan the room until he finds me, his full lips pull back in a smirk and I admit, I'm *not* unaffected by him and I hate that. He is *her* brother for Christ's sake and here I am eye-fucking him!

"I assume you are the asshole who stole my best friend's body?" The anger that laces each of Ro's words has my wolf wanting to roll over and submit to him. He may not be chief alpha, but Bexley could easily challenge Cass's wolf.

"How could I steal something that belonged to me?" Now that, gets my attention and has Kora pushing to the forefront growling, I feel my body vibrating with rage, trying to fight off the shift. My vision sharpens and my senses go into overdrive, I close my eyes taking in some deep calming breaths to gain control from my wolf. When I feel my shoulder pop, I know I'm done for, Kora is going to win this battle and I'll be in wolf form in a matter of seconds.

"Breathe." The whispered word and the feeling of his hands as they cup my cheeks is enough of a shock to stop the shift, I blink my eyes open and stare at him.

I want to kill him!

His eyes widen in shock, I didn't mean to open the mate link further by communicating with him silently. I try to pull out of his hold, but he tightens his grip on me.

Don't let him see that he is affecting you, find your poker face and be the cold badass that I know you can be.

Hearing his voice in my mind has me gasping. When the mate link first clicked into place months ago, I made sure to wall off my mind from his, I never wanted him to hear my thoughts. Now, I'm slightly grateful for the fact he can speak to me like this, his touch and words have stopped Kora from taking over. She is pleased that her mate is able to have a stronger hold on us, I don't hate the idea, but I don't relish it either. Cass releases me and moves so that we are standing side by side, I'm overwhelmed that he chose to treat me as an equal. I snarl and narrow my eyes at Tristan.

"She never belonged to you, she was mine and you took her from me." His mask of indifference never falters.

"My sister belongs with her people–." Cairo's growl has Tristan twisting his mouth, Belle and Creed grab an arm each to hold him back.

"You were never her people! She belongs with us, *we* are her family, I loved that girl since I was nine years old. You may share DNA with Skylar, but you are nothing to her, she was *my* sister, *my* best friend, *my* beta and my pack. She will return with us, if you won't willingly hand her over, then I will take her from you and burn this fucking house down if need be." Tristan nods his head, but his eyes betray him this time, I can see in the depths that Cairo's words have touched on his feelings.

"I think we have gotten off on the wrong foot–." Cairo cuts him off again.

"Give me Skylar, now!" Tristan's eyes harden as he stares at Ro, God the last thing we want right now is for Bexley to view his stare as a challenge.

"I am trying to help you!"

"How?" I bark out, Tristan swings his gaze back to me.

"Skylar gave away her power and it wasn't hers to give." I furrow my brow in confusion.

"What does that mean?" Cole asks.

"Can we sit down? I'll explain everything and I promise you, when you hear what I have to say you will be thanking me for taking my sister." Ro scoffs.

"Not fucking likely asshole." Tristan glares at Cairo.

"By all means then, top floor third door on the right is where my sister is." Cairo spins and heads for the door but Tristan's next words has him stopping in his tracks. "Take her and your child will die."

"The fuck did you just say?" Believe me when I say,

Hunter just took the words out of all our mouths. Jess being the peacekeeper that she is, breaks away from us and moves toward Tristan, but stops a few feet away when Creed releases a growl of warning.

"I'm Jess." Tristan smiles kindly and nods.

"I know who you are Mrs. Reeves." Jess cringes.

"Please don't call me that, it makes me feel old." Tristan chuckles and nods.

"Very well."

"Can you please explain to us what it is that you are doing with Sky and why it has anything to do with my brother's baby?"

"I will be more than happy to, why don't we have a seat, it's a bit of a long story I'm afraid."

I watch as the others move toward the couches, Cass remains beside me and I can feel the tension radiating off him in waves, I even feel it through the link we share. It's hard to differentiate between his emotions and mine, he leans down and whispers in my ear low enough for only me to hear.

"We can run?" A laugh bubbles out of me without my consent at his outlandish comment. "You may think I'm joking but I'm not." I smile and shake my head as I look at him.

"I need answers and he seems to have them, I have to hear him out." He nods solemnly.

"Then we hear him out, I'm here if you know...you need... something." I nod and quickly scurry away before shit gets more awkward between us. I stop as I scan for an available seat, I glare and groan internally, how fucking cliché!

You know in the movies when the girl is trying to avoid facing the guy but there aren't any seats left except for the one next to him or in front of him? Yeah, that's me right now. Ro and Belle share a seat, Kayla is in the single next to Creed and Jess who share as well. Cole occupies the other single seat next to Tristan, then directly in front of him is a three-seater with Hunter on one end and two spare seats. Deciding not to be that chick I move around Hunter and claim the spot at the other end leaving Cass to sit in the middle. Cass rounds the couch, looks at me and smiles before sitting and staring directly at Tristan.

Take that asshole!

Our mate could take him out.

Kora, I don't like the douche bag, but we are not asking anything of Cass.

He is our mate.

No, he is your mate and my...We'll discuss this later!

I close the link and fight the groan that wants to break free when I feel Kora laughing inside me, her mocking is starting to piss me off. I may have been raised to believe that when you find your mate that's it, you live happily ever after. That notion died months ago when the love of my life told the truth about her not being my true mate. I had an inkling before then, but I never questioned it, when Cass shifted for the first time in front of me, something changed. It was like Kora had woken up for the first time in years and wanted no–needed to shift and claim her place by her mate. I thought I was losing my mind until *she* told me the truth, I would always choose her regardless of this bond between me and Cass. Skylar Cage was my happily ever after.

"Why the fuck did you say my baby would die if I take her?" The threat is clear in Cairo's tone.

"She must remain here where she belongs–." Cairo cuts Tristan off.

"She belongs with me!" That's it, I have had enough of this shit. I release a growl which has everyone snapping their gazes to me, I look at both Tristan and Ro as I say.

"She doesn't belong to either of you, her rightful place is

with me!" I slowly climb to my feet keeping both these entitled assholes in view. "I loved her more than either of you could understand, there will never be another love story like ours. I fought for my place by her side and made sure she knew every fucking day that she mattered." I focus solely on Tristan as I say. "You may think because you are related that Sky belongs here, but let me tell you something ass wipe. Blood doesn't mean shit where I come from, love, trust and loyalty makes you family. Sky had that with us, not you or this fucked up coven." Tristan nods and slowly climbs to his feet, Cass, Hunt, Cole, Ro and Creed stand as well. Tristan eyes each of them and smiles knowingly.

"I see from how this lot protects you that my sister was well cared for–." Creed scoffs and cuts Tristan off.

"If you think Sky needed our protection then you really don't know who the fuck your sister was." Pride swells inside me at my brother's words.

"The name *Skylar Cage* had grown ass men and alphas shitting themselves at the thought of her coming for them. Your sister was one of the best warriors I have ever known, she taught me everything I know." Cairo's words have tears building in my eyes.

"Sky was someone you never wanted to cross; We all knew she couldn't shift, nor did we know of her magic, but she didn't need to. Her hand-to-hand combat and blade skills were unmatched by any and let me tell you something for free, Sky would have died happily for my sister and Ro. If you know what is good for you, you will give her to them before they tear this place apart." I smile at Cole and mouth a silent *thank you*.

"I can't give you Sky–." Cairo tries to protest but Tristan carries on ignoring his outburst. "We have her body in a stasis, the power Skylar held wasn't just her own." I furrow my brow in confusion.

"What does that mean?" I ask. Tristan focuses on me, seeing that heat in his gaze makes me hate myself even more, as my body begins to warm from that one look he shoots me.

"The night our parents were killed I was just a baby–."

"How old are you?" I blurt out, I cringe when he smiles, I'll admit I'm scared shitless that he may be a minor or worse a virgin, and I just...took advantage of him?

"I'm twenty-eight." A whoosh of air escapes me and I nod. I feel Cass's gaze burning a hole into the side of my head but ignore it, I don't owe him shit. "On that night they transferred their power to Sky, thinking she would return to the coven and our people would help her transfer it between the two of us. Without the help of a coven, having that much unchanneled power inside you is like a bomb waiting to go off." I reach up and cover my mouth as reality slams into me, my knees give out and I flop back into my chair.

He's lying, right?

No, I hear the truth in his words.

"Callie, what's wrong?" I can't answer Cole, my mind is reeling over what I just pieced together. I feel Cass drop down beside me, but I pay him no mind as I slowly lift my gaze to Tristan.

"She told me she couldn't remember how she ended up on her own, if she had of known this place existed, she would still be alive." A whoosh of air escapes Sky's baby brother as he reclaims his seat and steeples his hands in his lap.

"Yes." That one word has me vibrating with anger and Kora thrashing against my ribcage.

"Did you even look for her? Did you give a shit that she was out there on her fucking own?" Tristan opens his mouth but I'm too angry to allow him to get a word in and carry on with my tirade. "You lived in a huge ass house while she slept in the woods, you went to bed each night warm and content, but she didn't. She had no one until she found Cairo, you and this fucking coven are pathetic–."

"You know fucking nothing about me or my coven!" The anger in his voice is tangible. "The coven searched for their heir, when I came of age, I devoted all my time to locating my sister. The reason she is dead is because of him!" He turns angry eyes to Cairo and sneers, Ro reels back in shock but recovers quickly and lets loose a growl.

"Say that again you fucking pussy, I kept that girl alive–."

"You fucking killed my sister!" In a split second, Tristan is on his feet and rushing forward, Cairo has his arm cocked back ready to lay waste to Tristan's face. Belle inserts herself in the middle of them and places her hand out in front to ward Tristan off, Cairo is too slow to move her, her hand touches Tristan and then her eyes roll back.

Fuck, she's having a vision.

Cairo wraps his arm around her waist to steady her, Belle doesn't pass out anymore. Since she completed her transition, her visions haven't been as bad–well, that's what Hunter told me anyway. I see the anger swirling in Cairo's eyes, he wants to pummel Tristan but his devotion to his mate wins out, I look to Tristan and see his face is contorted with concern.

"I never touched her; I swear." Cairo growls in answer to Tristan.

"My sister has visions, these days human touch shouldn't affect her, but you did." Tristan looks to Hunter in surprise.

"I didn't mean to harm her!" Remorse is thick in his tone, but everyone ignores him as Cairo speaks to Belle.

"What do you see beauty?" The way Cairo can change his tone from a raging asshole and instantly switch to a doting lover is something I will never understand. As I stare at him and the way he holds Belle so lovingly, the remainder of my anger toward him flees. I had no right to blame him for what happened to Sky, I know aside from me he loved her just as much as I did.

"He searched, tried everything, coven left him because he wanted to find her. Sky has to be here." Belle's answers are confusing as shit.

"What else do you see?" Before she answers Cairo, her body trembles slightly and then her eyes close for a moment before she blinks them open. Her eyes are back to their normal color, her forehead is creased and when she finally looks at Tristan, heartache is clear in her gaze. She pulls away from Ro, much to his dismay and approaches Tristan warily. He stands tall and stiff as he looks down at the little vampire.

"You loved her more than anything and you love her still." His eyes narrow suspiciously. "Do you want to tell them why Sky is here?" If possible, his body stiffens further.

"I will not–." Belle cuts Tristan off.

"It will help them to understand that you are not a bad guy, I know now and I thank you for this Tristan."

"The fuck are you talking about beauty?" Belle turns and smiles lovingly at her mate before turning to face me. I climb to my feet slowly feeling like this conversation is going to reveal shit that I won't like.

"He took Sky because–."

"I took my sister back because she told me to." Tristan cuts in, we all focus our attention on him and wait with bated breath for him to continue. "I have never seen, spoken to or knew what my sister looked like until after she died. She appeared to me in a dream and told me what I had to do in order to fulfil her last wish."

"We're just supposed to believe that?" The bitterness that coats Cairo's tone doesn't surprise me. I admit it's pretty coincidental that Sky... vanishes after all these years with this insane amount of power she once wielded and now, long lost family members come out of the woodwork to *help* her out.

"I don't care what you believe–." Tired of this constant back and forth I cut in.

"What is the reason she gave you for taking her...body?" Tristin swings his bright hazel eyes to me, I expect to see some form of content in his gaze but instead, all I am met with is a blank stare–he's hiding his emotions from me, why?

"To preserve it until the time came for her best friend's baby to be born." That one sentence has each of us turning to Cairo, his face is a mask of rage, and his upper lip is pulled back in a snarl, his eyes have turned to the onyx of his wolf. Belle places a hand on her mates' chest, Cairo takes a shuddering breath, and his eyes begin to flicker between his normal ice blue and Bexley's. The last thing we need is for him to shift with Jess present, I dart my eyes to her and see Creed wrapping his arms around her whispering in her ear to calm her wolf. If Bex forces a shift, Jess's wolf–Sheba will take over, and given how far along she is, that isn't safe for her or the baby.

"Ro, calm down."

"I'm trying beauty." Cairo grits out between clenched teeth.

"What he did, saved our bean." Cairo stops trembling and Bexley recedes completely allowing Ro control of their body. Cairo looks between Tristan and Belle a few times before finally settling his sights on Tristan.

"Explain what my mate means, *now*." I can hear the alpha power in his tone, and it has Kora wanting to rise against him, I close my eyes and take a few calming breaths. Kora has always been a submissive wolf even when Sky came into our life, but since Cass marked me, Kora wants to prance around and show the world she is better than them. I hate the fact that she thinks her shit don't stink and it irks me.

Cut your shit out!

He is beneath us!

No, he isn't, Bexley cannot be led Kora. Cairo pledged his allegiance to Cassius.

He didn't pledge to me!

I slam the link closed between me and my insufferable wolf, she is out of control, and I can't deal with her shit at this moment.

"Sky told me that I had to keep her body in a stasis, when she died the funnel between her and your child was severed."

"What does that mean?" Cass asks.

"It means that if Sky had remained buried, the link between the two of them would have shattered and the baby would be overrun with the power of three witches, as well as being a shifter and *maybe* a vampire as well. Sky needs to remain in a stasis so that she has an open link with the child." Something isn't adding up, Tristan is hiding something.

SEVEN

CASSIUS

Callie lets loose a growl and moves until there is only a foot of space between her and Tristan, Atticus surges forward and urges me to yank our mate back.

She will rebel if I do that.

She has to learn her place and it isn't behind or in front of us—it's beside us.

Yeah, try telling the crazy she-wolf that.

I close the link between us and watch as she eyes Tristan with a look of trepidation, the fucker stands there with a blank look on his face. Why he is shielding off his emotions from us I don't know, I hate that we are out of our depth here. None of us know enough about these witches to even think of taking them out, if seeing the carnage Sky could cause is an indication to the power they hold, we are fucked.

"You're hiding something, and I want to know what it is. Why is my mate really here Tristan and don't even think about lying to me?" Hearing her freely refer to Sky as her mate has a bitter taste forming in my mouth, I'm getting sick and tired of allowing her free reign. I have given her space to grieve and mourn the loss of her thought-to-be-mate, I won't allow this tirade to continue much longer.

"Fine, but just remember I tried to free you of this pain." A pained look clouds his eyes as he stares down at *my* mate. "A spell was cast to allow Skylar's heart to beat again–." Gasps ring out then shouting ensues, no one can be heard over the other. I shout for them to shut the hell up, but no one pays me any mind, I'm the alpha fucking chief and they will obey me. I allow Atticus to come forward so he can put his wolves in their places. A growl of pure dominance comes from deep within my chest and in a matter of seconds the room is engulfed into silence with each of them looking to me. I meet each of their gazes so they can see the wolf in my eyes and know not to push me.

"Allow him to fucking finish what he was saying, or we will be stuck standing here for another fucking hour!" Everyone except for our mate nods in agreement, Callie lifts her lip in a snarl, and I don't miss how her eyes flicker between her own and her wolf's.

"Don't try to pull that alpha shit on me again, I will never submit to you Cassius–." I won't allow her to berate me or belittle me in front of the others any longer, so I cut her off.

"You will and you have already, is the mark of my wolf on your shoulder not evidence enough of your submission, *mate*." My voice is rough and allows no room for misunderstanding. Everyone here–the bitch ass witch included needs to know she is mine and I will deal with her how I see fit.

"Don't fucking threaten my sister–." I snap my gaze to Creed and growl, before more can come of it, Cairo blocks his best friend from my view, and I narrow my eyes.

"You may have the power to get them to submit, given your rank, but do not start off your reign as alpha chief by bullying your wolves into following you. Respect is earnt Cassius, not given, so show each of them that you are worth following or face the mutiny that will come." I clench my hands into fists at my side wanting nothing more than to punch Ro, but I know if I do, I will have to deal with my sister.

"Look, can we take a seat and I'll explain. I don't need any of you shifting in my home when my daughter is upstairs–."

"You have a kid?" Cole cuts in and asks, for the first time since arriving here Tristan's mask is gone and it is clear for all to see the love he feels for his child in his eyes and the way he smiles wistfully at the thought of her.

"I do, I would rather her first encounter with shifters be a pleasant one instead of a heated dick measuring contest."

"No contest needed, I got the biggest cock here and the only reason Jess and Belle are with these two is because they felt pity for them." Creed and Cairo glare at Cole while the rest of us chuckle, well everyone except for Kayla who seems like she would rather be anywhere but here, why?

"Duly noted, now have a seat and I'll explain." We all do as requested, Callie is stiff as shit next to me but I take this opportunity and use it to my full advantage. I splay my arm across the back of the cane lounger and fight my smirk when I see her shift forward slightly. "Okay, Sky does have a heartbeat but it is only because of a spell our grandmother cast." He looks directly at Callie as he speaks his next words. "My sister is not alive; we cannot raise the dead. In order for us to help the child we had to keep Sky...functioning so the child can funnel the power between itself and Sky and not be overrun by it."

"You owe my sister and Cairo nothing, why would you do this for people you have never met, because of something Sky said?" Tristan turns to Hunter and for the second time I see no mask, just sheer pain in his eyes.

"Witches believe that when someone dies and transfers their power to their successor, a part of their soul intertwining with their magic. For me, helping your sister and her mate means a part of my parents and my sister will live on through their child."

"What do you get out of this? How do you know Kayla and why is she here?" I blow out a frustrated breath, can't these people stay on fucking topic? Kayla scoffs at Creed but still remains silent allowing Tristan to explain her involvement.

"A chance to keep my coven's legacy alive, and help a child to not meet the same fate as my sister. I wish there was someone out there who could have helped my sister. Kayla is here because she got caught lurking in the trees, she explained who she is and why she's here. The rest of it is her story to tell, not mine." Kayla looks away from the group giving us a clear indication that she is not going to share what her reasons are for being here. "I'm happy to take you all to see Sky, but she cannot–." Callie cuts Tristan off.

"You have our word; we won't take her. *But.*" I tense beside her and wait with bated breath for her next words. "When this is all over and the baby is here safely, I'll be taking her back home with me." Tristan clenches his jaw and I hear him grinding his teeth as he fights to keep his composure.

"We'll cross that bridge when we come to it. Now, if you will all follow me." Tristan leads us from the room, I don't look around and take in my surroundings, my sole focus is on the woman who is swinging her hips side to side in front of me. My hands can grip them perfectly, her sways and my mouth waters at the thought of biting into the flesh of her cheek. I'm an ass man, always have been. Don't care if a woman has double DD's or bigger, it's all about the ass for me and let me tell ya, California Reeves has one hell of an ass. I feel my cock stir in my pants, I'm right behind her and when she gets to the stairs in front of me, her ass is right in line with my face. I groan internally and will myself to calm the fuck down, don't get me wrong I am fucking furious with her for allowing another man to touch what is mine. But I don't have to be happy with her in order to fuck her, it might actually help alleviate some of the anger I feel toward her right now. My ogling of her ass and hips comes to a close too fucking soon when we stop outside the closed door, Tristan stands there looking over each of us before finally settling his gaze on Callie. She has grown stiff and tense, I move until her back is plastered against my chest. She can deny it all she wants, but I feel the moment she allows her body to fall into me, I wrap an arm around her waist and anchor her to me. "Are you ready?" The question is for Callie, and everyone knows it.

"If you need to take some time sis–." I cut a look to Cole that has him clamping his mouth shut. I bend down and whisper in her ear, low enough for only her to hear.

"I'll be with you every second, I won't let you break in front of them. I swear." Her body deflates as she nods her reply to Tristan. The silence is deafening and the tension in the air is thick as Tristan turns the knob and slowly pushes the door open and steps inside, the others follow suit, Creed stops in the doorway and looks to his sister. He opens his mouth to speak but I shake my head urging him to leave it and allow me to deal with my mate, once we are alone in the hallway, I spin her around to face me. She refuses to meet my gaze, so I grip her chin and lift it until her eyes meet mine, it destroys something inside me when I see uncertainty shining in her eyes. California Reeves is a force, I mean for fuck's sake her brothers call her a hurricane, seeing this timid unsure woman standing before me, instead of the normal spitfire that chews me a new asshole daily feels all kinds of wrong. "Do you want to go in there?"

She takes a shuddering breath. "I-I don't know."

"We can get out–."

"If I see her again it makes all the dreams of me fooling myself into believing she just...went away...aren't true."

"I'm not gonna pretend to understand what you are going through, but what I do know is, if you don't go in there and see her, you will regret it." I can see I am getting nowhere with handling her with kid gloves so, I decide to take a harsher approach and hope to God, it doesn't bite me in the ass. "You are no meek submissive wolf *Alma*, take a minute and pull yourself together, then you march your ass in there and do whatever it is you need to do to get your closure." A fire blisters in her eyes at my words, we stand here a moment longer until she nods and pulls away from me. To my utter surprise she reaches out and grips my hand in hers, I snap my gaze to hers in questions.

"Thank you." Who knew two little words could bolster someone's ego so much, she releases my hand and heads inside the room that holds the body of the woman she loved.

EIGHT

CALIFORNIA

As I enter the room I feel eyes on me from every direction, their bodies block my view of her and for that I am grateful. I need to take just one more moment to prepare myself for the sight of her, I close my eyes and take in some deep breaths urging myself to hold it together. Skylar Cage was a fierce warrior who was respected by so many and chose to take *me*, as her mate.

I will not dishonor her strength and courage by standing here crying like a coward, even though my chest feels like it is caving in, and I can barely breathe. The sight of her is going to crash the walls I have built around myself, I won't be able to fool myself into thinking she has gone away for a while. The night Belle and Alex sent us to say our goodbyes to Sky, she told me she knew from the moment at the alpha challenge when Cass shifted that he was my true mate.

She knew I slept with him, and he marked me, I thought she would be pissed or hate me, but she didn't. She was happy for me that I had found my soul mate, what she didn't know was, I had already found my soul mate, you only get one of those, and Skylar was mine.

I still haven't had the strength to tear open her favorite Naruto plushie, she told me there were letters inside and they will explain everything. As dumb as it sounds, if I shred her plushie open to get the notes I'll be shredding a part of her and I can't do that—I just can't, well, not yet anyway.

"We're right here with you Callie, when you're ready to open your eyes, you'll be able to see her." I appreciate my bestie so much in this moment, Jess giving me a heads up means everything. I slowly blink my eyes open, and when I see her, another part of me breaks inside. My hand comes up to cover my mouth, I feel hands on me but can't tear my eyes off her to check who it is, I tentatively take a step forward and then another until I'm finally at her side. Cairo is kneeling on the other side of this makeshift bed thing cradling her head against his, I run my gaze over her, she has a silk throw over her waist but I see the band of her jeans just above it, she wears a plain purple shirt, I reach out to grab her hand but freeze when I spot something. The bite mark from Bex is gone!

I shift closer to her face and Ro reluctantly releases her head so I can see her, her beautiful pink lips are puckered like she is about to be kissed, her long lashes don't flutter open like I hope they would. I'd give anything to peer into those beautiful muddy brown eyes one more time! Her blonde hair is fanned out on the red silk pillow, I reach up and cup her cheek, I stifle a gasp, I expected her to feel cold but she's warm. I just stand here and stare down at the woman who gave my life a purpose, Skylar gave me a reason to fight for something better than just being the alpha's little sister. I was so spoiled as a child and she showed me I didn't need materialistic shit to be happy, she taught me to fight, showed me how to love and be one with my wolf.

I feel the tears begin to build in my eyes as I lean down and rest my forehead against hers. I don't care that everyone is watching me, I need this moment with her. I feel the tip of her nose against mine and I sigh as I brush my nose side to side against hers.

"Butterfly kisses baby." I whisper as the first tear falls; I gently place a featherlight kiss to her lips as the rest of the tears fall down my face. "I'll find who outed you baby, I'll make them pay for everything." I hiccup out.

"What happened to the...mark on her neck?" I hear the pain in Cairo's voice and a part of me wants to slap him for having the balls to ask that when his wolf, is the one who fucking did it!

"Witches have ointments that cure wounds, I applied it and my grandmother spelled it so the wound would heal and leave behind no blemishes." Tristan may have answered Ro, but I can feel his and Cass's eyes on me–watching. I ignore them and focus on the beauty before me, even in death she looks stunning.

"I wish there was a cream to bring you back to me." I whisper. I don't know how much time passes as I just stand here touching and holding her hand, I can't keep my hands off her because I just know this will be the last time, I allow myself to see her until we lay her body to rest–again.

"Hey sis–."

"You try to rush her Colton and I'll break your jaw." I roll my lips between my teeth to stop my smile from breaking free. I open the mind link between Cass and me.

Thank you.

For what?

Shutting my brother, the hell up. I hear him laugh inside my mind and when a warmth spreads through me I begin to get angry. I shouldn't be feeling anything for him while I'm fucking standing next to the body of my dead girlfriend!

Time is of no consequence, you take as long as you need,

your big mouth brother can fucking wait. I refuse to answer him, I won't disrespect her like that.

I peek up and see Tristan leaning against the wall next to the window, its then that I realize the sun has set, I've been in here for hours and he hasn't complained once! A small reassuring smile graces his face and I implore him with my eyes asking him to help me bring her back. He releases a breath and then deflates slightly as he shakes his head.

"You can make her heartbeat." I cry out, his eyes hold pain and understanding which just serves to raise my anger. "Why not?" I scream at him; I feel Cass creep up behind me, I peer over my shoulder and growl. He holds my gaze daring me to challenge him, *his* only saving grace is Tristan speaking, which pulls my attention back to him.

"I can make a heartbeat yes, but I cannot restore her soul back to her body. Think of it like she is on a ventilator and the only thing keeping her here is a machine. None of what we have done is okay, our elders have no idea what is happening inside these walls of my coven."

"Why?" Cairo asks.

"What we are doing here is against coven regulations and the penalty for this is having not only mine, but my daughters and grandmother's powers stripped. Witches believe that when you pass, your body must be returned to the earth immediately so that you can be one with nature again. Stealing my sister's body and preparing her body like this breaks every rule, as soon as your mate delivers your baby–."

"Don't say it!" I cut in; my battered heart can't handle hearing those words. Belle isn't due for at least three more months, which means, Sky will remain here in this stasis until then. A part of me wishes she could stay like this forever but then, the rational side of me knows that she isn't at peace. I focus back on her and how she looks so peaceful.

"I'm sorry California." I don't look up at Tristan as I answer.

"Don't be, you didn't kill her." The sharp intake of air from behind me causes me to cringe, I turn to face a guilt-stricken Cairo. "I didn't mean you, I meant whoever outed her to the fucking council." I run my gaze over all the men, including Cassius. "I have never asked any of you for anything, but I am now. Help me find the mole who outed Sky to the council, please, I need to know why they wanted her." Creed is the first to answer.

"You have my word sister; Jess and I are heading back tonight and we will do some digging."

"I've been looking for months and won't stop until I find out, whoever did this will die–slowly." Cairo's words call to the beast inside me. "I'm still trying to find Alex's mole, whoever it is must know something."

"Why do you say that?" Cole asks.

"Because the day we rescued Jess, Jacob was nowhere to be seen. I'm assuming it's because Alex had him distracted while we rescued my sister, his reasons behind that though, I have no idea what those are." Cole nods stiffly but remains silent.

"You are all welcome to spend the night and dine with my family and I, if you so wish?" He voiced it in a way that includes everyone, but from the way Tristan Cage is looking at me, I can tell that invite was meant solely for me.

"Thank you, but Cairo and I will be heading back with Jess and Creed tonight." Tristan pulls his gaze form me and focuses on Belle.

"Very well." Cole is heading back with them as well and Cass has sent Hunter back to pack his shit and fly back to the Wilder pack. Apparently, Cass is staying since his father is overseeing his duties as chief alpha for a few days. Hunter is pissy he has to return to his pack, but even he knows he can't run from his alpha duties forever. I don't think he ever wanted to return to his pack to be honest. I look around the room and that's when I notice someone is missing.

"Where is Kayla?"

"That snake of a bitch!" Cole growls at Creed's outburst, but Tristan cuts in before anyone has a chance to ask what the hell that was about.

"She is with Mera, my daughter." I furrow my brow in confusion but don't say anything, Kayla has always hated kids– maybe people do change? As Creed steps back from Sky, Cairo approaches and a part of me hurts for him when I see a look of devastation plastered across his face. He reaches down and clasps Sky's hand in his, he drops to one knee and nuzzles his cheek against her hand. Tears spring to my eyes, Cairo Cruz is one of the most fearless, head strong men who I view as indestructible and here in this moment he seems so small and lost. I used to get jealous and hate the bond between him and Sky, but now, I can see it clearly for the first time ever. Cairo and Sky loved each other so much because they were all each other had and viewed each other as family–siblings even.

"How does someone say goodbye to their soul mate?" A lump forms in my throat at Cairo's words. "You have been by my side since we were snotty nose kids, you whipped my ass more times than I can count. You are and will always be my saving grace Skylar, I love you so fucking much, and I don't know how I'm ever going to let you go." When I see a tear slide down his cheek, I'm done for, tears cascade down my own, as does Belle and Jess, watching Cairo break in front of them. "I want to be selfish and hold onto you forever but, out of everyone in this fucked up world you are the one who deserves peace the most. I want you to be the first to know this, Belle and I found out the sex of our baby." Gasps can be heard around the room; Belle has a loving smile on her face as she places her hand on her mate's shoulder in a show of her support. "We're having a girl, and we are naming her Skylar Blake Cruz."

"Belle–." She meets Cass's gaze but shakes her head, letting him know they will talk about it later, because, right now Cairo needs this time.

"She will know everything about her aunty Sky, I'll teach her everything you taught me. My daughter will never live like we did, she will be warm and loved from the moment she takes her first breath. I promise to not fuck this up, God knows if I do, you will find a way to come back and haunt me or some shit." Ro takes a deep breath and closes his eyes as he readies himself for his final goodbye. Like me, he won't come back again, it's too painful for the both of us. Ro climbs to his feet and gently places her hand back on the bed and cups her face. "As your alpha, it was my greatest honor to have a warrior like you by my side, there will never be another beta that will ever come close to filling your shoes. But as someone who has loved you for more than half my life–in a sisterly way of course." Light chuckles sound out around the room at that comment. "I want you to know that I owe you everything, I am who I am today because of you, so, give those sons of bitches' hell up there and take no prisoners." He leans and places a tender kiss to her forehead before pulling back, resting his forehead against hers whilst whispering. "I love you forever and always Skylar Cage, I won't say goodbye, because this isn't the end, I'll just say see you soon."

Him not saying goodbye heals a crack in my heart, he is exactly right, this isn't the end. I'll see her again, not today or next week, but I will see her again. Ro moves back and immediately pulls Belle to him and places a kiss to the top of her head, Jess makes her way toward me, and I smile at my bestie. Jess is one of the strongest people I know, and the fact that she kicks ass and stands her ground just adds to her character.

"Whatever you need, whenever you need it, you know I'm here." She smiles and then motions to her giant belly. "Well, until this wee one arrives, after that I may be run off my feet." We both laugh and the laughter helps break the tension that has been thrumming through me since we arrived. "Seriously though, I love you Callie and I'm always here for you no matter what." She leans in closer and stage whispers. "I may be mated to your brother but, *chicks before dicks, always!*" I splutter when Creed growls and begins to mumble under his breath, Jess and I are still laughing our asses off when Creed storms over and grips her hand hauling her from the room. She mouths to *call her* as my brother continues to storm out.

NINE

CASSIUS

After the others left, Callie and I dined with Tristan, but his ghost of a grandmother never showed and nor did his daughter. He told us that Kayla left as well, I don't know what it is with that girl, but something doesn't sit right. No one, I mean no one helps someone without their own gain, she is hiding something, and I am going to find out what it is!

I growl and roll over in this overly large bed punching the pillows to try make myself comfortable, the only fucking reason I agreed to stay and not go with the others is because *she* stayed. There's no way in hell I was leaving her here with that fucking prick Tristan, the guy rubs me the wrong fucking way and don't think I didn't notice the way he looked at her, all day he's been looking at her with fuck me eyes, trailing her every move.

I made sure that when he escorted us to our rooms that hers was next to mine, just in case he decides to take a walk. I want to rip the bastard apart for ever thinking he could touch what is mine but, Atticus doesn't seem to share my thirst for his blood. A creak in the hallway has me sitting up and straining my hearing, when another creak sounds out, I jump to my feet and rush to the door throwing it open. I freeze on the spot when Callie stands in front of me, I narrow my eyes at her as I lean against the door jam and cross my arms over my chest. She runs her heated gaze over me, I'm only wearing a pair of sweats, I smirk when I see lust lurking in her beautiful green eyes.

"Going somewhere *Alma*?" Her tongue darts out to moisten her lips as she shakes her head to clear her thoughts, I'd bet good money on where her mind had wondered to.

"I'm." She stops and clears her throat. "I was just going to get a glass of water." My eyes narrow to slits and a growl pulls from me, she stands before me in a pair of silk sleep shorts and a white sports bra. This girl is testing my fucking restraint!

"Want to put some fucking clothes on first?" The lust in her eyes is replaced by rage at my outburst. She places her hands on her hips and cocks her head to the side causing her long hair to cascade over her shoulder, thoughts of me gripping it and plowing into her invade my mind. I push the memories of fucking her back and shift slightly to hide my semi, blowing my load daily in the shower hasn't helped dull the ache of wanting to be inside her again.

"You sexist prick! You stand here shirtless and yet you look down your perfect nose at me?" She scoffs but I smile wide causing her to glare up at me.

"You think my nose is perfect?" She growls but there is no heat to it, then throws her hands in the air as she storms past me. I chase after her and reach out gripping the back of her neck as I yank her backward, she stumbles but manages to find her footing as I slam her against the wall. Her eyes flash to her wolf's and I growl in satisfaction, I apply enough pressure to slightly block her windpipe as I lean down until we are nose to nose. "You run; I chase." My voice is gruff, thanks to Atticus being so close to the surface, the thrill of the chase turns him on.

"Get your hands off me."

"Why? You don't seem to mind letting others touch what is mine." I lower my voice to barely above a whisper and I make sure she can see the threat in my eyes when I say. "You let anyone touch this." I cup her pussy in my other hand and relish in her gasp. "I will break every fucking bone in their hand and make you watch. I've let you stew in your sorrow for long enough, I'm done playing this game." I don't give her a chance to respond, I grip her waist and lift. Her instincts kick in and she locks her legs around my waist and rest her hands on the tops of my shoulders whilst glaring down at me.

"What the fuck are you doing, Cassius?" Hearing my name come out of her mouth only intensifies the hardness of my cock, I ignore her question and walk briskly to my room, kicking the door shut behind us. I grip her waist and throw her backwards, she shrieks but it's cut off when she bounces on the bed. She tries to push herself up but I'm faster, I climb on top of her and nestle myself between her legs, she strikes out and manages to land a punch to my jaw. I snarl and grab both her wrists in my hand and pin them above her head as I grip her chin in my free hand. She tries to turn away, but I squeeze hard enough to inflict pain until she finally meets my stare, anger and hatred shine in her eyes but so does lust. I scent the air and growl my approval when I smell her arousal.

"So, you like being treated like a common whore?" She growls and her eyes change to her wolf.

"I'm not a fucking slut!"

"How many people have you fucked California?"

"Fuck. You." She emphasizes each word. I curl my lip in disgust and scoff.

"Not until I know whose cock has been inside you since I shattered your fucking perfect reality." Her gaze morphs from rage and hate to disgust.

"You may be my mate, but you don't fucking own my body! I will fuck whoever I want–." I cut her off with a growl so vicious and loud I'm sure it woke the others in the house, I get right in her face until our noses are touching.

"I'll kill anyone you touch; you make fuck me eyes at anyone and they are dead." Her eyes gleam with triumph, I pull back slightly and make sure to keep the shock from my face when she smiles.

"Oh baby, what makes you think I've been fucking a man?" I glare down at her tightening my hold on her wrists as she thrust her hips up and grinds against my hard as fuck cock. "You know better than anyone that I had never been with a man until I fucked your brains out." I grip her hip to stop her from wriggling beneath me or risk looking like an amateur and cum in my fucking pants from her dry humping me.

"The fuck are you trying to say?" I grit out, she relaxes in my hold, and I see that mischief look in her eyes, she is about to unleash hell on me. I'm rendered fucking speechless when she lifts her head and brushes her nose against mine licking my lips! Because I am a fucking fool and allow my cock to override my rational side, I relent to her touch, the she devil clamps my top lip between her teeth, I pull back releasing a growl, the metallic taste of my own blood invades my mouth. "The fuck was that for?"

She smiles wickedly and licks a droplet of my blood from her lip. "I prefer to eat pussy rather than suck dick, so stew on that tidbit of info for a moment, *baby*." I peer down at her in confusion until the penny finally fucking drops, she must see it in my eyes when everything clicks into place. "What's that line again?" She pretends to think on it for a moment before continuing. "Oh yea, it wasn't you it was me. Or was it, right person wrong time?" She shrugs as her vindictive words yet again stab me in the gut. The expression on her face is enough to tell me that she will fight everything I throw at her, including not having the strength to let her go.

"From now on, you sleep next to me." She opens her mouth to bite back but I cover it with my hand. "If you run, I'll chase you down California and trust me, you won't like the fucking beast that finds you. Mark my words, you are mine and come hell or high water, you will stand by my side until the dirt covers my body when I'm six-feet deep."

She starts to shuffle so I tighten my hold across her mid drift, trying to let sleep claim me again, but then she shimmies her ass against my morning wood, my eyes snap open and a groan rises from my throat. She lay still and that's when I realize she's still asleep. After our sparing match last night, I held her firm against me in a spooning position in case she tried to bolt, I knew she was emotionally exhausted, literally falling asleep as soon as her head hit the pillow. I on the other stayed up for hours and watched her sleep like a fucking creeper.

"I have to pee." Her voice is course with sleep.

"Hold it, I'm warm and comfy." She huffs out her annoyance without saying anything further. I contemplate whether to tell her that she moaned my name three times last night? Instead, I opt to ask this question, which has been bugging me since yesterday. "What does *butterfly kisses* mean?" She stiffens in my hold and her breaths come in fast pants; I can tell this has a deeper meaning to her than I thought. Minutes tick by and I resign myself to the fact she isn't going to answer me.

Her voice is low and tinged with pain as she answers. "It was our thing, Sky found it hard to show affection in public, so she came up with *butterfly kisses*." She sniffs and I feel like a piece of shit for making her cry, I roll her over to face me climbing on her at the same time. She's too lost in her pain to register the compromising position she is in; I cup her face between my hands and wait for her to focus on me, grief is evident in her gaze.

"She was your person, I get that. I'm not trying to replace her Callie; I could never do that. You both shared a history that I cannot compete with, not that I'm trying to, I want to help you–."

"You can't."

"Why? Because if you smile or feel any remote kind of happiness you're afraid you might be shitting on her memory? She wouldn't want that–"

"How the fuck do you know?" The venom in her tone tells me that I have to be honest with her.

"Because, I know how you fucking feel! My brother fucking died, and I would give anything in this goddamn fucking rat shit world to bring him back. It kills me each and every day that I get to wake up and he doesn't! I hate that it was him and not me...it should have been me." I whisper the last part as I sit back on my hunches and drop my chin to my chest. I miss Blake so fucking much and the guilt of not being able to save him eats away at me daily. He was my younger brother and my one job as the eldest was to protect my siblings, God knows I couldn't even do that. Shame eats away at my insides; I find it hard to be in the same room with my family, purely because I feel like they blame me for his death. I'm so lost in my inner turmoil that I hadn't registered her hands cupping my cheeks and she gently lifts my head until we lock eyes. For the first time since marking her, she stares at me without any malice in her gaze, her thumbs stroke my cheeks, as if I'm a moth to a flame I close the space between us, then kiss her. She tenses and I pull back feeling like an asshole–.

"Do it again." My eyes widen at her request, I reach out and grip the back of her neck to hold her in place, as I slowly lean down, I search her gaze giving her ample enough time to back out. I smash my lips against hers and groan when our tongues entwine together, my cock strains against my sweats begging for release. I use my free hand to grip her waist and my weight to push her back against the bed, nestling myself between her legs, I groan when I feel the warmth from her pussy against my throbbing cock. A moan tumbles from her when I rock against her, I get lost in a frenzy of lust as I explore her body with my hands. I want to tear the clothes from her and lick every inch of her soft skin and bury my face right between her thighs. I pull back and grip the edges of her sleep shorts, slowly sliding them down whilst holding her stare, I wait for her to protest, throwing her shorts to the side indicates I'm good to go. I peel my gaze from hers and focus on her pussy, I dart my tongue out to moisten my lips, my mouth begins to water at the sight of it.

"If I start, I won't stop." She smirks and opens her legs wider; my thoughts dissipate as my chest starts to burn. I grip her waist and in one swift move I roll us over until she is strad-dling me, her gaze meets mine. "Get the fuck on my face and ride it." Her pupils dilate, she shuffles up my body and places her legs either side of my face, she grips the headboard as I slap her ass. She squeaks out her surprise, I do the same to the other cheek but this time she moans, I latch onto the globes of her ass and push her down onto my waiting tongue. She cries out as I moan at the taste of her, she tastes like honey, it's fucking addic-tive and I've been dying to taste her again. I lap at her opening and push my tongue inside her, she moans and pushes down against me. I lick my way up her slit and then suck her clit into my mouth.

"Fuck, shit, yes Cass." I continue eating her cunt like a starving man, tremors start to wrack her body so I pick up my pace flicking my tongue even faster, then she detonates, coming all over my face as she screams my name. I push her off me and climb on top, I push my sweats down enough for my cock to spring free. Her hazy eyes bulge at the sight of it.

"When the hell did you get your dick pierced?" I smirk down at her gripping my shaft, a couple of pumps and a bead of pre cum coats my head, she moistens her lips and her tongue darts out, in hunger to taste me. I swipe my thumb over the head of my cock and hiss, I place my thumb against her lips and smear it, she willingly opens her mouth and sucks my thumb whilst moaning at the taste. I want to drag this out and punish her body for everything she has done and put me through, but the truth is, I need to be buried balls deep inside her more than I need air right now!

"I'm gonna fuck you hard and fast, I don't give a fuck if you don't come again." I don't wait for a response as I line my cock up to her entrance, I slam inside her, she screams out. If I wasn't still so pissed at her for fucking Tristan, I might have given her time to adjust to the size of my cock, instead I thrust my hips and fuck her like she isn't my mate. I need this to release some of the pent-up rage I have inside me.

"Fuck, Cass. Just like that." I growl and place my hand on her face and push it to the side, I can't bear to look at her right now let alone hear her voice. Her pussy clenches my cock trying to milk it of its cum, but I'm not ready to let go yet I pull out of her and flip her onto her stomach.

"Ass up, face down, now!" She obeys me like a good girl, huh, so she is happy to be dominated in bed but not in day-to-day life.

Once she is in position, I massage the globes of her ass giving one side a good slap, she lurches forward before a moan spills from her treacherous lips. I grip her cheeks and spread them, at the same time leaning down to lick her ass, she tenses, but after a moment when she lets go of her modesty and allows herself to feel the pleasure I'm inflicting on her, she pushes back against my face. I quickly pull back and slap the other side, she yelps but isn't fooling anyone I can see how wet her cunt is from me eating her ass. "Next time, I'm fucking your ass and you're going to love every minute of it." A shiver runs through her, I can see the slight blush on the back of her neck and know that my words have excited her.

"Do it now." She taunts.

"I told you, this time is about me not you, so shut the fuck up and take my cock like a good girl." I slam my dick inside her, and we both cry out at the feeling, I fuck her at a ruthless pace, I feel her body begin to tremble as she is on the cusp of another orgasm, so I pull out and slap her cunt. She screams in pain, but it quickly turns into a horny moan, I lay another smack to each of her cheeks and relish in the red hue that coats her ass. I slam inside her again, the only sounds that can be heard is skin slapping and her cries of ecstasy. My balls begin to tighten, I know I said I didn't care if she came or not, but I need to feel her pussy clench my cock as I spill my seed deep inside her. I reach around and pinch her clit between my fingers, she screams out.

"Cassius, I'm coming." I use my other hand to grip the back of her neck to hold her in place as I fuck the shit out of her, she screams my name loud enough to wake the whole fucking house, I slam into her two more times before I roar out my release and shoot jets of my cum inside her wet cunt.

TEN
CALIFORNIA

After Cass pulled out of me, I leapt from the bed running to my room and jumped straight into the shower scrubbing myself raw trying to rid his scent from my body, I can't believe I was powerless to resist what just happened! What the fuck was I thinking? The only positive out of that ordeal was he didn't mark me again, I don't think I would have been able to handle being claimed by him, again, without my consent. I fear that Tristan or worse his daughter may have overheard us!

I sit here on the bed in nothing but my towel as guilt washes over me, I just got my brains fucked out while my dead girlfriend is just down the hall. What the fuck is wrong with me? I bury my face in my hands and try to fight off the feeling of shame and guilt that is welling inside me. I need to get my shit together–.

"Here I thought you would be glowing in the after effects of your mating." I leap to my feet in fright at the sound of his voice, I was so lost inside my own head, I didn't even hear him enter. I clutch my towel tighter and try to appear unaffected by his mere presence, yeah, I sure as fuck need help, clearly, I'm not well in the head.

"What are you doing here, Tristan?" He rolls his lips between his teeth, and I become a slave to my hormones as I zero in on his luscious lips.

"See something you like?" I snap my gaze back to his, a sly smirk graces his handsome face and I groan internally. He just admitted to hearing me fuck Cass and yet he stands here eyeing me like a starved lion, I shiver under the intensity of his gaze.

"Why are you here?" He leans against the door jam and crosses his arms over his chest, much like Cass did last night. He's wearing his three-piece suit like armor, stunningly handsome whereas Cass, is rugged and rough around the edges but that just adds to his sex appeal. I mentally facepalm myself, I have to get the fuck away from these two egotistical males before I wind up spit roasted—wait, could that be an option?

Stop it Callie, Sky lye's meters away and you're acting like a wanton slut!

I mentally berate myself and cringe when I see Tristan cock a brow. "Something on your mind?"

"What the hell do you want?" My temper is rising but I'm not angry at him, I'm pissed at myself for allowing the two males in this house get under my skin, unfortunately stirring something inside me, other than despair over the loss of my girlfriend.

"I actually came to see if you would join me in my study, we have a few things to discuss." His demeanor shifts from relaxed to on edge, the change in the atmosphere has me on alert and Kora rising to the surface.

"Is everything okay?" He runs a hand through his hair and sighs tiredly.

"Get dressed and meet me downstairs." He pushes off the door jam and enters the room smiling wide, his rapid mood change is giving me whiplash. Before I can question him, Cass appears in the open doorway, his eyes land on me and his lips pull back in a snarl glaring at me in just a towel. His gaze swings to Tristan and a growl tears from him, his eyes shift to his wolf's with each step he takes into the room. I act on autopilot as I move in front of Tristan and block him from Cass's impending approach, Cassius stops when his chest smacks into my face, I attempt to take a step back but freeze when I feel Tristan at my back, I gasp when I feel his hands on my waist, Cass releases another growl in warning.

"Get your hands off her before I break every fucking bone in your body." I feel Tristan's chest vibrate with laughter and groan; this guy has a death wish. Cass is a wolf and will kill Tristan in seconds!

"See, your words say one thing alpha but the intrigue in your eyes says another. She may be your mate but that doesn't mean, she belongs to *you*." The way Cass vibrates with rage and how his gaze is boring into Tristan shouldn't get me hot and needy, but it does–see what I mean? I'm fucking broken. Cass grips me under my arms and lifts me, I screech in shock and on instinct lock my legs around his waist, I'm well aware my bare pussy is plastered against him, my towel starts to loosen so I attempt to shift myself to hold it in place, but his growl stops me. Tristan let's out a dark chuckle, clearly, he doesn't realize the danger he's in when he steps closer, nearly flush against my back. Cass narrows his eyes to slits as he glares at him over my shoulder.

"Touch her and I will kill you." The warning in his voice is clear.

"Oh, but I already have and I'm dying for another taste." This time I groan out loud, Tristan is provoking Cass and I have to end this before they really do fight it out.

"Boys, I'm right here–."

"Shut the fuck up, *Alma*," Cass snaps, I still in his hold when Tristan begins to laugh like a maniac, I peer over my shoulder and furrow my brow in confusion as he points at Cassius.

"You possessive fuck, even your pet name is like a brand on her." I turn back to Cass and ask.

"What does he mean?" He grinds his teeth but doesn't answer me.

"It means *soul* in Spanish." My eyes widen in surprise, Cass's hold on me tightens at Tristan's admission.

"Go fuck yourself, dick." Cass turns back to me and the anger in his eyes calls to the darkest parts of me. "Pack your shit, we're leaving–."

"Not today you're not." Cass opens his mouth to rebuke his claim, but I cut him off when I grasp his face and turn him to meet my stare.

"Tristan has information he wants to share with us, we need to hear him out." I plead. He shifts his gaze back to Tristan and grits out.

"You have five minutes."

"Should we let *our* girl change first?" I gasp at the audacity of him to claim me as *their* girl, I'm no one's! I was someone's girl once, but that stopped when she died months ago, the reminder of her has me tensing and struggling to get out of Cass's death hold. Yet again, I'm reduced to a horny bitch in heat by these two men. Cass reluctantly sets me on my feet with a grunt and flick of his head toward the adjoining bathroom. I roll my eyes but don't argue as I grab my yoga pants and a white crop tee and sports bra, I ruffle through my bag for panties and discreetly pull them out tucking it into the pile of my clothes, the hiss that escapes them tells me they saw the red thong.

Sitting in Tristan's study only intensifies the awkward silence, Cass and I each occupy the two chesterfield chairs while Tristan sits behind his desk in a leather wingback. His fingers drum against his desk and it's beginning to unnerve me, I've never been one to wait and my patience is running out.

"Can we get on with this?" I snap, Tristan's frosty stare meets mine and the emotionless mask he has on his face has me fighting my urge to cringe. Gone is the playful sex crazed man I willingly gave my body to and now in front of me is the arrogant club owner I propositioned for sex the night I found out who he really is.

"She'll be here in a moment, don't get your lacy thong in a twist." I narrow my eyes, Cass growls in warning electing a smirk from Tristan. I hear the chesterfield screech under the pressure of Cass's death grip and tense waiting for him to strike out at Tristan for being an ass, before it can escalate further the door opens and our head's turn toward the intruder. My mouth drops open in shock when a brown-haired little girl waltzes into the room unaware of the tension and beelines for Tristan. He smiles wide as he pushes back from the desk and holds his arms out for her, she leaps into his arms and snuggles into him. When her gaze lands on me I still, a lump forms in my throat as her muddy-brown eyes lock with mine, her cherry colored lips hitch up into a wide care-free smile, its then that I realize who she is—she's Tristan's daughter. "Mera, meet my friends Cass and Callie." She turns to Cass and a blush begins to coat her cheeks, she waves shyly at him before giggling and burying her face in her father's chest.

"He's really pretty, daddy." She mumbles against his chest, Tristan's face contorts into a disgusted look, Cass grunts and smirks cockily back at him. My god, these guys egos are bigger than their...heads?

"He isn't pretty, he looks like a cross between Shrek and Donkey if you ask me." I choke on my own spit and try to mask my laughter by coughing, obviously failing miserably feeling Cass's gaze boring into the side of my head.

"She's the lady, isn't she daddy?" Tristan's gaze snaps to me before he quickly averts it and gives a subtle nod. Her eyes capture mine and I'm immediately transported into abyss of pain.

She has her eyes.

She isn't her!

I know Kora, I know.

I wish I was able to shield you from your pain, allow me to shift and I can give you that reprieve.

The thought is very tempting, with Cass here, Kora won't try to run. We haven't shifted in a while, and I know that we need to do it soon or I run the risk of Kora forcing the change and that is never pleasant.

"Yeah, she is." Tristan's softly spoken words pull me back to the present.

"How do you know me?" I ask. Mera beams and claps excitedly in her father's lap, I look to Tristan, he shrugs and smiles down at his baby girl.

"You're California, aunty Sky told me you were really pretty." I gasp and sink back into my chair.

"You said none of your family has ever met Skylar!" The accusation in Cass's voice is clear, Mera's tiny button nose scrunches up in confusion. Tristan glares at Cass, the frosty look in his eyes has shivers sliding down my spine.

"You may challenge me at any given moment, but you will

not raise your voice again, whilst my daughter is present. I never lied to you, Cassius." A growl tumbles from Cass and Mera shy's away huddling into her father further. I reach over and place my hand on Cass's arm, his gaze snaps to me, I shake my head urging him to calm down. Regardless even if Tristan lied, his daughter doesn't have to bear witness to grown men fighting.

"Daddy." Tristan pulls his glare from Cass as he strokes Mera's back soothingly and shushes her. I need answers, so I push on.

"I'm sorry about Cass, his wolf doesn't like being left in the dark." A small timid smile touches her lips. "Can you tell me how you saw your aunty...Sky?" My voice pitches slightly saying her name, the feeling of the guy's gaze boring into me tells me they didn't miss it. Mera peeks up at her father, he nods encouragingly for her to tell her story.

"Aunty Sky visits me." My brows jump to my hairline and my eyes widen.

"How?" Cass asks.

"Mera isn't like myself and Sky, I have the power to manipulate nature like my sister but obviously not as strong. Mera on the other hand can communicate with spirits; she is what we call a shadow walker." My mind is reeling after listening to Tristan describe what his daughter is able to do.

"You can see her, like now?" I hear the hope in my own voice, she smiles sadly and shakes her head. "What does that mean?" I urge, Tristan cuts glare to me in warning and I instantly feel like a bitch for pushing a child for answers.

"Merz, why don't you go find Nona and then I'll come get you once I finish up here?" She smiles and places a kiss to her dad's cheek before scurrying out of the room. My focus is solely on Tristan as I wait for him to elaborate more, I need to know everything! "Mera stopped seeing Sky the night you and I slept together." The pity in his voice, even the growls coming from Cass can't stop the sob that breaks free. I bury my face in my hands and weep, of course she would stop coming, why the fuck would she stay here when I fucked her brother? I feel Cass's hand on my shoulder, ignoring him as I do Tristan when he places his hand on my other shoulder. "It isn't what you think Callie." I drop hands and glare at him, he rests against his desk with a smug look on his face that makes me want to slap him.

"How the fuck do you know what I'm thinking?" He raises his hands as if surrendering.

"Let me explain before you have a tantrum and storm off, you're a grown ass woman for Christ's sake, pull yourself together." My mouth drops open in shock, but it quickly bleeds to anger, I strike out and slap him. My hand stings from the pressure but I ignore it as I lock eyes with the devil in a three-piece suit.

"You get that one for free, do it again and I'll punish you in a way only I will enjoy." It's meant to be a threat but even I can decipher the sexual innuendo in his words. I feel Cass press up beside me but don't take my eyes off Tristan.

"Try it and see–." Tristan cuts of Cass's would be threat.

"She stopped coming to Mera because her business here was finished. Witches are not like wolves or vampires; we don't die and go to heaven or whatever the fuck it is."

I throw my hands up in frustration. "What the fuck does that mean?" I scream at him, Tristan pushes off the desk and gets in my face, Cass pushes against his chest in warning. It does nothing to deter him though, his next words are like a bucket of ice to my bloodstream.

"It means Cassius isn't the only man you will be with; you are as much mine as you are his!" I choke on air; Cass drops his arm and I feel through our mate link his confusion. "Skylar's last bit of business on earth was making sure that you and I met." I shake my head trying to deny his claim. "Did you notice how your wolf never tried to attack me when I fucked you? and never rises up to kill me when I get too close? Or even since the moment you walked through those front doors having both Cass and I here that you and your wolf felt at peace for the first time in months?"

ELEVEN

CASSIUS

After Callie ran from the room and took off outside to shift, I have been sitting on the back patio waiting for her return. I know I can access the mate bond to track her but I need this time to process as much as she does. It sickens me that his words held truth, the fact Atticus hasn't forced a shift and torn him apart for touching our mate makes me wonder if he is right. It isn't unheard of for a wolf to have two mates, it's just extremely rare. I scoff to myself, nothing about my family or hers is normal so why doesn't this turn of events shock me?

"He never wanted this; you know." I'm on my feet in a split second as I spin and come face to face with an old woman, her gray eyes shine with wisdom, wrinkles cover her face and hands, the sundress she wears falls to her feet and the sheer cardigan she wears wards off the nip in the air. Her gray hair is piled in a bun atop her head, fluffy pink slippers poke out of her dress as she steps toward me. This woman resembles all the naughty nanas from TV shows I used to watch as a kid, she pats me on the chest as she claims the wicker beside the one, I just vacated. "Sit down, I'll explain what my grandson did not." I hesitantly claim my seat eyeing her at the same time; I haven't forgotten that she is the one that cast the spell on Sky. Tristan said this woman is strong and the fact that she is appearing to me as meek and weak tells me she is up to something.

"You can drop the act." She cuts her gaze to mine and a sly smirk touches her lips.

"What gave me away?" I scoff.

"The fact that your eyes shine with cunningness, your hair is too neat for a nana who plays dolls with her great grand-daughter. The stale scent of cigarettes doesn't help either, but the winner was, the stench of whiskey on your breath and it isn't even eleven in the morning yet." She throws her head back and rasps out a laugh, I have no idea why, but I laugh a long with her, she pats my arm and winks.

"You're good, really good. I haven't met many shifters in my lifetime, but my god, your races reputation proceeds you, alpha." Her nod of respect toward my status tells me this woman knows a lot more than she portrays.

"You have me at a disadvantage, *mistress*." With all the research the packs have done on witches we learnt that the elder generation of witches or warlock's titles are master and mistress.

"Oh, don't play coy with me boy, you may read a lot of books about us, but half of that stuff is horse shit." I choke on my own laughter, her eyes gleam with mirth.

"You are not what I expected...?"

"You can call me *kitty*." Fucking hell, I throw my head back and bark a laugh. I haven't laughed this hard in so long, this woman is a fucking hoot. "Shh, or else king stick up his ass will find me." I cough to try and control my laughter as I quirk a brow at her.

"*King stick up his ass?*" She rolls her eyes.

"I love my grandson, lord knows I do, but that boy is a fun-sucker!" I splutter.

"A *fun-sucker?*"

"He sucks the fun out of everything, that boy needs to get his balls drained more often." The reminder of *who* last drained his balls washes the lightness I was feeling away, replaced by unease. "Why do you look like I punched your dick?"

Jesus Christ! This woman is worse than a bunch of teenage boys at a party.

"No one punched anyone's dick, I was just reminded of something."

"Well, do you care to share with the rest of us?" I scrunch my face at her forwardness, I hate to admit it but it's...refreshing. "I'm a bored old woman, give me some juicy gossip to keep me entertained." *Fuck it.*

"Apparently my mate is also your grandson's and I want to tear his fucking throat out."

"I see." I glare at her.

"You *see* what?" She smiles and it irks me that she has a knowing look in her eyes.

"Are you more pissed that your wolf knew about this before you did or the fact that the idea of spit roasting your mate appeals to you?" I open my mouth to berate her but pause, do I want this? What the fuck, no I don't want this, Callie is mine and only mine!

"I've had my fair share of threesomes *Kitty*, but the idea of sharing Callie doesn't appeal to me one iota." She rolls her lips over her teeth and nods.

"Open your mind, alpha. Don't view life the way humans do, we are not held to their standards, witches don't normally end up in a monogamous relationship. I had three men once and let me tell you, the things those men could do with their tongues–."

"Okay." I cut in not wanting to hear the rest, just the thought of her getting railed has me shuddering. The sound of footfalls alerts me someone is approaching, when I catch a whiff of their scent and groan. Tristan appears a moment later, he darts his gaze between Kitty and I and scrubs a hand down his face before locking eyes with me.

"She told you about her harem, didn't she?"

"Yeap." I pop the *P* to emphasize my discomfort, Kitty on the other hand just laughs.

"Geez, both of you need to find that girl, strip her bare and fuck her until her pussy is a mold of your cocks–."

"Jesus! That is enough of that."

"Amen to that." I interject agreeing with Tristan. Kitty smirks at each of us and winks.

"See, I knew you two would agree on something." She pats my arm twice before standing to go in search of Mera, telling Tristan to stay with me and sort out our *shit*, as she put it. He sighs before dropping into the seat Kitty vacated, I don't even look at him, I can't. The silence stretches between us, we both have our legs stretched in front gazing out at the manicured lawn.

"How long did you know about her?" He doesn't perceive to not understand who the *her* is in question.

"I didn't find out until the day after I slept with her, if I had of known..."

"Would it have changed anything?" A whoosh of air escapes him, I peer at him out the corner of my eye, his face is etched in pain.

"I don't know, I want to say yes because of who she is to my sister. But I don't know. I thought I had found my ever after with Mera's mother but that was just a fucking lie." That piques my interest.

"What happened?" His head rolls to the side as he eyes me.

"I'm only going to tell you this because I'll spell you afterward so you can't share this with anyone else, I can't risk Mera knowing the truth."

I scrunch my face but nod none the less. "I'm a bastard, but I will never do anything to harm a child, you have my word on that." He nods but I can see he still doesn't trust what I say.

"Mera's mother was a power seeker–."

"A what?"

"It means she only sought me out because she wanted the power I had, if truth be told I never did, Skylar had it all. Gemma didn't find this out until a couple of months after we started dating, she left me and I was heartbroken. Nine months later she shows up on my doorstep with a baby and says its mine, I'm man enough to admit that I was more excited to see her back than question the paternity of the baby."

"Is she your daughter?" I cut in, his eyes harden and his muscles coil.

"I never took the test; I didn't need to. Mera is my daughter and that is all there is to say on the matter." I nod in understanding, I hate to admit it, but I respect him for the decision he made, he cared more about his daughter than DNA and that goes a long way in my books.

"What happened to her mother?"

"She wanted my power for my daughter." I suck in a sharp intake of air, what the fuck kind of person trades their child for power?

"How do you do that?"

"My kind choose their successor, so when we die our power goes to them and the elders of our own coven help us balance the influx, so we don't combust...like Sky."

"You gave her your power?" A haunted look crosses his face as he shakes his head.

"No, my grandmother wouldn't allow me to." It hits me.

"Kitty took your place; she gave up her power so you didn't have to." He nods solemnly.

"Yeah, something like that." Silence descends once again but this time it isn't uncomfortable.

"How do you know she is your...mate?" He chuckles.

"We don't call our partners *mates*; we call them our betrothed or bonded. I didn't know until Mera told me, when we meet our betrothed and bond with them as one, our power gets a... boost, I guess you can call it. The day after we slept together, I felt my power growing and when Mera told me, I knew."

"What if she doesn't want this?"

"*Keep it real*, what you really want to know is, if you can deal with sharing her. I can't answer that for you Cassius, what I will state is I won't give up without a fight. My whole life has consisted of fighting for my family, when Gemma came into my life, I thought I had found the one, but we both knew after we slept together that there was no bond. I was okay with that because I loved her, Mera gave it meaning again. I was okay being alone to sow my wild oats at my clubs when the need struck, until I met Callie. Something about her called to me, I shut down the idea of a betrothed years ago, until she broke through that barrier without even trying." I snort.

"She has that effect on people."

"I don't want to fight you on this–."

"Then don't." The heat of my words isn't lost on him. "I am the chief alpha, and she is my mate."

"So, this whole cock measuring contest is because you are worried about your wolves finding out that your mate is bonded to another?" I grit my teeth and clench my fists, Atticus stirs inside me and that's when it hits me, if my own wolf won't challenge him for her, then he must be linked to us somehow.

"I don't give a fuck what others think, I'm here for her and that is it."

Time passes as we sit and wait for her return, Kitty was kind enough to serve us supper out here, Tristan disappeared to snag us a bottle of whiskey and a couple of tumblers. The whiskey warms me from the inside, I admit, spending this time with Tristan has given me a chance to know him a bit better, he isn't such a fuckwit like I thought.

"She'll come back, right?"

"Her wolf won't allow her to run from me, Kora will bring them back."

"How does that work? With your wolves I mean, do you all name them?"

"Nah, when we unlock our shifter side our wolves already have their names, they are like us in much the same way. Callie is fire and snappy, so is Kora, I'm headstrong and dominant, so is Atticus."

"Atticus, so that's your wolf's name."

"Yeah, so do witches have other halves?" He chuckles and shakes his head.

"Nah, we're not that cool. Each of us are born with our powers, the elders help us master our gifts and they determine which element we fit into."

"What does that mean?"

"Witches are fueled by nature, like earth, wind, water, fire and it is very rare to be born with the ability to control both. It's not like the movies where we can cast a spell, and someone disappears, nor can we blink to transport ourselves. There are some witches who can cast spells, but they are very *very* rare." He lifts his hand and mumbles something under his breath, the wind around us begins to pick up and the warm night breeze turns frosty in seconds. Tristan closes his hand, and the wind starts to slow down, the slight breeze returns to its normal warmth. "I have control over air."

"What did Sky have?"

"She could control, air, water and I believe she was able to tap into our father's magic. Our mother controlled water, our father's gift for example was he could uplift a tree and move it with the flick of his wrist, so I am told."

"So, did Sky have the ability to control all three?" Again, he shakes his head.

"No, I would have inherited my father's and she, our mothers. The elders would have helped the both of us with our control and eventually with guidance we would have learnt to master it."

"I need to know, my sister's baby–." He holds my gaze as he cuts me off.

"You have my word, Cassius. No harm will befall your sister's child, when it is safe for us to move Sky, I will personally assist in the birth and make sure that child is trained until it can handle the power that's inside her. I'm pulling every string I have to work out if I am dealing with a witch baby or a baby from three different races."

"Why would you do that?"

"Cairo Cruz gave my sister a home, her only request aside from making sure California was taken care of, was that I keep his baby safe and guarantee it lives." I hold my hand out to him; he stares at it for a moment before placing his in mine. We shake as I hold his gaze and offer him the one thing I can.

"I, Cassius Wilder, chief alpha to all wolves, grant you Tristan Cage safe passage across all my lands." I feel the alpha decree pass through me, knowing that each alpha under me will feel it too, any alpha that comes in contact will now be able to sense he is off limits and not to be harmed.

TWELVE
TRISTAN

I stare at him in shock, after our encounter earlier this is the last thing I expected him to do. He has just given me access to all the wolf packs. If only I can offer him the same thing with the covens and tell them the truth about why we are hiding out at my grandmother's house, but I can't, I'm just making headway with him. They have no idea what grams has done, she did it with good intentions but it blew up in our faces a couple of months ago.

"Well, this is unexpected." Both Cass and I stand and turn to face her as she stands at the far end of the patio, stark naked. Sticks and debris are scattered throughout her hair, mud is smeared all over her delectable body. Cass pulls his shirt off and chucks it to her, I instantly hate the sight of his shirt on her when she puts it on. Not out of jealousy, but because his fucking shirt just blocked my view of her pert tits. "I'm...uh, I'm gonna take a shower."

"Want a hand?" Her gaze snaps to me and I can see the unease creeping into her eyes, she has to let go of this guilt she is fucking carrying.

"We should talk, Alma." Callie skirts her gaze to Cass, her shoulders hunch forward, and she gives him a curt nod.

"Can I take a shower first and put some clothes on?" Wanting to push her boundaries even further and shatter this shell of grief she has around her I say.

"We can carry this on in your room, I mean, it's not like either of us are strangers to what lay beneath that shirt." Cass groans and pins me with a dirty look, I refuse to back down. Him handling her with kids gloves and giving her space clearly hasn't worked, it's not in my make up to allow someone to get away. When I want something, I won't stop until I have it and, I want California Reeves.

"You think because we fucked that you know me, newsflash asshole, you don't, not that I give a shit what the ghost of my girlfriend tells your daughter, I may be mated to him, but I sure as fuck am not mated to you, so please, go fuck yourself." Cassius shifts subtly to try and shield her from me, I decide if this *arrangement* is to have a chance, I need to stamp out my place now, or risk being pushed out. I lift my hand and call on the power inside me, it circles around us and I shift it to Cass, I control it to shove him against the side of the house and hold him there. He glares at me, his shock quickly bleeds way to rage as he thrashes against his invisible binds. Callie stares at him, clearly at a loss as to what is happening–. "You can control elements like she did." I take it back, she isn't confused, she's in shock that I can control air like my sister did. Cass tries his best to fight against my restraint, I tighten my hold on the air to stop him from shifting, I may be able to push the man so far but I'm not ready to try that with his beast.

"All I want is to talk, that is it, no hidden motives." Her eyes narrow suspiciously.

"Fine, let him go and then we can talk, *after* I shower and change!" I scowl at her but agree to her terms and pull the power back inside me. Cassius drops to the ground like a sack of shit, he's on his feet before Callie can reach him to check him over, he charges at me and I call on my magic again but he's too quick. His hand grips my throat, I lift my arm and ram my elbow down his arm causing his grip to loosen giving me the chance to swivel out of his reach, he comes at me again with fists raised. I dodge the first hit but the second connects with my ribs–Fuck! I groan but don't go down, I strike out faking a hit to the left, he shifts to block his face, but I snake out with a right jab to his jaw. He growls, his eyes shift to the blue of his wolf, black fur begins to dot his arms. "Stop it!" I hear Callie scream, Cass and I trade blow for blow, he lands a good hit to my jaw that has me stumbling back a few steps. I right myself ready for the next round.

Too late, the sound of material ripping has my eyes widening, I watch in fascination as Cassius shifts before me, his face contorts as his snout begins to grow, his change to that of his wolf's, his arms become legs, his back arches and fur sprouts out all over him as he lands on all fours. His huge black wolf stands before me growling and snapping its jaws, I stand here stupefied as to what I do next, fighting him on two legs is one thing, but facing him in wolf form is another. I call on my magic lifting my hand as he sails through the air with his jaws open ready to take a bite. The wind picks up and I don't hesitate when he is an inch from my face, I swipe my arm in front of me and watch as the wind slams into him and sends him crashing through the window, glass shards fly out and I duck and cover to protect myself from being hit by them. Callie rushes forward and steps in front of me as Atticus climbs to his feet and shakes out his coat ready for another round.

"That's enough, the both of you." She shouts. I stand here panting as adrenalin courses through my veins, I haven't been this pumped in a *long* time. Atticus growls as he eyes me. "I don't care Cassius, shift back now!" I furrow my brow in confusion but then it clicks, wolves can communicate through their minds. The fact they seem to be having a private chat that I am not privy to, grates on my fucking nerves, I'm ready to put an end to this–.

"Daddy?" Everything inside me shifts, I snap my gaze to my little girl who stands mere feet away from the raging wolf. Atticus turns toward my girl and my blood turns to ice, I push in front of Callie to garner his attention. He angles his body so Mera and me are in his sights, I raise my hands to show him I surrender.

"Don't hurt her, please." I beg, his head cocks to the side and I see the war in his eyes. Cass is trying to gain control back, but the wolf still sees me as a threat and won't back down. Callie presses up beside me and lays her hand on my arm, still eyeing the wolf.

"Cassius is an asshole, but he and Atticus will never harm a child Tristan." Her words do nothing to soothe the fear inside me, Mera attempts to move but freezes when the wolf focuses on her, I gulp and ready myself to jump through the window and take the wolf down. "Tristan?" I reluctantly peer down at her from the corner of my eye. "He won't hurt her; Cass can't gain control right now because he is too angry." She grips my hand in hers and nods at the wolf as she pulls me toward the back door and enters the house. She moves us until we are near the black wolf, I do as she instructs aware of the danger my daughter is in. Callie releases my hand and kneels down, cautiously avoiding the glass, she then motions for Mera to come toward her. Mera looks to me for guidance, I war within myself of what I should do. "He won't hurt you sweetheart; Atticus only wants to scent you, so that...if you get lost, he will always be able to find you." I dart my gaze between Callie and Atticus, the blue eyes of the wolf meet mine and that's when I see it, he won't hurt her. I drop down next to Callie and wave Mera over encouragingly; she tentatively comes toward me, but I see the uncertainty in her gaze. When she is close enough, I pull her into me wrapping my arms around her as I place kisses all over her face. I can feel their gazes on me, but I don't give a fuck, I may want this bonding to work between the three of us, but Mera will always be the most important person to me, *always*.

"Can I pat the doggy, daddy?" I snort a laugh, Callie chuckles while Atticus chuffs his annoyance at being called a dog. I release my daughter and cup her face between my hands as I look at her.

"You listen to what Callie tells you, okay?" She beams at me and nods her head eagerly, I smile back but flinch, the fucker split my lip. Callie reaches out for Mera's hand and gently pulls her over.

"Hold your hand out, like this." Callie holds her arm out with her palm up and Mera mimics her move. "Atticus will come over and sniff you."

"Will he bite?" The tinge of fear in her voice guts me, what the fuck have I just got my daughter involved in?

"No, I promise you, I will never let a wolf hurt you." The conviction in Callie's words has a warmth spreading through me, she may resent me but clearly that doesn't bleed over into my child. Atticus comes forward slowly, Mera stiffens when he is an inch away. The wolf crouches down to try and make himself look less frightening, I scoff internally, nothing that fucker does will make him look less scary. He sniffs her hand and then darts his tongue out to lick her fingers which pulls a giggle from her. I wait with bated breath and I'm tense as shit as he gets closer and starts to sniff her face, I tilt forward slightly, but Callie snaps her gaze to me and shakes her head. With her moment of distraction, Mera breaks away from her and heads for the wolf, I quickly dart forward but stop in my tracks when the wolf releases a growl. Mera wraps her little arms around his neck and nuzzles into his fur, Atticus keeps his gaze on me as he allows my daughter to poke and prod him, he never once snarls or growls even when she yanks on his tail.

"What the hell is going on?" I voice aloud.

"This is Atticus's way of showing you he will protect her, we may not understand this *thing* between us, but Atticus seems to, and he wants to prove he is no threat to Mera." Her words resonate with a part of me that I thought died when Gemma broke my heart, I meet the cold blue eyes of Atticus and nod, showing my respect for what he is doing.

I stand in the doorway and smile as I watch my little girl sleep soundly, Mera is so fearless and not much fazes her. Tonight though, was one of the scariest moments of my life since becoming a father. For the first time I felt powerless to stop anything from happening to her, I sigh and run a hand through my hair as I quietly close the door and head to my study. I'm so lost in my own thoughts that I don't even notice Cassius and Callie sitting in the chesterfields in front of my desk until they stand. I dart my gaze between them wondering why they are here, each of them has showered and changed, like me Cass sports some blemishes on his face, unlike me though his will be gone within a couple hours thanks to his shifter healing.

"What are you doing here?" I ask as I head toward the liquor cart and pour myself two fingers of Whiskey knocking it back, I pour another three glasses handing one each to Cass and

Callie, The silence stretches and I sigh, I'm too tired for this shit.

"I would never harm your daughter." I focus on Cassius, I hear it in his words and see it in his eyes, he's telling the truth. "I may not like you, but your child is innocent." I nod my head.

"Thank you, now if that is all? I got shit to sort–."

"No that isn't it." I narrow my eyes at her.

"So, you can fuck off for hours having a tantrum and then come back and expect me to hear you out?" Fire swirls in her green eyes, Cass may handle her with kid gloves, but I won't.

"You can go fuck yourself–."

"I'd rather fuck you." Cass groans and shakes his head, but I ignore him as I focus on Callie.

"You will never fuck me–."

"I bet you said that to pretty boy over there, in yet I heard you screaming his name this morning." Her eyes widen and her jaw slackens, but I'm not finished here, she needs to hear this. "You're mated to him and feel guilty because you're near him, you belong to the both of us and unlike him I will not pussy foot around you. I'll break every fucking one of your walls down and make you see that your life hasn't ended because Sky's did." She is on her feet in seconds, her eyes shoot daggers at me, Cass stands beside her and tries to coddle her. "Let her have her tantrum, you do nothing for her by shielding her from her feelings."

"You don't know shit Tristan; you didn't even know Skylar and yet you think you have the right to have an opinion–." My phone rings and I watch as her eyes warn me not to answer it, I grab it off the desk and answer.

"Caleb, what happened?" Caleb is the general manager to my clubs, witches normally join incomes to help the covens, I refused. None of those fuckers tried to help me look for my sister, they wanted me to find her so they could claim her power. Our parents were two of the strongest and the fact that Sky had both their power inside her meant she could over throw the elders.

"Another of your *friends* came looking for you." I grit my teeth.

"And?"

"I told them you found a piece of ass a couple of nights ago and haven't seen you since." I ignore the two wolves as they growl.

"Keep that up, I'll be back soon."

"Got it." I hang up and drop my phone on the desk. Their gazes bore into me; I shrug and motion for them to take their seats.

"You think being a dick helps this situation?"

"You think treating her like she is made of glass helps, Cassius?"

"Stop talking about me like I'm not here!" I cut my gaze to her and ask.

"What will it take to stop you from killing yourself each day?"

"You don't know me!"

"You're right I don't, I just read a file a mile long on every-thing about you. Plus, I have all the information from Kayla concerning you, for instance your fascination with girls instead of boys. Cassius Wilder shattered your hymen and now look, you have two cocks to play with at your beck and call." My crass words hit their mark, she slouches back in her seat and drops her gaze from mine.

"I don't like you!" She mutters, I smirk.

"You don't have to like me to fuck me." Cass laughs and holds his fist out to me, I bump it and wink, electing a groan from Callie.

BRUTAL BEAUTY 103

"So, what? You're both friends now or whatever this is?" Cass shakes his head and says.

"Hear what he has to say, keep an open mind." I tell her everything I told Cass about being bonded and what it means, I told her about Gemma and it startles me when she white knuckled the arms of the chair.

"She sounds like a right bitch!" I smile and nod my agreement. "Does she see, Mera?"

"No, ever since Kitty made the deal she hasn't come back." The lie tastes bitter on my tongue, I need to finish this transfer fast before they find us. Silence encases the room, both Cass and I watch her as she mulls over what I have just said. I get this is hard for her, but it wouldn't be if she just accepted the mate bond and allowed me to bond with her as well. I can see she loved my sister and I know her loss eats at her daily, but she has to move on.

"I heard everything you said, I know this isn't an ideal situation." She meets me and Cass's gaze before she continues. "But I can't just turn off my feelings for Sky. You both have to know that, I thought she was it for me." She sighs and runs a hand through her hair trying to find her next words to better explain. The look on Cass's face tells me this is the first time she has opened up about her feelings. "I loved Skylar from the first moment I saw her," Her voice turns watery and her eyes rim with tears. "That woman taught me how to be *me*, she loved me flaws and all. The kind of love we shared doesn't just go away." I nod my head in understanding as I stand and head toward the large panting of Mera that sits on the wall behind my desk. I grip the side of the painting and pull it back till it swings to the other side to reveal my safe. I enter the combination, 4-12-13, Mera's birthdate. I open the safe and grab the plushie, as I turn to face Callie she gasps and covers her mouth with her hand.

"Before you tear me a new one, just know Mera informed me that Sky wanted to make sure I had this to pass onto you."

THIRTEEN

CALIFORNIA

My eyes are wide as I stare at the Naruto plushie he holds. "I thought I lost that." I whisper. He smiles sheepishly and shakes his head.

"I had Kayla snag it from your apartment, I wanted to make sure it was here when the time was right." I see the relief in his eyes when I don't scream at him, I don't mean to be a bitch to either of them but it's so hard to not feel guilt. If Sky was still here, neither of these two would even be on my radar.

"What am I missing here?" I turn to Cass, the worry in his eyes makes me feel like shit. I have been so busy trying to hurt him my shame overwhelms me right now and yet, here he sits trying to help me find closure.

"When I last saw Sky, she told me that she hid letters in that plushie for me. I don't know how she knew what was coming, but I never had the strength to go through them."

"What if we help you?" I dart my gaze back to Tristan slightly taken back by his offer; I don't know him, but I feel like I do. I don't know whether it's because this *bond* is true or if it's because I'm trying to latch onto him because of who he is to

Sky. I'm so fucking confused and just need to shut off my mind for a bit, maybe he is right. What if these letters help? What if they don't?

Then they will both be here to help.

Kora?

Yes.

Can you feel a bond or something with Tristan?

Yes, which is why he wasn't killed the moment you shared his bed.

So, is he like our mate?

No, I don't know what he is, but I feel a kindred spirit inside him that calls to me, sort of like Atticus.

I close the link and look to each of the guy's as I wrap my arms around myself and speak. "Okay."

I was expecting Tristan to lead us to a lounge room, not his bedroom! Cass and I stand here side by side as we look around, this room doesn't seem lived in, old paintings of houses and landscapes adorn the walls, a fireplace and loungers take up a part of the room. Red velvet curtains are drawn to block out the moonlight, Tristan's shoes clink against the wooden floorboards as he passes by us.

"Make yourselves at home, I'm gonna grab a quick shower." The words die in my throat as he shucks off his suit jacket and unbuttons his shirt giving me a full view of his tanned skin and those abs–.

"I'm standing right here!" I shake my head and turn to face Cass as I smile impishly. He rolls his eyes and continues to observe the room, I turn back but Tristan has disappeared. Cass being the non-caring ass that he is forgoes the loungers as he makes his way over to the...you have got to be shitting me!

"He has a *California* king bed." I place my hands on hips and watch as Cass pulls his shirt over his head and kicks his shoes off, he stands there in nothing but black basketball shorts. I can't stop my gaze from drinking in every part of his exposed skin, I bite my bottom lip to stop the appreciative moan from tumbling out of me.

"Come on." I shake my head and focus back on his face; a knowing smirk graces his face and I mentally facepalm myself. I have the urge to use Roger tonight after seeing both of these men shirtless–.

"The fuck is Roger?" My eyes widen focusing on Tristan standing in the open doorway behind Cass with steam billowing out around him, he stands there in nothing but a towel.

Jesus take the wheel!

"I believe Roger is someone she planned to use tonight." I dart my gaze between them, Tristan looks murderous whilst Cass looks intrigued.

"Two not enough for you, kitten?" I glower at the arrogant warlock.

"How do you even know about Roger?" Cass cocks a brow, and I can't stop staring at both of them and how fucking eatable they look standing there.

"You were thinking out loud babe." I glare at Cass when he laughs, Tristan still looks confused, well fuck them I can play this game. I grip the hem of my shirt and yank it over my head, standing before them in nothing but my sports bra and yoga pants. I sway my hips as I walk toward the bed, feeling their heated stares on my body, as I slowly climb on the bed and crawl up until I rest against the pillows. I meet their lustful looks as I say.

"Roger is my vibrator and I plan to use him tonight."

"Fuck."

"Jesus." They both say in unison, I can't help the chuckle that burst out of me at their expense. Tristan storms off toward the walk-in closet across from us, Cass jumps up next to me and doesn't even try to hide the fact he is adjusting his semi hard cock. My mouth waters at the sight of it, a deep growl comes from him.

"I'm trying hard here not to pin you down and fuck you, I can scent your arousal." I bite my lip and meet his gaze; Cass slowly leans toward me and right now I don't have it in me to reject him. His lips ghost over mine and I close my eyes waiting for him to kiss me, I slowly open my eyes to find his gaze focusing over my shoulder, I turn and that's when I see Tristan standing at the edge of the bed in nothing else but shorts.

I groan. "Can we get this over with, I have an appointment with my battery-operated friend to keep." Cass chuckles as Tristan shakes his head and climbs on the bed, all my bravado flees my body as each of them settle on either side of me, Tristan reaches over to grab the plushie from the side draw, but it's not the plush toy that has me on edge and wanting to run. As if in sync with the other, they both shift closer touching the skin on my arms, I fly off the bed with hopes of escaping this torment, a squeal escapes me when both of my ankles are yanked backward, and I fall face first on the bed.

"Going somewhere, kitten?" The humor in his voice makes me want to punch him.

"Come back Alma, you have to hear this." At the reminder of the letters, I tense and nod as they release my ankles. I sit up and cautiously crawl between the half-naked gods and reclaim my position in the middle trying to keep as much space between me and them. Tristan hands me the plushie and I stare at it like it like it's an alien, I know I need to do this, but I also know that whatever those letters contain will break me and shatter any progress I have made these past couple of months. I peer over at Tristan to find his gaze is already on me, whatever he sees in my eyes has him nodding. He grips the plushie between his hands and prepares to rip it open, but I lash out and grip his hand to stop him.

"Please don't destroy it...it...it was her favorite." He nods, I close my eyes not wanting to bare witness to this carnage. I clung to that thing every night until it went missing. The sound of it tearing makes me cringe and unknowingly reaching for Cass, he grips my hand with a slight squeeze letting me know he is here with me. At the sound of crinkling paper, I look up to see a small stack of envelopes in Tristan's hand, he gently lays the plush toy back on the side draw and counts out seven letters.

Seven letters, once those letters are read, I will never hear from her again.

That thought alone has tears clouding my vision, I take a few deep breaths to compose myself as I reach for the first letter with shaky fingers, Tristan opens the first envelope and hands it to me. I pull my hand from Cass's grip to unfold the letter; the sight of her messy handwriting brings a sense of happiness and sadness swirling inside me. I take a deep breath before reading the first one aloud.

California,

If you are reading these letters then that must mean I'm gone, or your nosey ass found my secret hiding place. A watery chuckle escapes me.

I know you must feel betrayed by me, I should

have been honest with you from the start, but I couldn't, I was too much of a coward. The thought of losing you killed me; I know your true mate is out there and I hate myself for deceiving you. I need you to know, if I'm still breathing when you find that bastard, I won't give you up. I'll fight till my dying breath to keep you Callie, because you are my reason for breathing and striving for peace.

Your brothers and Jess will be with you through this, don't push them away baby. They love you and only want to help. I need you to do something for me though, okay?

Please don't blame yourself, none of this was your fault baby, I knew this was coming for years, even now I feel the power inside me growing unstable.

Shit!

I hear you coming, I'll write again soon.

Love always,
Your Sky-Sky.

By the end of the letter tears start to cascade down my cheeks, not wanting to dwell on my feelings I reach for the rest of the envelopes. I scan through the dates on each of them, pausing when I see the last three aren't addressed to me. One is to Cass, I turn in shock to see he is just as confused as I am. I flick to the next and I'll admit, I expected to see his name, I knew Sky wouldn't have just written me letters without including Cairo.

A sharp intake of air can be heard from my other side when the next name comes into view, I turn to him.

"Why the hell would she write you a letter?" Tristan opens his mouth, but no words come out, he snatches the letter from me before I can protest, he rips it open and begins to read aloud.

Hello, brother.

This feels strange, I didn't even know you existed, let alone get to know you! And yet, here I am writing to one of the men who will end up with the love of my life.

If only I had of known about you, or even had the chance to meet you, did you know about me? Did you ever search for me?

I don't even know why I am writing this, a part of me wants to kill you because I know where you end up, and it kills me that you get to be with her, and I don't.

I've been told you are good man, you're a father I hear. I had no idea I was an aunt, not that I would have been a good example of one, unless she wants to hunt, play with knives and fight? Then I would be the woman to teach her.

Bullshit aside though, I wish things had been different, I wish I had of known you and our family. Just know, I had a great life, and I found a brother *when I least expected it. Cairo and I grew a pack, we made a home, and we bloody did it all on our own.*

We each have fallen in love, I never thought that day would come.

Look after her, cherish her and treat her well. California is the only reason I have fought as hard as I did the past years. She is stubborn and won't trust easily, but she is a Cage through and through. Love her like I do, and I promise you she will be the best thing to ever happen to you and Mera.

Take care of yourself and that niece of mine.
Your sister,
Sky.

Tristan's eyes keep scanning over the letter rereading it, I can't make sense of any of this until Cass chuckles and shakes his head. I glare at him, but the asshole just holds his index finger up and snatches his letter from me, he tears it open and reads his out loud.

Cassius fucking Wilder,

Of all the goddamn wolves in the world, it had to be you, didn't it?

I want to stab your throat and watch you bleed out.

The thing I don't understand is how you and Callie don't know yet?

From the moment we entered your pack I could see this...link binding you to her, neither of you seem to notice it!

I hate you!

I hate that your fucking sister confirmed what I already knew! The only bonus for me is that she will also end up with a Cage, so eat shit asshole.

Here is your one and only warning, Cassius,

You fucking treat her like a queen, you adore her and cherish the fucking ground she walks on. You protect her like you do Belle, you put her first before your pack, always. She is not some trophy to be won. You work for her love; you show her that you care and make damn fucking sure she knows she is loved daily.

I may not be able to kill you, but rest assured, Z and Ro both know about your little mate link. You fuck her over and I have tasked Z with ending you, Ro will help hide your body and both of them have practiced their alibies, so Belle won't know a thing.

Love her well Cassius, I hate to admit it, but I have seen nothing but good in you. I know you will be a good fit for her, don't let her push you away, fight for your place at her side.

Sky.

Fucking Belle!

She knew this whole time and never uttered a goddamn word; I am going to wring her fucking neck!

"I can see the blood thirsty look in your eyes." I glare at Cass. "Just remember, my sister is an immortal original vampire and is also heavily pregnant. You know she can't tell you everything she sees, or it will alter the outcome." Is he fucking serious?

"Your sister knew! She knew this whole fucking time and never said a word, to anyone. She knew about Tristan; let alone you being my mate and chose to tell Sky and not me!"

"I can't speak for her, but you know Belle would never intentionally hurt you California. She doesn't have a malicious bone in her body, please, don't take this out on her–."

"Who the fuck should I take it out on then, Cassius?"

"Me." Both Cass and I turn to face a guilty looking Tristan, he stares at me with regret shining in his eyes.

"Why?" I growl out.

"Because I should have found her, I should have...I should have done more! You're mad because she knew about you two." He scoffs, the guilty look is gone and replaced by anger. "She fucking knew about *me*! She never came to find me, called or even sent a fucking letter, and yet she came to me for help! My whole life has been fucked up because of her, I thought she had died, and we did–." He pauses, I narrow my eyes at him, he is hiding something, and I will find out what it is. I try to calm myself as I stare at the last three letters which are addressed to me. I have to do this now while I'm still angry, at least I can focus on my anger instead of the pain inside me.

Did you know you snore?

I want to record it so I can play it back for you in the morning, but I also don't want you to claw my face off. You look so beautiful; I should be helping Ro plan our attack on the council but instead I sit here staring at you as you sleep.

Fucking hell California, I love you so much it physically pains me.

I don't want to leave you baby, but I don't have a choice. Finding Belle and casting a spell on her today confirmed I don't have long.

I know enough about my power to know I shouldn't be able to perform spells, and yet here I am. I cured Jess's injuries and granted Belle the privilege to go outside. I don't even know what I am anymore, and that scares the shit out of me.

Fuck, Ro just summoned me, Cassius has news apparently.

Forever yours,
Sky.

I swipe the tears from my face as I tear the next one open.

My time is coming baby,

I feel it the closer it draws near; I want to tell you the truth about everything, but I can't. I won't risk losing you, I just want to hold onto you for as long as I can.

I hid these letters in the hopes you would never have to find them, but I know that was a pipe dream. You will need these letters.

I'm so sorry I betrayed you and tricked you into thinking I was your mate; God I wish the bond was real, but even you have to know now that I'm not a shifter.

How much easier would our life had been if I was?

I'm so sorry Callie, if I could spare you the pain of what is to come then I would.

Please don't hate me.

I love you always,
Sky.

I close my eyes and allow the tears to fall unchecked as I clutch the letter against my chest and weep for my lost love. Fuck the pain is crippling, I feel like my heart is breaking all over again knowing that she went through this alone, she knew the whole time and never once confided in me. I'm angry at her for leaving me in the dark for so long, but how the hell do I stay angry at a ghost? Cass places a comforting hand on my shoulder and Tristan places one on my thigh, it pisses me off that their touches soothe the pain inside me. I want to wallow in this misery and let it consume me, but I know they won't let me.

"Do you want me to read the last one to you?" I shake

my head, I appreciate Tristan's offer, but I have to do this, I want to see the words myself. I open my eyes and fold the letter as I gently place it on top of the others, I grab the last one and stare at it. This is it; this is the last time she will speak to me.

"She will be with you always, she hasn't truly left you, Alma. You will meet again one day." Cass's words give me the strength I need to open the final letter.

Hello, my love.

I'd like to hope this isn't the last letter, but I know in my heart it is.

I saw it today, the moment he shifted, and you saw him. Cairo isn't the only one who found their true mate today, don't get mad. It's okay baby, I knew this day would come, and I have dreaded it for years, but not now. Because I know that when I'm gone, he will be there for you, he'll put the pieces back together and build you back up.

He won't be the only one, there will be another. I don't think you will like the connection he has to me though.

My time is up baby.

Do me a favor though, okay?

Don't give up on love, they're out there waiting for you baby. God, I wish they weren't, I wish it was me. Let them help you, allow them to love you and worship you, because you deserve that.

I've had a great life, been so blessed to have

found my chosen family, but above all that baby, I was blessed with the best when I met you.

Be happy, live wildly and just fucking live! Don't hide away and shut yourself off from the world. Take some time to grieve, even if I told you not to, I know you won't listen to me.

Don't hate Cairo, this has to end Callie, he is the only one who can do it. It is going to destroy him to do what needs to be done, he'll need your forgiveness more than anyone's.

Much like you, he'll push everyone away, please don't desert him as he will need you the most, be there for each other.

I don't care what you do with my body, I don't want you to sit at my grave and mourn every day, so burn me, do whatever you have to, but DO NOT cry over me daily.

I'll always be with you California, always. I will never completely leave you, you'll feel me, either in the subtle change of the wind, or at the beach when the waves change direction around you. You'll know it's me.

I'll love you always in this life, and I will search for you in the next, and ten thousand worlds more, until I find you.

You are mine and I am yours.

With all my love and so much more, baby.

Yours now and always,

Sky-Sky.

I couldn't contain the sobs that wrack my body, even if I wanted to, I hold the letter close to my chest as I break apart, I let the tears flow freely. This time I cry for the woman who was robbed of loving me until we were old and gray, I cry for the love that never had a chance to flourish to its full capacity. Cass wraps his arms around me and hauls me against his chest, he whispers words of love, but they don't register. I'm too lost in my own head to focus, *she knew*, she knew this whole fucking time and never said a word!

FOURTEEN

TRISTAN

I twirl her hair between my fingers and marvel at the silky feeling, she sleeps soundly between us, her eyes are red and puffy from all the tears she has shed. Cass held her for over an hour until she finally cried herself to sleep, I didn't realize how deep her connection was to my sister. I see it now, there didn't have to be a mate link in order for them to love as deeply as they did. I'm still reeling over the fact that she knew about me, why didn't she ever try to find me?

"She is going to fight us more than ever now." I blow out an exasperated breath at Cass's words. I lull my head to the side, he stares down at her with nothing but love in his eyes, we are so different.

"Then don't let her—."

"She's grieving, she needs this time!" His gaze meets mine; I see the anger in the depths of his eyes, and it irks me further. She doesn't have time to grieve, she needs to be prepared for what is going to come. I've got reports from some of my sources that the elders are closing in our location, Gemma the power-hungry bitch is with them. We will need to find another safe location in a couple of days. "What's your rush?" A whoosh of air escapes me, everything inside me is saying not to trust him, but if this thing is going to work, then I have to try.

"I haven't been completely honest." A growl sounds out and I glare at him. "Don't fucking wake her!"

"Why?"

"Because she isn't ready for the truth, Cassius."

"Tell me everything now, or I take her, and you never see her again!" The threat in his tone is clear, I don't doubt he will back his words.

"Kitty never offered up her power to Gemma." His eyes narrow and he opens his mouth, but I push on needing to get this out. "We thought Sky had died years ago, so as a ploy we offered Gemma the power Sky held. The elders have been trying to find a way to end my family for years, like I told you earlier, it is rare for a witch or warlock to be able to cast spells. Kitty can cast as well as wield two elements. Skylar and I come from one of the strongest lines–."

"What are you getting at?"

"Let me go back to the start, Kitty was promised to marry Henrik, he is the son of the last high warlock of our elders. Long story short, Kitty ran from her coven and met my grandfather, she returned years later, married and pregnant with my father. The elders were outraged so they ordered the death of my grandfather and Kitty's unborn child, my grandfather was poisoned. To punish my grandmother further, they decided to wait until the child was born to kill it, what they didn't expect was for my grandfather to name kitty as his successor. Kitty has the power to control fire, water and cast spells. Needless to say, Henrick's father was found dead, and kitty agreed to never use her power against the elders again if they allowed her to leave and live in peace."

"Why the hell did they allow that?"

"They had planned to steal my father once he was born."

"Why?"

"Because my grandfather was the last fire elemental in existence. They thought if they take my father, it would be easier to transfer his power to Henrick, making the elders unstoppable. The thing is, when they came for him, Kitty didn't go down without a fight. She had taken in stray witches and warlocks and offered them a safe haven here, in this house. They all fought against the elders and the only injury Henrick had walked away with, is half his face was burnt, Kitty never sought revenge for her husband's death or even when they came for my father."

"Is her name really Kitty?" I chuckle and shake my head.

"No, her real name is Doris. She was nicknamed Kitty because apparently her pussy is the reason why there is such a divide amongst the covens." Cass's face scrunches in disgust and a shudder rolls through him.

"I think I'll call her Doris."

"Unless you want half your face burnt, I wouldn't."

"What happened next?"

"Nothing, she was left to raise her son in peace as long as she followed coven law, which she did. Nothing happened until I met Gemma, I didn't know at the time that, she was a plant."

"What?" This part is hard to admit.

"Gemma was planted, she never loved me or wanted a life with me. Her getting pregnant was just part of their plan–."

"*Their?*" I meet his gaze and hold it as I admit my greatest failure.

"Gemma is Henrick's daughter, Kitty and I never knew until it was too late."

"Wait, so Mera?" I nod.

"They thought Mera would be a fire elemental like my

grandfather, Mera can't control elements or even cast, she's a clairvoyant."

"Huh?"

"Mera can speak to the dead; Gemma must have had her tested when she was born. If she held power, there is no way Gemma would have traded her."

"So why are they coming after you now, after all these years?"

"They know I found Sky; it wouldn't have been an issue if Sky's power was sent to someone of age, but it was sent to a babe in the womb, which means she needs a beating heart to keep that funnel open."

"What are you getting at?" The tension in his voice tells me he knows where this story is going.

"If they find Sky and realize that none of us have her power, they will go after the child." Growls tumble from him.

"You bastard! I'll kill them all before they get near my sister–."

"How? Don't you think I have been trying to find a way out of this?"

"Why the fuck are you helping my sister, really?"

"Because the power that child inherits, means part of my family lives inside her, I will not lose them again. This I promise, I will train the child and protect it."

"What else are you hiding?"

"We have to move Sky soon; they are closing in on our location."

"What happens if they find Sky?" I grind my teeth, his eyes narrow. "Tell me!"

"They will sever the connection to the child in order to reroute it, they have casters in their midst and with their power they can take her's. Sky might not have been able to access the fire inside her, but they can."

"I thought your parents could only manipulate water and earth?"

"They did, but my father could also wield fire. It is something that was hidden from everyone, it would have made him a target. I believe one of my kind tipped your council off about my sister."

"So, should they get to her, what are their intentions?"

"They will be stronger than all of us, your wolves wouldn't stand a chance against covens, nor will vampires. Up close, maybe, but if we attack from a distance you wouldn't stand a chance." He scrapes a hand down his face and sighs.

"I thought Sky taking out the council was the end of this type of shit, clearly, I was fucking wrong. We have to warn the others, Cairo is going to lose his shit when he finds out. Why are you not trying to steal the power back from my niece?" If I take a chance in telling him and it backfires, I run the risk of putting my family in danger–.

"I can answer that." Both Cass and I stare down at the little devil who duped us both into thinking she was still sleeping.

"Are you okay?" She smiles up at Cass, but it doesn't reach her eyes, she shrugs her shoulders.

"I guess."

"What do you think you know, kitten?" Cass shudders.

"Dude, after what you just told me about Kitty, you need to think of a new pet name." We both chuckle.

"You won't hurt the baby because you already have fire magic inside you, you let us believe that you were weak to test us." I smile down at the clever she-wolf. "You won't allow the baby to possess all three elements though, you plan to transfer one to Mera." I roll my bottom lip between my teeth as I hold her gaze.

"Why?" I don't take my eyes from her as I answer Cass.

"Because I didn't know if I could trust you."

"What changed your mind?" I don't get a chance to answer Cass, Callie answers for me.

"When Atticus didn't harm Mera, you and I both proved our worth to him, when our concern was for Mera and not hurting her to get to him." Cass eyes me expectantly.

"Yes, I couldn't risk you using Mera against me, so I hid my true power from you. Just know, I would have burnt you to ash without batting an eye if you were within an inch of her. Out of the three elemental powers, Belle's child will pass on one to Mera, otherwise she will end up like Sky. No one can control three elements, I can't do it because I already have two, as does kitty."

"Which means, Mera is the only option?" I nod.

"Yes kitten. Now, how much of that conversation did you hear?" I eye her expectantly; she doesn't cower or even seem embarrassed about listening in to our conversation.

"All of it." Her eyes flicker to a turquoise color, her wolf is close to the surface. "Just know, I'll let that shit slide because I understand you wanting to protect your daughter, Sky always kept me in the dark so, I will not be lied to again."

"You have my word." I hope she can hear the truth in my voice.

"Is there anything else we should know?" I shake my head. "Okay, then as Cass is the chief alpha he can offer you, Mera and Kitty a safe haven amongst the packs. My brother and Cairo will make sure you stay hidden, I swear to you they will not let any harm befall your daughter, neither will Cass and I." My eyes widen in surprise as Cass nods his head and growls his approval.

"Why?" I whisper, I've never had friends let alone people I trust aside from Mera and Kitty, this is all new to me.

"Because Sky trusted you enough to tell you about me. We protect our own, and you Tristan Cage...I guess are our own." I bite my bottom lip to hide the smile that wants to break free. She moves until she is kneeling in the middle of the bed and faces both of us. I can see how tense she is, as nerves begin to wrack her body, I refuse to comfort her. She has to find the strength within herself, she nibbles on her bottom lip and it takes more strength than I care to admit not to groan at the sight. My cock twitches in my pants at the memory of what those lips felt like wrapped around it. "I don't know how this is going to work, just because she wrote some letters doesn't mean I don't love her. Sky is...was everything to me." She meets Cassius's stare. "We're mates." A whoosh of air escapes him at her acknowledging their bond. "I feel it, so does Kora but that doesn't mean I can wash away my feelings for her." She turns to me next; my breath stills in my throat. "Kora feels something with you as well, I don't know what that *something* is, but clearly it is there."

"What are you saying?" Cass stole the words from me.

"I'm saying, give me time. I need to process this shit on my own time and I don't need either of you pressuring me. I'll help with hiding Sky and protecting her from your elders, we all will, but as for anything else." She motions to herself and then to us. "We'll cross that bridge when we get to it."

FIFTEEN
CALIFORNIA

Five days have passed.

Cass, Tristan and I seem to have found a common ground, we even work well together. Doris, or as she prefers to be called, *Kitty* has been great, she has encouraged us to do whatever we think is best. She is a funny woman; she makes crude comments all the time and wasn't the least bit shy of moving mine and Cass's meager possessions into Tristan's room.

Tristan and Cass left early this morning to collect my stuff from my apartment in NYC. Tristan told us during this time that it's best we all stay together, of course I was inclined to agree. The guys organized movers to pack our entire apartment and for it be transported back to Rosewood. They aren't expected to be back until late tonight, Tristan has some things to sort out at his clubs and honestly, I could do with the break.

Neither of them have pushed me for more, we all share the same bed each night. Aside from them sleeping half naked and making me envision all types of dirty things, I have kept my hands to myself. It isn't through their lack of letting me know I can touch them *anywhere* I please. Last night was the first-time

I nearly caved and gave into the lust inside me, Tristan spooned me from behind and Cass pressed against the front of me. Having them both so close and feeling the heat of their bodies against me, meant I got zero sleep! I needed to give Roger a workout, I'm adamant I packed it, and if memory serves me right it should be in my bag! I'm that fucking horny I'm not above asking Kitty if she saw my vibrator whilst moving my stuff into Tristan's room. The fact that Cass and Tristan, both found it amusing and laughed at me rummaging through my bag, makes me think they took my fucking vibrator!

"Callie, want to come play in the garden?" I swivel around on my stool and smile at Mera, she looks beautiful, her long brown hair is in Dutch braids, she's wearing overalls and chucks. Her eyes beam at me, and for the first time in days, a sense of longing shoots through me. Every time I look into Mera's gaze, I see *her*.

"Sure thing, kiddo." I dump my mug in the sink and smile at Kitty as we make our way out back, Mera and I have been hanging out daily while the guys try to devise a plan on moving Sky, without telling the others the whole truth. Cass and I don't want to tell them until we are face to face, I know shit has been hard for Cass being away from the packs. He spends hours on end in a makeshift office near Tristan's study making calls and trying to do his job from a distance is wearing on him. Tristan has been just as busy organizing his clubs and *hotels*, yes, hotels! Turns out that the man is mega rich and has establishments all over the freaking world! Both guys are stressed out and working their asses off while I sit around and play board games with Mera.

"Callie!" I shake my head to clear my thoughts and smile down at the sweetest little girl, I'll admit I'm already so enthralled by her. She even has Cass wrapped around her finger; I can see he adores her, but Miss Mera seems to be crushing on one of my guys.

My guys? Where the fuck did that come from?

After helping Kitty clean up from supper, I opted to do bath time with Mera at her request. I read her a bedtime story and she was out within minutes; we had a big day today and I'm stuffed. Who knew an eight-year-old kid had that much energy? We played outside for hours, I even shifted and let her meet Kora, Mera loved it. When Kitty called us in for supper, I'm woman enough to admit I was thankful for the reprieve. I can't tear my eyes off her, how could anyone, let alone her own mother trade her? Mera is such a beautiful, kind, caring kid and I've only known her a few days and yet I would protect her with my life, if I ever get the chance to meet this Gemma, I'll break her fucking nose. I brush her hair back and place a soft kiss against her forehead.

"Sweet dreams, kiddo." I stand quietly and tip toe to the door, closing it quietly behind me and head to my room—Tristan's room—our room? I groan and stab a hand through my hair, only to cringe when I feel debris from my shift, shower it is.

Tristan's shower is heaven, the waterfall shower head has the best pressure! My brother may build houses for a living but compared to this baby his showers are shit. This is the first time in days where I haven't rushed my shower because I didn't want the guys to wait.

As I brush the conditioner through my strands, a pang shoots through me at the scent. My hair smells like Tristan, admittedly I kind of miss the broody bastard, I even miss having

Cass here. They spend most of their days tied up in their daily duties, but they always make time to see if I'm okay, Tristan mentioned if I wanted to spend time with Sky, but I can't, her letters gave me strength to try and heal and move on with my life. I have to honor her wish and live, not just exist anymore. I rinse my hair and then hop out of the shower pat drying my body and wrapping my hair in a towel. I take a good long look at myself in the mirror, my eyes don't hold that same carefree expression anymore, nor do they look dull and lifeless. I have color back in my cheeks and my appetite has picked up, I couldn't stomach the thought of food much less eat it after I lost her.

A smile graces my face, I loved her so much and because of that love I have a life I never knew I wanted. Losing her has been the hardest task I will ever have to endure, but because of her I also found two great men. I turn away from the mirror and drop both my towels in the hamper as I exit the bathroom to acquire a clean shirt from Tristan's closet, I freeze in my tracks.

"Fuck."

"Jesus." I stare at both of them with bulging eyes, what the fuck!

"You aren't supposed to be back till late!" I shriek trying to cover myself with my arms. Tristan stands there with his suit jacket open and tie loosened, his muscular legs strain against the fabric of his slacks. Cass's mustard colored shirt is taut across his chest and jeans fit his thick thighs like a second skin, his black Raiders snap back is hung low over his forehead.

"Kitten it's after midnight." The gruff tone of his voice and the lustful look in his eyes sends a shiver down my spine. I dart my gaze to Cass seeing the heat in his gaze, time has slipped away from me which means I spent hours watching Mera sleep!

Fuck!

I spot one of Tristan's button up shirts on the bed and flick my head toward it as I ask. "Can you pass me that?" Their gazes follow mine, Tristan shucks out of his jacket and tosses it on the bed next to the shirt, he lazily picks it up by the collar using his index finger. The shirt swings side to side as he eyes me, I grit my teeth as I look to Cass for help. The fucker just shoves his hands in his pockets and shrugs.

"You want the shirt?" I grind my teeth together and nod. "Too bad." The bastard flicks the shirt over his shoulder and smiles. "Whoops." My mouth drops open in shock, I look between the both of them and shudder when I see the raw need in their gazes. It astounds me that both these red-blooded males stand before me, willing to put aside their differences just so they can have *me*! Six months ago, I would have laughed in your face if you told me my destiny was to end up with a man, let alone having two of them who are now looking at me like they are starving. I've never slept with a man until Cass, now look, I fucked him twice and slept with Tristan once!

"Get out of your head, baby. I can hear you overthinking from here." I shake away my thoughts and stare at Cass, the challenge in his gaze has Kora rising inside me.

We don't submit.

You got that right, we'll show them, Kora.

With a renewed sense of determination thanks to my wolf, I drop my arms, Tristan sucks in a harsh breath and Cass whistles between his teeth, holding my head high I strut toward them, the closer I get the more tense they become. Cass must have learnt from last time, he quickly covers his cock with his hands, I smirk triumphantly at him. I stop an inch away keeping them both in my sight, I feel their heated stares all over my body and fight the shudder that wants to roll through me, I close the space and push between them as I bend over, making sure they have a nice view of my naked ass as I retrieve the shirt from the floor. I stand and smile to myself as I spin around to face them. The smile drops from my face immediately when Cass is right there and has my face clasped between his hands. I don't have a second to process before he slams his mouth against mine, I gasp in shock, and it grants him access. I moan at the taste of him when his tongue swishes across mine, I reach up to rest my hands on his shoulders as he deepens the kiss. I get so lost in the taste of him that I forget about Tristan being here until he presses up against my back. I break the kiss with Cass and peer over my shoulder at him, he doesn't seem the least bit deterred at the fact I was just sucking Cassius's face off.

"Do it again." I furrow my brow in confusion.

"What?" A heated look enters his eyes, before he can say anything more Cass grips my hips and lifts me off the ground. His hands squeeze the globes of my ass, I decide to shut off my brain and live in this moment because God knows I need this release. I lean down to kiss Cass and do as Tristan asks, all of a sudden I'm yanked back by my hair, I turn to glare at Tristan and before I know it his mouth is on mine and all thoughts flee my mind, his hold on my hair tightens until I'm partially leaning on him, I feel myself getting wetter by the second, full well knowing my arousal will be soaking through Cass's shirt. I cry out when Cass sucks one of my nipples into his mouth, I break the kiss and watch as he swirls his tongue around it, his eyes are locked onto mine.

"You like that kitten?" A part of me wants to hide my face in embarrassment as I lap up the two men worshipping me, but the another part feels so empowered that these two alpha males desire me.

"Yes." I moan out as Cass switches sides; I try to grind against him to find some sort of friction to alleviate the ache, but his grip on my ass holds me still and I growl in frustration.

"Want his tongue somewhere else?" *Oh Jesus.* Tristan yanks my hair harder, and the slight touch of pain mixed with the pleasure Cass is inflicting on me has a moan tumbling from my lips. "Answer me." I meet his heated stare with one of my own.

"Yes, I want him to eat my pussy." Tristan hums his approval; Cass releases my nipple with pop.

"Your wish is my command baby." Tristan releases his hold on my hair as Cass carries me over to the bed, I search his gaze trying find any sign of him not wanting this, I see his need for me which has my chest tightening and in some small way wondering if I'm ready for this. Cass lays me on the bed and hovers above me for a moment before he leans down and kisses me, this kiss isn't like the others, this one is almost like he is claiming me, at the same time telling me I will never be able to hide from him again. Before I get to lost in the kiss, he breaks away and begins to trail kisses down my neck before reaching my tits, he reaches out and cups them in his hands before tweaking my taut buds pulling a moan from me. He continues down my body, I sit up and lean on my elbows watching as he kneels between my legs, he places tender kisses to my inner thighs causing me to squirm. I peer just above his head to see Tristan standing there directly behind Cass with his heated stare focused on my pussy.

"Open her up for me." Cass doesn't fuck around; he parts my dripping pussy for Tristan, who groans at the sight. "Tell me what she tastes like?" Cass uses his other hand to rid himself of his hat and then blows on my clit, I shudder at the feeling. Anticipation courses through me as I wait for him to take me over the edge. He flicks his tongue out and swipes it over my swollen nub, making me cry out, he licks through my folds until he reaches my entrance. His tongue probes inside me and I scream out his name as he fucks my greedy cunt. The pleasure ends to quickly when he stops and peers over his shoulder at Tristan.

"She tastes like fucking honey."

"Hmm." Tristan licks his lips and the sight alone has me clenching my thighs together. "Make her come on your face." Cass's wicked gaze meets mine before he smirks and sucks my clit into his mouth, I drop back against the bed without trying to fight the shivers that roll through me. I feel the bed dip a second later watching Tristan shuffle toward me, he lifts the top half of my body so he can slip in behind me, I'm leaning against his chest whilst staring down at my chief alpha on his knees eating my pussy. I moan out loud when he pushes his tongue inside me, Tristan lifts my arms and wraps them around his neck. "Don't move them." I nod, too lost in the feelings coursing through me to form a coherent answer. He reaches around and flicks my nipples causing me to buck against Cass's face.

"Fuck!" I cry out.

"Not yet kitten, I want to see how many times he can make you come before we fuck you." His words are my undoing, he pinches my nipples between his fingers as Cass inserts a finger inside me and sucks my clit into his mouth, I cry out as shudders wrack my body and I come harder than I ever have before. I dig my nails into the back of Tristan's neck as I ride out the aftershocks of my orgasm. "Make her come again!" Tristan's voice is rough and raspy, I can feel his hard cock poking me in the back, Cass wastes no time, he buries his face into my cunt and I scream out, it's too much, my pussy is too sensitive from just coming.

"I can't stop." I literally beg, but he doesn't let up, Tristan twists my nipples electing another moan from me. "Please." I don't know whether I'm begging for him to stop or to continue, I'm too lost in the pleasure they are inflicting on me to understand what the fuck I want right now!

"Ride his fucking face, I don't have to be a shifter to smell how fucking wet your pussy is." Cass pushes two fingers inside me, and I moan, his pace quickens and my body takes on a mind of its own as I ride his fingers and fuck his face chasing my next release, Tristan tweaks my nipples harder causing me to arch off the bed. He grips my chin and turns my face to him, I hold his gaze as another moan tears from me, he smirks before smashing his lips against mine. I groan at the taste of him, this moment is so surreal, I'm kissing Tristan while Cass is between my legs eating me out, just the thought of this moment has me clenching Cass's fingers and screaming my release into Tristan's mouth. I break the kiss and slump back against his chest, boneless and in a foggy state of euphoric bliss. Tristan shifts behind me and lays me flat against the bed as he hops off, I smile to myself as I replay what just happened in my mind. That was the hottest sexual encounter I have ever had!

"Oh, kitten, we're so far from done with you." I struggle to sit forward and rest back on my elbows as I stare up at them, they both stand at the end of the bed with hungry looks in their eyes. Cass grips the back of his shirt and pulls it off, my greedy eyes drink him in, I bite my lip trailing my eyes lower to see that delicious V. My attention is snagged when Tristan begins to unbutton his shirt, letting it drop to the floor.

Jesus Christ.

His body is sculpted and mesmerizing, his six-pack is on full display making my mouth water. I marvel at the sight of him when he begins to undo the button on his slacks, my over-sensitive clit begins to throb at the thought of what pleasure his cock can bring me. I may not remember how good it was last time, but I do remember the ache between my legs the next morning relishing the idea of feeling that again.

"This time, you're going to get us one at a time but, the next time, it will be the both of us, at once." My eyes widen at Cass's words, I nod like an idiot. Call me crazy but I'm already excited about the next time this happens. I watch in wonder as both guys drop their pants and stand before me proudly with their cocks fully erect, Cass's cock is thick and wide, you feel every inch of him when he is inside you, those piercings only add to the pleasure that his monster cock can pull from you. Tristin's dick is huge, like the size of a fucking baby's arm! Unlike Cass, Tristan is circumcised. I bite my lip and anxiously wait to see what they have planned next; my cunt begins to clench on nothing but air! Cass hops on the bed and takes the same position Tristan did moments ago, his cock prods my back, without needing to be prompt I wrap my arms around his neck and pull him down to me, as soon as my lips touch his, he opens for me. The thought of Tristan watching us has heat coursing through my body, I peek my eyes open and peer over at him, I gasp into Cass's mouth when I see him stroking his cock.

"Open your legs wider." Without breaking my kiss with Cass, I do as he asks, he steps forward and stands between my legs. He runs a finger through my folds, and I begin to shake involuntarily, he hums his approval before lining his cock up with my entrance. I tense in anticipation, he grips my hips as he slowly inches forward, the tip of his head pushes inside me and I gasp. I pull back from Cass and watch as Tristan's cock slowly starts to disappear inside me, inch by inch, we both moan out in pleasure once he is fully sheathed inside me. "Fuck. You feel so fucking good, your pussy is squeezing the fuck out of my cock." My breaths are coming in rapid pants.

"I need you to move." I grit out, he pulls nearly all the way out of me before slamming back in, I cry out in his pleasure, fuck this feels so good. He starts to quicken his pace and I yell at him to fuck me harder. Cass captures my lips and fucks my mouth with his tongue as Tristan punishes my pussy with his skilled thrusts. Cassius rolls my nipples between his fingers as

Tristan grips my ankles and raises my legs until they are near my head, Cass assists him by taking hold of my ankles and holding them in place as Tristan climbs on the bed and quickly lines himself up with my opening and then slams inside me. I scream out in pleasure as he fucks me hard, from this angle he is so deep inside me I can taste his cock in the back of my throat. "Fuck, like that." I cry out, I can feel my orgasm cresting trying to latch onto it, he pumps faster and I can feel my orgasm building, just as I'm about to peak he pulls out of me. I growl out in anger that he would deny me what I want, I'm rendered speechless when he smacks my ass and I yelp. Cass drops my legs as I stare at Tristan in shock.

"You may call some of the shots outside this room kitten, but in here, we rule the roost and you will do as we fucking say, got it?" I'm speechless and to fucking horny to rebuke his state- ment so I nod my head. "Good, now roll over." I do as he commands and lay flat against the bed, he grips my ankles and pulls me back until I'm bent over the edge of the bed. He kicks my legs apart and I'm left standing half folded over the bed and on my tip toes. "I'm gonna fuck you while you suck Cass's cock, I think it's only fair he comes in your mouth since you came in his." I bite my lip to stop myself from moaning at his dirty words, I lift up slightly as Cass shifts forward, I place my arms on either side of his thighs, his cock juts up in my face proudly. He grips the base of it as he lines it up with my mouth, I dart my tongue out and lick from the base to the head, as his pre cum dots my tongue I growl my approval at the taste of him.

"Fuck baby, fully open your mouth and take all of me." I oblige him by taking in as much of his cock as I can, but it's too big. I start gagging trying to pull back but he grips my hair holding me in place as he thrust his hips, spit drips from my mouth and my eyes begin to water. I lift my hand ready to tap his thigh to let him know I can't do this, Tristan slams inside me and all thoughts dissipate from my mind, I scream around Cass's cock. "Fuck, do that again!" He demands, Tristan pulls out of me repeating the same movement causing me to cry out once more, Cass moans his approval. Tristan continues to fuck the shit out of my greedy cunt, laying smacks to my ass every second thrust, I manage to find a rhythm of pushing back against him whilst sucking Cass's cock like a porn star.

"Fuck your pussy is so fucking tight!"

"Suck it just like that baby. You're gonna make me cum and I want you to swallow every fucking last drop of me!" God their dirty fucking words turn me on, I dig my nails into his thighs trying to take him deeper. His grip on my hair tightens as his thrust grows more erratic, I've never swallowed a man's cum before, so I don't know what to expect, I'm slightly nervous but also excited to taste it for the first time. "Fuck yes, get ready baby." Two more thrusts and I feel his warm cum in the back of my throat as he grunts out his release whilst moaning my name. I try to swallow as much as I can but some of it spills down the shaft of his cock, Tristan stops moving behind me as Cass pulls his cock from my mouth, I suck in large lungsful of air, my moment of reprieve is shattered when I see Cass swipe his fingers down his cock and then presses them against my lips. "I told you to swallow every fucking last drop."

"Open your dirty mouth and suck his cum." Tristan grips the back of my hair and yanks my head back, I gasp in surprise, Cass uses that to his advantage as he pushes his fingers in my mouth. Tristan shoves his cock back into my cunt and I cry out around Cass's fingers, moaning at the taste of him, his salty release has Kora growling inside me. Cass pulls his fingers out and then runs his knuckles down my cheek.

"Good girl, now milk his cock for all its worth baby." *Fucking hell*, just their words seem to do the trick, Tristan reaches around to rub my clit which causes me to scream out and clamp down on his cock as I come for the third time tonight, I flop forward absolutely spent. He releases my hair and grips my hips as he fucks me, four thrusts later he roars his release with my name on his lips. I feel the jets of his cum shooting inside me and clench the walls of my pussy trying to hold him there forever.

Their cocks are going to be the fucking end of me!

SIXTEEN

CALIFORNIA

Tristan flops forward and rests against my back, the only sounds in the room are our ragged breaths. I've never come as hard as I did tonight, that was the most erotic and mind-blowing sex I have ever had. Fuck, even watching porn and using Roger never made me come that hard before.

Tristan moves and I breathe easier without his weight pressing on me, I flinch slightly as he pulls out. I'm so boneless and debilitated that I don't have the energy to close my legs—fuck. As if shocked by an electrical current I stand and cringe when I realize it's to late, his cum starts to drip down the inside of my thighs. I feel the blush as it heats my cheeks, I must look like a sight.

Cass shuffles off the bed and disappears into the bathroom, I begin to doubt myself, was that to much for him? I stifle a gasp when Tristan wraps his arm around my waist and places a soft kiss on my shoulder.

"Don't overthink it, we both enjoyed what just happened. He'll be back in a second." Sure enough, Cass appears a second later holding a washcloth, I swoon a little as he drops down in front of me and cleans the mess between my thighs. I hiss when he wipes between my folds, his worried gaze meets mine and I feel like shit when I see the guilt in his gaze.

"I'm fine, I promise."

"We were to rough!" I reach down to cup his face between my hands and smile reassuringly.

"It was amazing, I'm sore but in the best way possible."

"I told you she can handle it." Cass scoffs but doesn't acknowledge Tristan speaking, once he's finished, he dumps the cloth in the hamper. Tristan leads me to the edge of the bed before pulling the covers, I hop up and shuffle to the middle. The guys each use the bathroom and then pull on a pair of shorts before joining me in bed. I turn to each of them and glare, they are both in shock by my heated stare. "What'd we do now?"

"I didn't hurt her, that was all you!"

"Like fuck, you nearly broke her jaw with how hard you were fucking her face." I groan and slip lower down the bed until the comforter covers my face. What the fuck have I gotten myself into? They just fucked me senseless and now they're bickering over who did what, they are like children! I growl my annoyance when they flip the covers back, it pisses me off as they hover over me trying not to laugh.

"I hate you both!" I grit out.

"You don't have to like us to fuck us kitten." I scowl at the smart mouthed warlock.

"Bite me asshole!"

"I would but that's more of Cassius's kink not mine." I growl in warning which just causes him to laugh.

"How about you tell us why you're hiding under the covers?" I focus on Cass and pout slightly as I say.

"How is it that you two get to wear shorts and I have to stay naked?" Both their faces contort in confusion, they exchange a look with each other before they both throw their heads back and...laugh! The bastards have the audacity to fucking laugh at me! I reach up to grip their ears and yank on them hard, each of them cursing beneath their breath as I continue to pull harder.

"Fucking stop you little she devil!"

"Jesus, fucking hell stop your crazy shit." They both cry out in unison. I release their ears and shove them back so I can sit up, I try to crawl off the bed but an arm wraps around my waist and hauls me back against a naked chest. I growl and allow Kora to come to the surface, she doesn't like to be subdued.

"Let me go!"

"Not until you explain why you are pissed." I fight against Tristan's hold but it's futile. I cross my arms over my chest and exhale a loud huff.

"Baby, why are you mad?" I hold Cass's gaze as I growl, his eyes flicker to his wolf's and Kora preens inside me at the thought of riling her mate up.

"Why do I have to remain naked and you both aren't?" I shout, Cass looks to Tristan before focusing back on me.

"Uh, because we would rather stare at you naked all night long and not each other's dicks?"

"I'm all for fucking you together, but I draw the line at swords touching throughout the night." I can't stop the laughter that bubbles out of me at Tristan's words, both guys join me and the tension in the room starts to disperse as the anger flees from me.

I'm having the best dream!

God, I don't want to wake up, it feels so good.

"Not a dream Alma." At the sound of his voice I snap my eyes open in surprise, Cass leans over me and places a chaste kiss to my lips. A moan escapes me, I lift the covers startled, Tristan's hazel eyes stare back at me from between my legs. He swipes his tongue through my slick folds as Cass throws the covers off us. Not one to be left out, Cass pushes me back till I'm lying flat and then sucks my nipple into his mouth whilst tweaking the other.

"Fuck!" I cry out, holy shit. My body is burning up and thrumming with need as they inflict the most delicious torture. Tristan's tongue is like a weapon, hitting the perfect spot, the warmth of Cassius's mouth as he laps at my nipple and flicks his tongue across my harden bud has me arching off the bed. I feel my orgasm building and reach out to grip Cass's arm to ground me, I fear if I don't, I'll explode into a million pieces and never be whole again. Tristan prods his tongue in my tight hole and I gasp, he parts my pussy and circles his finger over my clit as he fucks me with his mouth. "Oh god!" Cass releases my nipple with a pop and quickly rids himself of his pants before throwing one of his legs over me and straddling my chest. I peer up at him and watch as he holds his thick cock in the palm of his hand, a dollop of pre cum coats his head. I dart my tongue out to moisten my lips, suddenly starving for a taste of him. He strokes himself in rhythm with the moans coming from me, he grips the base of his cock as he swipes it across my face smearing his pre cum all over me.

"Open." The gruff tone of his voice sends shivers down my spine, I open my mouth and he pushes his cock inside. He throws his head back groaning my name. "Lick it as you suck baby." I try to focus on my task but it's so fucking hard when Tristan is literally tongue fucking my wet cunt. My climax is building, and I want this release more than my next breath. I bob my head on Cass's cock whilst thrusting my hips on Tristan's face trying to find my looming release, Tristan grips my hips and holds me in place as Cass shifts to his knees so he can ram his cock further inside my mouth. Spit flies out of my mouth as I gag around his wide girth.

"The sound of you choking on his dick has me rock fucking hard kitten." I groan around Cass as Tristan's dirty words cause my liquid to gather at my center. Cass begins to find his rhythm as he fucks my face, Tristan sucks my clit into his mouth whilst he finger fucks my pussy. I cry out around Cass's cock; my orgasm is right there.

"Come all over his fucking face and let him taste your come baby." Cassius's words are my undoing, I scream around his cock as I come so fucking hard on Tristan's face. I clamp my thighs on either side of Tristan's head as aftershocks wrack my body, Cass yanks his cock out of my mouth, and I inhale ragged breaths trying to come down from my high. Tristan pulls free of my hold and I peer down at him like a stalker watching him push his shorts down, his glorious cock springs free, it's red and hard and in serious need of release. I don't wait for their instructions; I leap up and crawl to the end of the bed on my hands and knees. Tristan watches my every move; I grip his cock and relish in the pained hiss that escapes me. I don't hesitate as I open my mouth trying to gulp as much of him as I can, I feel the bed dip behind me, and I shiver in anticipation. Cass grips the globes of my ass, I expect him to slam inside me but gasp when he spreads my cheeks and I feel his tongue swipe across my puckered hole. I release Tristan's cock and peer over my shoulder ready to ask him what the fuck he is doing, and then Tristan grips my chin and turns me to face him. I'm mortified when and unchecked moan escapes me as Cass's tongue breaches the barrier of my forbidden hole.

"He's going to eat your ass while you suck my cock. When your hole starts to relax, he'll lube his cock and fuck you there while I bury my cock deep inside your pussy. By the time we are finished fucking you, you won't know where you begin and we end. We'll be so far inside you that you will never be able to rid yourself of us, now suck my fucking cock and relax so I can destroy your fucking pussy." I moan, not just from the feeling of Cass tongue fucking my ass but from Tristan's crass words. I never knew I was into dirty talk but fuck me, it turns me the hell on. I suck him back into my mouth as I push my ass back against Cass's face, a part of me knows I should be shy about the fact he is literally eating my ass, but it feels so good I just can't bring myself to care. I grip the base of Tristan's cock and suck him as deep as I can whilst pumping him, Cass pulls back and I groan at the loss of him, then I feel cold liquid slide between my cheeks and clench.

"Relax, it's lube. I'm going to stretch you out, if I don't it will hurt you." Tristan pulls free of my mouth and looks to Cass.

"Do it." Cass doesn't hesitate, he rubs the gel around my hole before probing one of his fingers inside, a chuckle escapes me and both guy's freeze. "Why are you laughing?" I look up at Tristan and then peer back over at Cass.

"Just because I ate pussy doesn't mean we never used dildos. I may have been a virgin to *real* dick Cassius, but I'm no virgin to my pussy *or* my ass when it concerns a dildo." Cass's mouth drops open, Tristan has a shit eating grin on his face as he grips me under my arms and pulls me from the bed. Cass slides off behind and within a second he grips my hips and lifts me into Tristan's hold, I try to wrap my legs around him but he stops me, Cass grips me under my knees and spreads my legs wide. Tristan steps forward and smirks sexily as he grips his cock and lines it up with my greedy cunt, that is already clenching on air in anticipation. He pushes inside me slowly, I moan each time he buries himself further inside me, he groans once he is fully sheathed inside me. I want him to move but he won't.

"Take her legs." Tristan's hands replace Cass's, I wrap my arms around Tristan's neck, I close the space between us and capture his lips in a kiss that steals my breath. Cass parts my cheeks as I get lost in the feeling of Tristan tongue fucking my mouth and the feeling of his cock inside me. "That's it baby, just relax." I feel the head of his cock at my hole, I may have been fucked by a dildo in the ass, but it doesn't compare to the size of Cass, my body has a burning sensation knowing there are two cocks inside me at once. This is a whole new experience for me and I'm fucking living for this moment. I break the kiss when he begins to push inside my ass, I unwittingly tense which causes Cass to stop. I take a few deep breaths as I turn to him, he leans forward and kisses me, I melt into the kiss, I cry out when Tristan captures my nipple between his teeth and bites down. Cass uses my moment of bliss to push further inside me, a cold sweat begins to coat my body as I try to relax. Tristan grips my chin and yanks me to face him, effectively breaking my kiss with Cass, only for him to take over kissing me, he rocks his hips and I moan into his mouth. His thrusts are lazy and unhurried, I get so lost in the feeling of Tristan fucking me that when Cass pushes inside me again, I barely feel the sting. Cass cries out when he is now balls deep inside my ass.

"Hold her legs and spread them wider." when Cass takes all my weight and I slide further down onto his cock, a moan tears from me, Tristan's cock feels so much bigger inside my pussy thanks to Cass's cock in my ass. I wrap one arm around Cass's neck and the other around Tristan's, I kiss each of them and then use my grip as leverage to push myself up and down on their cocks, we all moan at the feeling. I get the feeling that the guy's are getting tired of me being in charge, Cass tightens his grip on my legs as Tristin grips my hips to keep me in place so they can fuck me.

"Jesus Christ, your pussy is fucking milking my dick already!" I throw my head back and moan, I'm to lost in the pleasure to bother answering him.

"Her fucking ass is amazing, it's so tight. You like me fucking your ass Alma?" I meet his gaze.

"Fuck yes, now fuck me harder so I can come." A devilish glint enters their eyes, I have no doubt they're up for the challenge. Their thrusts turn from slow controlled ones to hard, punishing thrust and I scream out, Tristan grips my hair and yanks me forward until we are nose to nose, I cry out again and he glares.

"Shut the fuck up before Mera hears you." He snarls before smashing his lips against mine to keep me quiet, I scream into his mouth as I feel my orgasm building, just before it crashes into me, Cass clamps his teeth into my mate mark and stars explode, with the euphoric bliss of him claiming me again and both their cocks bringing me to orgasm, I nearly pass out from coming so fucking hard. Cass roars his release behind me, screaming my name as he comes inside my ass. Tristan breaks our kiss as he cries out my name and slams into me one more time before he comes deep inside my pussy. Shudders flow through me as I lean back against Cass, the only sounds that can be heard is our heavy breathing.

"You okay?" I lull my head to the side and smile at him.

"Hmm." Is the only coherent thing I can say. Tristan leans forward and places a soft kiss against my throat before he slowly starts to pull out of me.

"Alma, I need you to wrap your arms and legs around Tristan." I nod my head and do as he asks, once in Tristan's embrace, Cass slowly pulls out of me and I flinch at the sting, my ass is going to be sore for a couple of hours until my healing kicks in. Tristan carries me into the bathroom and sits me on the counter, I cringe when I feel Cass and Tristan's cum start to drip out of me, I quickly hop off the counter and cringe when I feel it dripping down my legs, Tristan grips my hand and ushers me into the shower, I stand straight under the spray and sigh in contentment, who would have thought that I would be here months ago, not me that's for damn sure. I startle when I feel his arms wrap around me, he pulls me flush against him and rests his chin atop my head. I slowly reach up and circle my arms around his waist and relax into his hold.

"We'll never replace her, and we will never try to. This is all new to the both of us as well as you, it's going to take time to work things out, but please let us try. We can make this work if you allow yourself to feel half of what we do, I know you feel something for us, I also know you feel more for Cassius than you do me. Allow me the chance to prove to you that I am just as worthy as Cass." Before I can process his words or even respond, he releases me and leaves, I stand here alone and so unsure of *everything*.

How can I go from being so content and...*happy* to, unsure and feeling like utter shit in the space of a few minutes?

SEVENTEEN

CASSIUS

Was it something he said?

Is she distant because I marked her again?

These thoughts have been running through my head all day, I haven't been able to focus on anything other than her. Atticus is content for the first time in months at having his mate back with him, I feel the same. Last night and this morning was fucking amazing. I always thought that if I was ever fortunate to find my mate, never in a million years did I ever think I would share her, I knew Callie would be it for me the moment I shifted, if sharing her with Tristan is what it takes to keep her, then I will endeavor to make it work.

Whatever it takes to make sure she is happy; I don't know Tristan very well, but the fact that he shared his secret with me last night goes a long way in earning my trust. The added bonus is, we both have the same kinks when it comes to fucking, I like to fuck rough and hard as does he. I'm man enough to admit that it turns me on when he commands her, bending her to our will. I thought taking my time and letting her grieve was the right move, but I was wrong, she had put herself in a dark hole and Tristan was on the money when he said we needed to push her.

"If you frown any harder your face will stay like that." I turn to the doorway of my makeshift office and glare.

"What do you want Tristan?" He pushes off the door jam and saunters into the room like he owns the place–fuck–he really does own the place. He drops into the wingback chair in front of my desk as I close my laptop and twirl my pen between my fingers. The fucker sits there with his tailored suit and leather shoes looking like a stick up his business guru. We are so different, I'm a jeans, shirt and hat kind of guy, and he's all about perfect hair, suits and dress shoes, I shake my head and laugh to myself at the thought of him on pack lands, if we do return Sky to Creed's pack, he is on for a harsh reality check.

"Why are you laughing?" I shake my head and wave him off, I pull my hat off and run my hand through my hair as I meet his gaze.

"Did you need something?" He narrows his gaze; Atticus thrashes against my ribs urging me to put him in his place. "Keep pushing me, the next time we throw hands, Mera won't save you."

"Say my daughter's name again."

"*Mera*." We move as one and jump to our feet ready to lay waste to the other in a show of our dominance.

"So, you get along when it concerns sex." We never break our stare off as Kitty enters the room. "But, when she isn't around you want to destroy each other, oh, what fun times." She moves to the vacant chair next to Tristan and drops down crossing her legs, I watch her as she eyes us expectantly. "Sit your asses down and hear what I have to bloody say." I refuse to be the first to yield, I growl, warning Tristan to back the fuck down before I make him. The cocky fuck smirks at me before slowly lowering himself back into his seat. I follow suit and place my hat back on my head as I lean back in my chair and wait.

"What is it kitty?" She sighs dramatically, I roll my eyes at the old woman. She may appear like the grandmother from next door, but it's all smoke and mirrors, she has a tongue like a whip and quick wit that can rival half of the packs. She eyes her grandson before turning to face me.

"I assume you know our whole origin story?"

"Yes." I expect to see anger in her gaze at the fact of me knowing the truth; she surprises me when she smiles and nods.

"Good."

"Good?" I query.

"Yes, now I don't have to beat around the bush and risk his wrath for spilling the beans." She jabs her thumb in Tristan's direction and rolls her eyes which draws laughter from me, does this woman fear no one?

"Get to your point kitty."

"Shut your cake hole Tristan!" I choke on my own laughter; the bastard narrows his eyes at me which just causes me to laugh harder. "My grandson can be..."

"A cocky bastard?"

"Overbearing, I won't sit here and pretend to understand the dynamics of your relationship but, I will say you need to work it out fast." The hairs on the back of my neck stand up in warning.

"Why?"

"What happened?" Tristan and I ask in unison.

"Callie shifted this morning and refused to take Mera with her into the woods, when she returned, she asked me if she could help with cleaning Skylar tonight." I look to Tristan in question, he seems just as confused as I am. "Oh, for the love of God you are both dense. California wouldn't have asked me to see Sky if she didn't plan on not seeing her again, she went into the woods alone because I suspect she was trying to find her quickest escape route!"

Fuck!

Tristan and I are both on our feet and rushing for the door as kitty's laughter follows us out. "You're welcome." She shouts as we round the corner and race down the stairs, we're shoulder to shoulder as we enter the sunroom, only to find it empty, I dart my gaze around and that's when I spot Mera in the back yard running around giggling.

"There!" I say as I rush for the backdoor, I pull it open and race down the stairs heading for Mera with Tristan hot on my heels. The little girl stops and peers up at me with wide eyes as I draw near.

"Mr. Cass." I cringe, I hate that she calls me that, but Tristan says *it's a sign of respect.* If you ask me, he only makes her do it because he knows I loathe it. Tristan crouches down in front of Mera, he brushes his knuckles over her cheek electing a giggle from her.

"Darling, where is Callie?" She furrows her brow in confusion.

"You're going to get mad if I tell you." I see him tense; he takes a calming breath trying to control his panic.

"I pinkie swear I won't, Cass and I have to find her." She looks between Tristan and I before focusing on her dad again.

"I'll tell you on two conditions." Tristan groans.

"Now is not the time for your bargaining–." She crosses her arms and lets out a huff.

"Fine, Callie said I shouldn't break girl code anyway." He looks up at me and I can see the annoyance in his gaze, Callie is going to pay for teaching his daughter that. I can see he is getting nowhere, so I shove him out the way causing him to fall on his ass as I assume the position he was just in. He mutters curses under his breath, but even he knows I'm our best chance at finding her. I know it's wrong of me to use her little crush to my advantage, but I need to find Callie, I tried through the mate link, but it's blocked somehow.

"Sweetheart." A slight blush coats her cheeks, and she cringes, I feel like a pervert right now. "Can you please tell me where Callie is?" She smiles and I start to relax, I knew I could get her to talk–.

"Fine, but you have to play dolls with me and take me to dinner." I reel back in shock, Tristan splutters beside me.

"I think not!" I nod my head in agreement.

"I agree with your dad–."

"Fine, good luck finding her." She tries to pull away, but I grip her arms to stop her, I feel Tristan's gaze boring holes into the side of my head but ignore him.

"I'll do both of those things–." Tristan tries to cut in, but I push on, ignoring her triumphant smile. "But your dad has to be with me, those are my terms, take it or leave it." She pretends to ponder it for a moment before sticking out her hand to shake.

"I'll take it." She singsongs. We shake on it; I quirk my brow and wait for her to spill the beans of Callie's where abouts. "She went to say goodbye to aunty Sky." I'm on my feet again and moving toward the house with Tristan behind me, we race through the house and climb the stairs two at a time until we reach Sky's room, Tristan reaches for the handle, but I stop him when I hear her voice. He glares at me, but I shake my head.

"Why is she talking like she didn't hear us coming?" His face contorts.

"Sky's room is spelled by Kitty; you can't hear anything from the inside of that room." Oh, I lean in closer, as we shamelessly eavesdrop.

"I can't, not anymore. What happens when they can't do it anymore, will I be like this again?" *What is she talking about?* "I can't keep doing this babe." Jealousy rises inside me at the term of endearment, from the way Tristan clenches his hands into fist, I see I'm not the only one. "I enjoyed…no, not enjoyed, I fucking loved every minute of it. That's why I'm scared, I won't survive this again, I'm barely fucking surviving without you! God, and those fucking letters, why Skylar, why?" I can hear the anguish in her voice and know she is close to tears. "I would have given you everything if you had just fucking fought for me! I wanted you to fight a bit longer, to give me enough time to get to you and bring you back. Why couldn't you fight?" Sobs are tearing from her; Tristan moves to open the door, but I stop him.

"She is breaking down." He grits out.

"I know, she needs this outlet Tristan. I want to go in there and comfort her as well, but she has to release the anger she has." I put my ego aside to tell him the harsh truth. "She is still in love with your sister but she's so angry at her for leaving and not fighting. She needs to yell, scream or whatever it is to finally let go of Sky. She's angrier at herself for being pissed at Sky, that's why she hasn't moved on."

"What?" I sigh in frustration.

"California is angry because Sky died. She has suppressed her anger for so long and clung to her grief, so she didn't tarnish her love for Sky being angry with her for dying. She needs to do this; she has to let go of the last part of Sky she is clinging to." His eyes widen in understanding, he opens his mouth but clamps it shut when Callie starts screaming again. Atticus whines inside me wanting to go to our mate and comfort her. Fuck, it kills me to hear her so broken and not be in there to hold her.

"I fucking need you and you're gone! If you were here, I wouldn't even be in this place or thinking about them, I hate you for leaving me! I hate you for making me love you, you were it for me!" The pain in her voice is devastating, my chest aches painfully for her. I can understand how she feels, losing Blake shattered me and changed me in ways I never knew. I'm not obsessed with being alpha or ruling over my family's pack, I see there is more to life than duty now. "You were my fairytale fucking ending Skylar Cage, and then you fucking chose to die for your best friend! You chose Cairo over me; you said that if there was a choice, you would have picked me, but you're a fucking liar! You did have a choice, and in the end, you chose to save him and his fucking baby." She screams out and I slam my eyes closed, I don't know if I can take much more of this. "Why doesn't anyone ever choose me?" Her quiet broken whisper shatters everything inside me. "Creed chose Jess, Dad chose Davina over mom. Cole, he chooses whoever warms his bed–." That's it, I burst through the door, her shocked red rimmed eyes dart between the two of us, I'm panting and furious at her as I make my way around Sky to grip her face between my hands, she opens her mouth, but I cut her off.

"Did I not choose you over everything? I gave up my family, my pack, everything I have ever known, because I chose you. I will always choose you California, in this life and the fucking next, until we finally rest together for eternity. I chose you because I fucking love you!" Her eyes widen to the size of dinner plates at my declaration. She searches through my gaze for any sign that I might be lying, she won't find it because it's the truth. I'm in love with her and have been for a while now, I just had to man up enough to tell her.

EIGHTEEN

TRISTAN

I feel like I'm intruding on a private moment as I stand on the other side of my sister watching Cass kiss her. When her shock melts away she grips his arms in a way as if to stop him from ever leaving. I never knew how deep her pain was until just now, I tear my gaze from them and stare down at my sister. She looks so peaceful and content, thanks to the spell kitty cast, Sky won't decompose until we lay her to rest.

Why didn't you choose her?

That one question is circling inside my brain, I would always choose her, except where Mera is concerned. My daughter is always my first choice, no matter what. I also know Callie doesn't feel the bond like I do, because she isn't a witch, but the connection I feel toward her is bone deep and engraved inside my blood. I need her to feel half of what I feel for her, Cass and I are always at each other's throats but I know he loves her, and will protect her at the cost of his own life.

"Never doubt my feelings for you California. I'm not your dad or brothers, you are always my first choice. I even think your that dickhead over there's first choice as well." I snap my gaze to them and glower at the fucking cock sucker, her gaze slowly filters to me. The pain is still evident, but I see now, her insecurity to let go and allow us in isn't because she is fighting it per se, it's because she is terrified that Cass and I will leave her like my sister did. I make my way toward them and nod my head in thanks when Cass steps aside allowing me space with her. We stand here and hold each other's gazes; I see her eyes slowly start to flicker to her wolf's, but she fights for control again.

"Tristan–."

"Just...give me a second." She sighs but remains quiet, as I try to gather the words I need to say. "I'm not Cassius or, Skylar. They would each allow you to hide from your feelings and take the time you need, but I'm not them." I feel Cass's eyes on me but ignore it. "I'll push you past your boundaries, I'll make you face your demons head on and never let you hide." Her face begins to fall, and I see more tears gathering, she thinks I'm about to walk away from her. "But." Her eyes slowly lift to mine again. "I'll be by your side the whole time and help you through it, I can't make the same promise Cass did. Mera will always be my first choice, in every life. My little girl is everything to me, but know this, I vow to never leave you like Sky did. I will always fight to come back to you. You may not feel the bond on your side, but it thrums through me daily, you're like a drug to me kitten. I also can't confess my love for you, not because I don't feel anything, but because we're still new at this, but when it is time, everyone in this fucking world will hear me tell you those three little words."

"I–uh–I." She takes a deep breath and squares her shoulders. "Thank you, can you guys give me a sec?" Cass and I exchange a glance before nodding, we watch as she makes her way toward Skylar, she gently grips her hand and lifts it to her lips. "I don't hate you, I'm just angry that you're not here anymore." She lays Sky's hand back at her side and turns to face the both of us, Cass moves until we stand shoulder to shoulder. "I'll always love her." The conviction in her voice is awe inspiring.

"We know." Cass answers for us.

"I can't forget her."

"We're not asking you to, anyone whoever asks that of you will wind up dead, I promise you." She smiles appreciatively at me causing a warmth to spread through my veins.

"We have to move her; Ro has to let her go before his baby is born. She may have chosen him and it fucking sucks to admit that, but he loved her just as much as I do. He has to see her again and read that letter, can you make that happen?"

"Yes, but I'll need some time." I answer, it's the truth. Transporting a body isn't as easy as the movies make it out to be. There are a few loose ends that need my attention, I have to prep my businesses, sort out Kitty and Mera to travel with us, and make sure the elders aren't alerted to our departure, we've been lucky to stay hidden for this long, the last thing I want is for them to find us now while Mera is with me. She turns to Cass and asks him.

"None of the others know about us coming back, right?"

"I haven't said anything but that doesn't mean my sister hasn't had a vision."

"Okay, I think it's best if we call Creed and swear him to secrecy, I don't want to turn up when Jess is about to give birth and stress him out."

"Aren't we better to go to Cairo's pack lands, he's hidden in the mountains." She shakes her head.

"That was my first choice as well, but Creed and Jess have the biggest pack which means more protection for Mera and Sky in case the elders catch wind of our where abouts." My heart soars at the fact that she thought of Mera first. "Can we discuss the logistics of moving her, tonight?"

"Fuck." We both turn to Cass who is rubbing the back of his neck nervously and hiding his eyes under the brim of his cap.

"Cass?" He slowly lifts his gaze to her, looking very sheepish.

"Babe, I would love nothing more than to hang with you and talk shop, but Tristan and I have plans tonight." I balk at him.

"We do?" He turns and pins me with a look that says I'm stupid, I bristle at that implication.

"Doing what?"

"Yeah Cassius, doing what?" I snap, he narrows his eyes at me before facing Callie.

"His demon spawn hustled us." I can't help it, I throw my head back and laugh, Mera is very good at getting her own way, what can I say she takes after her daddy.

"I'm not following." Cass growls and then shoves me away from him, his aggression still doesn't deter my laughter.

"In order to find out where you were, because apparently this room mutes all magic so I couldn't track you through the mate link. We had to make a deal with the devil." She peers around to look at me, I shrug my shoulders and smile, allowing Cass to take the lead on this one.

"What did you do?" Cass's shoulders droop hanging his head as he speaks.

"I had to agree to dinner and playing dolls with Mera or she wouldn't break *girl code*. I agreed under the condition that Tristan had to be there as well." Callie rolls her lips over her teeth and tries to contain her laughter, Cass growls again. "It's not funny, she fucking hustled us, and that dipshit let her!"

"Fuck you! She's a great negotiator, it will come in handy

when she runs her own empire." Cass spins on me and points an accusing finger in my face.

"You'll be fucking paying for this; I draw the fucking line at dress up." Cass and I end up in a verbal sparring match, before we get too carried away Callie whistles drawing our attention back to her.

"Fucking hell, you are both worse than Kayla and the bitch squad back in high school."

"I take offense to that." I smart.

"Me too!" She rolls her eyes at us.

"Go do dinner with Mera and play dolls, who knows the two of you might actually bond over something other than my pussy." My mouth drops open, Cass stares at her like a deer in headlights as we watch her leave the room without uttering a single word.

"The fuck just happened?" I voice aloud.

"I think she just took our balls with her is what happened."

Dealing with my board members and running the club and hotels is less exhausting than playing dolls and having a *high tea* type dinner party. Callie served us all our gourmet meals in Mera's room, she gave Cass and I each a kiss and adding a wink before scurrying out of the room. Don't get me wrong, I love spending time with my daughter, but I don't do it often enough, no thanks to my workload let alone trying to conceal us from the elders and her power-hungry cunt of an egg donor. Mera was more interested in gaining Cass's attention than mine, I was pissed at first, but Cass handled her little crush with ease, and explained to Mera how he is in love with Callie. It was awkward as fuck when she asked if I loved Callie as well, explaining the dynamics of relationship to an eight-year-old is a lot harder than you think. I don't like secrets, and I never want my daughter to think it's okay to hide things from me, so I lead by example.

Nerves got the best of me as I waited for her outrage knowing that Cass and I are with Callie. I was in awe of her when she hugged each of us, plus having to explain to her that Callie wasn't some toy I bought her. She was just excited to have a girl around who could be like a mommy figure to her. That one comment had my heart breaking for my little girl, Cass placed his hand on my shoulder trying to comfort me in that moment. I wish things could have been different for Mera's sake.

Cass and I slowly tip toe out of her room after she made each of us read her a bedtime story, I pull the door closed quietly behind us and we both release a whoosh of air before chuckling quietly.

"Swear to god, being chief alpha is less taxing than playing dolls and having to eat with my elbows off the table." I laugh and shake my head as we head toward our room, *our*, it feels right saying that. "You raised a great kid Tristan." I pause, he stops and stares at me perplexed.

"Thank you." He seems taken back by my gratitude. He meets my gaze and I tense when a serious look takes over his features.

"I love Callie, but I also know you love her too." I try to brush him off, but he carries on. "I'm good with all of that, as long as it makes her happy. What I'm trying to say is, her being with you means your kind of with me in a way." I cringe at his choice of words.

"I'm never sucking your dick." I jest.

"You wouldn't be lucky enough to even taste my cock." My

eyes start to squint which just causes him to laugh before he finishes. "Comes you comes Mera; I want you to know that I'll protect her like she is my own. I know Callie is already smitten with her and believe me when I tell you, California's love for her is second to none. I've seen it with her nephew, if anything had to happen and you two didn't work for whatever reason, she would be coming for that girl and there isn't a fucking thing you could do about it." His words call to the deepest part of my soul, the part I locked away when Gemma broke my heart and chose power over the love of her daughter. Cass reaches out and places a hand on my shoulder. "She isn't your ex, give her a chance to love you both, and I promise she will be the best mother to your daughter if you allow her to be."

We remain silent the rest of the way, Cass opens the room door, and I can't fight the smile that breaks free. She lay on her stomach with her legs crossed swinging them back and forth, air pods in and a book in her hands. The bottom of her ass cheeks are hanging out of her sleep shorts, my cock hardens at the sight, I push past Cass to move in closer, she can't hear me coming thanks to her music blasting so loud in her headphones. I lean over and yank the book from her hands and hold it above my head as she leaps up on the bed, I smirk triumphantly.

"Give it back, Zayn was just about to pop Amelia's cherry!"

"Her fucking what now?" She glares at Cass before focusing on me again.

"Answer his question kitten." She huffs and crosses her arms over her chest in anger, all that does is push her tits up further and make me hunger for a taste of her.

"Zayn Bronson was about to fuck Easton's little sister and you ruined it." I flip the book over to see the cover has a half naked guy on the front, *Corrupt my mind by Kelsey Clayton*. My moment of distraction costs me, she leaps from the bed, and

I drop her book in order to stop the both of us from tumbling to the floor, once she realizes I've dropped it, she tries to wiggle free, but I tighten my hold around her waist. Cass saunters over and plucks the book from the ground and waves it in front of her, she reaches for it, but he snatches it aways. "Give it to me now Cassius."

"What are you going to give me in return?" She growls a warning; I bury my face in the crook of her neck and inhale her scent.

"Not a goddamn thing!" I bite down on the soft flesh where Cass's mate mark is imprinted on her skin, she gasps and tenses in my hold, I suck on it and this time a moan escapes her.

"You were saying babe?" When her arms wrap around my neck and her legs lock around my waist, I know she is up to something. I pull back and stare up at her as a devilish glint enters her eyes.

"Tristan?"

"Hmm?" I'm loving where this is going and want to play along.

"Fuck me while Cass watches." Cass chokes on air.

"The fuck? He snatched the book not me!" I roll my eyes and snort.

"Shut up Cass and sit your ass down, the adults are talking." A girlish giggle escapes Callie and for the first time since meeting her I don't see the haunted look in her eyes. Maybe Cass was right, she really did need to release her pent-up anger. I'm not stupid to think that her grief has magically disappeared, but I can see she is learning to cope with it, I'm fucking proud of her.

"Eat shit you fucking Harry Potter wannabe, she's mine." I pull my stare from her and focus on Cass, the little devil leans down and begins lick from the bass of my neck to my ear, causing a shudder to run through me.

"Ours, she is ours and if I recall, and I quote '*I'll do what-ever it takes to make her happy*'. I believe you watching me fuck her will make her delirious with happiness." He reaches out and smacks my arm away from her waist, grips her hips and tries to yank her backward, she tightens her hold around my neck and grips me tighter with her legs. All Cass is doing by yanking her is causing her to grind up and down on my dick and I'm down for that! Cass growls and his eyes change to his wolf's, he cages her between us, and I see a smug smile on Callie face. She can't see the way Cass is looking right now and I know he is up to something.

"Fine, have it your way Alma." Callie opens her mouth to retort but is silenced when Cass grips her shorts and tears them from her body, her shocked scream is the only sound in the room before Cass smacks her ass and a resounding *thwack* sounds out.

"Ow!" She cries out.

"Tell me *no* again." He dares her.

"You don't get to tell me–." He grips her ponytail and yanks her head back until she is arched backward and slams his mouth over hers upside down. His dominance over her and the way he is demanding control is causing my cock to stir inside my slacks. He breaks the kiss as fast as it began, Callie's breaths are coming in rough pants.

"I tell you what the fuck I want, now be a good girl and get on your fucking knees and suck both our cocks." My brows jump to my hairline, Cass pushes her up and she peers down at me. Her pupils are blown wide, I don't have to be a shifter to smell how fucking wet she is just from his words, the fact she is soaking through my shirt is proof enough. She releases her hold on me and I help her to her feet, she peers up at each of us as she slowly lowers herself to her knees. "You don't touch your-self; you take what the fuck we give you." Her eyes cut to me in the hopes I'll side with her, I shake my head in answer and tentatively stroke her cheek with the back of my hand.

"If you're a good girl, we might let you come after this." I say with a wink, a frown mars her beautiful face as Cass begins to undo his pants, I do the same. I grip myself and slowly stroke my dick hissing at the feeling.

"Open." I snap my gaze to her as she obeys his order, he grips the base of his cock as he pushes inside her mouth, she attempts to suck him, but he pulls back. "Wrap your lips around it every time I fuck your mouth." She squirms as she tries to rub her thighs together to gain some friction, she nods her head as Cass begins to fuck her face. I allow them to carry on for a few minutes before I grip the back of her hair and pull her to me, she opens willingly.

"Fuck." I hiss, the feeling of her wet mouth wrapped around my cock has my balls tightening, ready to cum like a pubescent teen. She disobeys Cass's order when she reaches up and strokes his cock with her hand, he throws his head back in ecstasy. She pulls back and grips my cock in her other hand as she returns to sucking Cass off, she continues to alternate between us literally grabbing our balls trying to suck us both at once. Any other time or if she was any other girl, I would never let my cock get this close to another mans, but it's different with Cass. I don't feel anything for him, I mean it turns me on to watch him fuck her, but that's it. Having my cock sliding against his as well as across her face and mouth just adds to the pleasure of this situation, I'll never fuck him, but I won't say no to having this happen again.

"Fuck yes!" Cass shouts, she sucks him, and I can tell from his erratic thrusts he's about to cum. A few seconds later he grips her head and holds her in place as he roars his release and shoots jets of cum down her throat. Like a good girl, she swallows every drop of him before he lets her go to continue sucking my cock. "Finish him off, I'm going for a shower." Cass disappears into the bathroom, and I use this moment of alone time with her to my advantage, I pull out of her mouth and yank her to her feet. Confusion is written all over her face, I lift her and carry her to the far wall. She locks her arms and legs around me as I slam into her, she screams.

"Fuck, Tristan."

"I need you to come all over my cock kitten." She groans, I fuck her like a man possessed, she captures my lips in a heated kiss, I taste Cass on her tongue and the dark monster that lurks inside me is loving the mixture of him and her both on my tongue.

"I'm not gonna last." She moans out, I pick up my pace and fuck her harder than I have ever fucked before.

"Get there, I'm about to cum." I grit out through clenched teeth. It's a euphoric moment when we come together, her screams can be heard for miles as she shatters all over my cock. I lean forward and rest my forehead against hers, something inside me splinters as I look into her eyes. In this moment, I can say with certainty that I will destroy anyone who ever tries to take her from me, California Reeves is mine, now and for always.

NINETEEN

CALIFORNIA

It's been nearly five months, five glorious months since we came to Tristan's home. We've worked at our relationship and the guys even get along, almost like they are best friends. I spend my days with Mera when I'm not helping the guys, they are teaching me how to run the packs and the skills to running a successful hotel and nightclub train.

I have to pinch myself sometimes, it's hard to believe that this is my life now. Don't get me wrong, I miss my family so much and they were ever so kind to fly my mother here. Having her and the guys with me as well as Mera and Kitty was surreal. My mom never once judged me, she was content because I'm happy.

My brothers don't know the exact situation between Cass, Tristan and I, mom thought it was better if I told them in person rather than over the phone. I was inclined to agree, I would agree to whatever she says, if it means I have more time to avoid *that* conversation with Cole and Creed, they will not handle that well.

Cass, Mera and I travelled back with my mother for the

birth of my niece, Tristan couldn't come with us as it would have left kitty alone. Not only that, he refuses to leave Sky unguarded until the elders are dealt with and she is finally laid to rest. My whole family and the pack were amazing with Mera, her and Cass have an amazing bond. We caught up with Ro and Belle while we were there, Belle is so over being pregnant and having Cairo's overbearing ass mollycoddling her daily. We let them all know what we had planned for Sky and bringing her back here. Everyone agreed that Jess and Creed's pack would be the safest place for us to be with Sky, Ro, Z and Belle will return to the Hasting-Reeves pack when we do.

After leaving my family we had one more stop, and that was to check in on Cass's pack, Mera and I made ourselves scarce, as Hunter, Gabriel and Cassius worked out what had to be done in order for Hunt to fully take control of the Wilder pack, in order for Gabriel to hand over the reigns and move to Cairo's pack lands. He wants to be with his daughter and first grandchild, Gabe has been helping Cass rule over the packs and even I can see the stress of it all has worn on him. I know Cass's responsibilities are here, but in order for him to maintain his leadership as chief alpha, a lot of traveling will be involved, what about Tristan? He has his whole life in New York, what happens when this is all over? That one question has been bugging me since we returned.

Tristan and Cass haven't said a word about what we are going to do and that scares me, I've finally let them in and I can't lose either of them. Cass tells me he loves me daily; I even told him the same thing a couple of months ago. It felt so weird to say those three words to someone other than Sky, a part of me felt like I was betraying her. Cass and Tristan reassured me that nothing I do or say would ever betray or belittle what we shared together. Tristan hasn't said he loves me yet, I get it though. He was fucked over so bad by his ex, I can relate to his feelings, it's hard for me to let anyone in after losing Skylar.

"You packed babe?" I shake my head to clear my thoughts and smile at Cass as he stalks into our room.

"Yeah, this is the last of it." Cass grabs my case and leaves me alone with my thoughts, I look around our bedroom and smile, so many beautiful moments between us have been shared in here. We made it a rule that every Wednesday is movie night in our room and Mera gets to pick. She selects the same movie every week and the guys hate it, but they know the rules, what Mera says, goes, or I don't give them a happy ending when she's asleep. They of course punished me by taking it out on my body in the most delicious ways, I was not complaining and took my punishment like a fucking champ.

"What's that smile for?" I spin around and bite my lip to stop myself from groaning, Tristan stands there with his hands in his pockets, slick as ever, his eyes burning with lust, just that one look has me clenching my thighs together. "Stop looking at me like that or I won' be able to say goodbye to my daughter without having a fucking hard-on." I giggle and slowly make my way over to him placing my hands on his chest. He narrows his eyes at me as I trail my hands down to the top of his pants. He grips my wrist stopping my downward decent and glares at me which causes me to pout. "I would love to fuck the shit out of you, but we have to prepare Sky so we can follow after them." His words are like a bucket of ice water, I nod my head as he grips my hand and leads me from the room. Mera and Kitty are traveling ahead of us on a separate plane for safety reasons, If their elders are tracking us, they will follow Sky not Mera, we will prepare Sky and take her to a private airstrip.

Mera launches at me as I round the corner into the foyer, Tristan reaches out to steady me. Mera clings to me like a monkey and buries her face in the crook of my neck, I look to kitty for an answer as to why she is upset.

"She doesn't want to leave you." My brow furrows in confusion. "She thinks you're not coming back." He whispered words that have my chest aching, I kneel down with Mera still in my clutches and gently urge her to stand, she does reluctantly. Her tear-stricken eyes bore into mine and my heart breaks, I swipe away her tears and try to smile reassuringly.

"I'm not going anywhere–."

"Then why can't I come with you?" She begs, Tristan drops down beside me.

"Darling, Callie, Cass and I will be there–."

"No, I don't want her to go daddy, she can't leave." She screams and launches at me knocking me to my ass, I look up at Cass and Kitty only to see murderous looks on their faces. I feel the exact same way, this sweet girl is terrified that I'll leave her, because her piece of shit mother did. I hold her tight in my arms, peering over at Tristan and my heart skips a beat at the defeated look on his face. "Don't leave." She sobs.

"I swear to you, I will never leave you." She pulls back and sniffs whilst swiping her tears away.

"What if you and daddy don't love each other anymore." I don't falter in my response.

"Then so be it." Her face falls but I push on. "But that doesn't mean I will ever stop loving you. I may not have given you the gift of life sweetheart, but I love you as if you were my own. Your dad would have to build a whole new world to stop me from finding you."

"And me." Cass says with such conviction that makes me love him even more. "We'll never leave you Merz, you're stuck with us forever." She nods her head as she drives back in to cuddle me quickly before rushing over to Cass. He picks her up and holds her close inhaling her scent.

"Promise?" His eyes harden.

"I swear to you on my honor as alpha chief, that I will never abandon you Merz, you're stuck with me."

"I love you." She sobs against Cass; tears threaten to spill from my own eyes as she declares her love for him for the first time. His shocked gaze meets mine and I smile encouragingly, Mera has professed her love for me continuously, but she's never said it to Cass before. Tristan reaches over and grips my hand in his, I look over and see an unreadable look on his face.

"I love you to the moon and back kiddo." A whoosh of air escapes Tristan hearing Cass's words.

After reassuring Mera that we would see her in a few hours, she was content enough to leave with Kitty, I know her daddy is on edge and worried because he isn't with them. Tristan stops outside the door to Sky's room; we have to transfer her into a coffin in order to travel. I hate the thought of her being in a box while her heart still beats, but we don't have a choice.

"What you both did...for Mera–." Cass cuts Tristan off when he places a hand on his shoulder.

"You never have to thank us for loving her, she is an incredible kid T. We would both lay our lives down for her without a second thought." He gulps and nods repeatedly at a loss for words.

"Cass and I know you and Mera, hell even Kitty is a package deal. We don't care for her because of you, we care for her because she didn't give us a choice but to love her." Not wanting to linger anymore I step forward and place a chaste kiss on his lips before opening the door.

"Didn't think you would be doing this on your own did ya?" Tears gather for the second time this evening as I race forward and launch myself at him, he wraps his around me as I soak in his comforting scent.

"If he wasn't your twin, I would burn his ass alive."

"Preach, brother." I pull back from Cole and smile up at him only to find his gaze fixed on my guys, I turn slowly to find Cole is eyeing out Tristan.

"Cole, what are you doing?" He pulls his gaze from Tristan to stare at me and then back to the guys. I tense, fuck, does he know? A growl tumbles from his lips and I dart out in front of him to garner his attention, I won't have my guys and my brother fighting. My brothers cold stare bores into me and I cringe.

"I should be the one asking, *who* are you doing here?" Fuck!

"Watch your mouth Colton!"

"Shut the fuck up Cassius." Cass growls and I hear him move behind me, I wheel on him and hold my hand out.

"Move!" He snaps, I growl as I feel the power of his alpha run through me. It wasn't a direct order, but I still feel the power of it thrumming through me, Cass promised me he would never take away my free will by using an alpha's order.

"Cass, he's my brother." I plead.

"He doesn't get to stand there and fucking judge us." The icy tone of his voice tells me Cass is furious, I knew my brothers wouldn't take the news of me being with the guys well. Cass and Cole begin to shout and trade insults, I wind up like a sandwich between them and look to Tristan for help, but his gaze is focused out the window. I tune Cole and Cass out as I watch Tristan walk toward the window, when I see him tense, I know something is wrong.

"Shut the fuck up! We need to move now, they're here."
Instantly Cass and Cole stop their snide remarks as they turn to
Tristan.

"Who?" Cole asks, Tristan ignores him as he heads for Sky,
he gathers her in his arms.

"We have to move now." He snaps.

"What about the coffin?" I ask as he heads for the door.

"There's no time, they're at the tree line." The three of us
follow Tristan in a line, my heart is pumping and fear thrums
through me. I may be a shifter, but after the horror stories
Tristan has told us about what witches and warlocks can do,
three wolves and a warlock don't stand a chance against all of
them. Cass darts in front of Tristan as we near the front door,
he flings it open and rushes toward the SUV that sits in the
drive, he quickly opens the back door for him to place Sky
inside. The wind is whipping around us, it's so strong that Cole
has to grip me around the waist to stop me from falling over.
Rain begins to pelt down on us as Tristan closes the back door,
the heaving water has us drenched in seconds. I move toward
the other side of the car, but Tristan reaches out to stop me, I
hear Cole growl but ignore him.

"I can't go with you." He shouts over the wind and rain; I
reel back and shake my head. He cups my face and peers down
into my eyes, tears begin to fall when I see the resolution in his.

"No, we have time–." He shakes his head.

"I'll hold them off, get Sky to kitty and she will do the
transfer to Mera when the baby is born." A sob tears from me, I
strike out and slap him.

"You promised you wouldn't leave me!" I scream. He
smashes his lips against mine and I cling to him hoping he will
change his mind. He pulls back and the look of love in his eyes
breaks me. "Look after my little girl, thank you for being the
mother she never knew. I love you California." He releases me

and takes off toward the back of the house, I race after him but Cass snakes his arm around my waist to hold me back as a sense of déjà vu races through me.

"Let me go!" I scream, he spins me around until I face him. I gasp when a sad smile graces his lips, I shake my head denying what I see in his gaze. "Please–."

"I love you with all my heart California." He intensely kisses me, but before I can cling to him, he pulls away and looks down at me, his eyes change from green to blue and I struggle in his hold.

"No, Cassius don't you dare fucking do this to me!" I scream.

"It's because I fucking love why I am doing this. Get in the car, board the plane and go to your brother's pack. Do not come back here, you stay safe!" His alpha order washes over me and Kora whines in agony, even she can't fight against his order, we may be his mate, but we aren't above his command.

"Cass–." He cuts me off.

"Take her now and don't stop!" As soon as Cass releases me to chases after Tristan, Cole is dragging me into the car kicking and screaming. I watch out the back window as Cole drives us away from the two men I have fallen madly in love with, I have never felt for anyone like this before, not even Sky. Losing them will destroy me.

TWENTY

CALIFORNIA

Everything inside me is hurting, my heart even beats at a lazy rate, almost like it knows it's no use beating anymore without them. Once we landed Cairo and Z were there to greet us, Caro carried Sky to the car. I slide in next to her and cuddle into her side, I know some will think it's weird being broken hearted over two guys, I have faced the fact that Sky is gone, but even right at this moment when I need comfort, she's right here beside me.

Tears leak silently from my eyes, Z slides in next to me but doesn't say a word, Cairo and Cole are in the front. I over hear Cole filling Cairo in on what happened outside the car, but I tune them out not wanting to relive that moment the guys ripped my heart out. I know they chose to stay behind because it was the only chance Cole and I had making it out of there safely with Sky, I feel like I have nothing to live for now...Mera. I jolt up in my seat and ask.

"Did Mera and Kitty get here safely?" I demand. Cairo meets my gaze in the rear-view mirror.

"I assume so, I left to come and get you lot. Creed and

Asher were the ones picking them up." I sigh in relief and snuggle back into Sky's side as I let the tears and grief wash through me thinking about Cass and Tristan.

I startle awake when I'm jostled to find Cole carrying me. "What are you doing?" I ask.

"You fell asleep, I didn't want to wake you, so I thought I'd put you to bed." He may be angry at me, but right now he knows I need my twin; I snuggle into him as a fresh wave of tears hits me. I bury my face in his chest when we enter Creed's house, I hear the others and can't handle the thought of them pitying me again. "I got you." Cole whispers as he keeps walking past the others.

"Callie?"

"Leave her brother, Cairo will fill you in once he has Sky settled." At the reminder of Sky, I feel even worse. She's dead and I haven't even let her go yet, now I'm going to have to do the same with Cass and Tristan. A sob breaks free, and I cling to my brother praying he can rid me of this pain. Cole lays me on the bed gently, I curl myself into a ball wrapping my arms around my middle trying to hold myself together. I feel the bed dip and when her scent assaults me I sit up and pull her into my arms as I break down.

"I'm right here baby girl." I cry out.

"T-their g-gone, t-they left me, mom!" I sob out, she pushes me back and caresses my cheek Her face is filled with nothing but love and understanding. "It hurts mommy, it hurts so bad." Tears pour from my mom's eyes as she stares at me.

"I know it does, I know everything hurts right now and you're broken inside baby girl. I'm so sorry that you are going through this pain again, you never should have gone through this the first time. You're California, so strong my girl, but I want you to pull yourself together, because there is a little girl out there who needs you, you have to be strong for her." I shake my head denying her claims.

"I can't, I can't mom!" Her eyes harden.

"You can and you will, your brothers and I will be here with you every step of the way."

"How the fuck am I supposed to bury all three of them? I loved her mom but..."

"Don't say it darling, you don't love them more, you just love them differently. Skylar was your first love, and you never forget your first sweetie, I saw the connection between you and the guys. You are their gravity that holds them to this earth, don't cry over them when there is a chance–."

"Not against the elder's mom–."

"Don't count them out, those boys will walk through hell for you Callie, don't doubt their strength. If there's a will there's a way, I promise you that."

An hour later, mom helps me clean my face and tidy myself up before leaving the confines of my room. Dread pools inside me as I follow my mother, I tighten my hold on her hand as we enter the living room. Everyone is here, Cole, Creed, Jess, Z, Belle, Cairo, Vince and even Alex. I look around and that's when I spot Kitty in the corner with Mera huddled on her lap, I take a deep breath and bypass everyone as I make my way to them. Kitty meets my gaze; I answer her unanswered question with a shake of my head. Her face hardens as she nods hers, she understands that the guys didn't make it. I fight against the sob that wants to break free as I reach out and pull Mera into my embrace, she clings to me as sobs wrack her body. I slam my eyes closed trying to reign in my own pain, mom is right, I have to be strong for my girl.

My girl.

She is ours Callie.

C-can you feel him?

No.

I close the link with Kora and slowly lower myself to the floor with Mera still clinging to me, I feel the others stares but ignore them as I rock her and place kisses on her head. When I feel Jess drop down beside me, I smile at my best friend, she wraps her arm around my shoulders and we lean into each other resting our heads together.

"Whatever you need, Creed and I will do it." She speaks.

"Technically she rules your pack now anyway." I snap my gaze to Z; he looks around the room and furrows his brow. "What?"

"What do you mean?" My mom asks.

"She's the chief alpha's mate, that makes her the new chief, right?" I tune out Z and the others as I ask Jess.

"Why is Alex and Vince here?" Jess stiffens slightly.

"He says they're here for the birth, Gabe and Hunter are on their way as well." I cringe, how the fuck do I tell Cass's dad and brother that he isn't coming back, and Gabriel has to bury another child? "Hey, don't worry about any of that okay. Just focus on Mera and what you need." I love Jess so much, since I met her years ago, I knew we would become best friends forever. She just gets me and knows what I want, Belle slowly lowers herself on my other side.

"Beauty, the wooden floors–."

"Shut the hell up Cairo, I'm fine." She snaps, I fight my smile.

"My brother still treating you like you're made of glass?" Belle groans in answer to Jess.

"He won't even let me shower alone in case I slip, next thing I know he'll be wiping me after I pee." Jess and I chuckle as Belle throws her hands up in frustration.

I startle awake when I hear shouting, I blink my eyes and notice its daylight. I didn't fall sleep till nearly dawn this morning, I just lay here watching Mera sleep and marveling at how much she looks like her father and aunt. When the shouts grow louder, I slowly detangle myself leaving her in a blissful sleep, she has been through enough. I pull the covers over her and place a kiss to her head before creeping from the room and closing the door.

"You are not getting anywhere near her!" I make my way toward the living room and freeze at the sound of his voice, The anger in Cole's tone sends a cold shiver down my spine.

"Have it your way then." A smile breaks free, and I take off running, I round the corner and plough into someone, Z reaches to steady me but drops his hold when a growl sounds out.

"Don't fucking touch her!" I dart around Z ready to run for them but freeze when I see both my brothers pinned against the far wall by an invisible source, I look straight to Tristan, he shrugs his shoulders.

"I warned them, they tried to keep you from me–." I cut him off as I take off toward them, I leap through the air, Cass catches me with ease, I wrap one arm around him pulling Tristan in at the same time. They both hold me in this awkward three-way hug, but I don't give a fuck. My guys are alive, and they came back to me!

"I thought you were dead." I cry, I feel them both flinch at my words and hold them tighter. I didn't think I would ever see them again; I pull back and stare down at each of them. They look so tired and worn out, I can see bruises and cuts that mar Tristan's beautiful skin, Cass doesn't sport any thanks to being a shifter. I lean down and kiss Cass before turning to Tristan and doing the same.

"Yeah, wow, nope. Did not see that coming." I pull back from Tristan to look over at Z, both him and Cairo are in shock.

"Let me the fuck down." I turn back to see my brothers are still stuck against the wall from Tristan's air magic. I look to Cole, and he bares his teeth. "I'm gonna tear you apart you little bitch." Tristan clicks his fingers and they both drop to the ground, I wiggle free of Cass's hold and stand in front of them, ready to face off against my brothers.

"Move Callie."

"Get real Colton. I'm not letting either of you two touch them."

"Him." Creed shouts whilst pointing at Cass. "I can deal with, but him I don't know, and I won't have him near you." I balk at the audacity of both my brothers, how dare they! I will not allow them to dictate my life, I am a grown ass woman, I open my mouth to give them a good tongue lashing but pause when I feel Z and Cairo close in beside me. "Stay out of this Cairo."

"Pull your head out of your ass Credence." Ro rebukes, I'm startled by his defense for me.

"She isn't your sister; I'd like to think after her being with Sky you might be inclined to agree–." I cringe, Cairo releases a ferocious growl in warning, Cass shoves to the front and moves to stand mere inches from my brothers. Low growls come from Cass; I can see from how tense he is that he is fucking pissed.

"Cassius–."

"Stay out of this beauty, she's his mate and it's his right to defend her." Out of everyone, it means so much to me that Cairo is accepting of me and Cass, I would like to hope that acceptance extends to Tristan as well.

"He's my brother." Kora takes control, she forces a partial shift as she turns us to face Belle and growls in warning. Belle's eyes widen and Kora chuckles, amused that an original vampire is frightened of us.

"He may be your brother, but he is mine." A slow smile spreads across her face and she nods happily, that I have finally accepted Cass as mine.

"You will both bow the fuck down and keep your thoughts to yourself, I don't give a shit if you don't know him! Tristan loves her and will lay down his life for your sister without a thought, don't ever try to come between us and her again." Cass's alpha tone is enough to silence the room.

"How are you okay with this?" Cole asks.

"He makes her happy, she loves him, and I love her, that's all you need to know, because frankly, it's none of your goddamn business. If you can't accept the way we choose to live, then I'll make sure she never returns here." Growls come from both my brothers.

"Are you threatening–."

"Tristan, Cassius, I'm so glad you are both okay." We all turn toward the back door to see my mom and kitty, they rush over and embrace each of the guys.

"It's good to see you again Mrs. Reeves." Mom blushes and smacks Tristan on the chest, I groan and roll my eyes when I see her cheeks turn slightly red.

"You smooth talker, you."

"Mom!" I scold, she shoos me like I'm a fucking fly.

"Why are you all standing here like you're in some sort of Mexican standoff?" I snort, waiting for Creed or Cole to explain themselves, but they don't get a chance.

"It appears your sons are not happy with the fact Cass and I are both with California." Mom wheels on my brothers and pins them with a look only a mother can muster, they may be full grown males but they both pale under the pressure of her glare.

"Mom–."

"Don't you *mom* me Credence." Jess, Belle and Vince chuckle behind us and I admit, even I have to fight the smile from spreading across my face. "How dare you both act this way; I did not raise either of you to behave in this manner or treat our guests like this." Cole scoffs.

"He stopped being a guest when he made himself at home between my sister's legs." Cass winds his arm back ready to hit Cole, but was intervened when Cole goes sailing through the air smacking into the far wall before landing on the ground with a resounding thud.

"Speak about her like that again and I promise you, next time you won't get up." My mouth drops open in shock at Tristan, he sets his sights on Creed next. "Think what you want, and say whatever it is you want to say, I don't give a fuck. Your opinion doesn't mean shit to me, but it does to Callie. I won't bat an eye at never seeing you again, but she will miss you, hear me when I say this. Don't make her choose between us and you, because you will fucking lose every time." The walls I had built around my heart since losing Sky have slowly started to come down, these two have broken through them each day. The remaining shards I had around my artery was just obliterated by Tristan's words, I reach and clasp his hand in mine, he meets my stare and smiles lovingly.

"California, take your men to see Mera, I'm sure she will be overjoyed to know they are okay." I don't argue, I grip Cass's hand with my free one and lead them toward where Mera is. We're stopped by Belle when she practically throws herself at her brother earning a growl from Cairo.

"Don't ever scare me like that again." Cass pulls free of my hold and wraps his arms around his sister.

"I'm sorry I worried you sis, d-does dad and Hunt know?" Belle stands back, bites her lip and shakes her head.

"I didn't want to say anything over the phone, they will be here later today, and I was going to tell them then." A whoosh of air escapes Cass as he nods, he places both his hands on her shoulders and bends, so they are eye to eye and smiles at her.

"Let's not stress dad more than he already is." Belle chuckles.

"Deal, he's been fussing and driving Hunter nuts about taking over so he can leave."

"Yeah, he told me he wanted to be here before the baby is born." Belle blows out and exasperated breath.

"God, I want this baby out now. Between him and Cairo constantly checking on me I'm done." Cass chuckles and Cairo storms over to her scoffing.

"I do not fuss!" She pins her mate with a death glare.

"You monitor my fucking temperature and have to taste test everything I eat first." Cairo throws his hands in the air.

"I do it because you might be in labor and not even know, plus, how do you know someone hasn't spiked the food?"

"Because you fucking cook it for me, you ass!" She shouts, Cairo grins sheepishly and rubs the back of his neck.

"Told you her moods will worsen the further along she gets." Belle wheels on Zeke and snarls exposing her fangs.

"You know Z, I haven't drunk from a vein in a while, keen to oblige me?" Z growls and narrows his eyes, these two bicker so much but I see nothing but love and adoration between them.

"Fuck no you little demon, you have a mate, suck that fucker dry." Cass splutters.

"I'll rip his fucking head off Gabrielle if you do that shit in front of me!" Cass snaps whilst glaring at Z, Belle rolls her eyes.

"Please, Cairo won't touch me because he thinks his dick is going to leave an imprint on the baby's head." Everyone breaks out into fits of laughter at Ro's expense, he scowls at his mate for voicing their private business.

"His dick isn't that big." Creed teasingly shouts.

"Fuck up asshole, your sister is still getting dicked by two guys." My mouth drops open as Creed growls, before this can continue and turn into another fight, I grab both my guys and lead the way to Mera.

TWENTY-ONE

CASSIUS

The three of us thought it best that we stay with Meg rather than at Creed's, Jess is pissed off at her mate because of how he acted and none of us want to bear witness to him getting a new asshole. Plus, this way I don't have to look at Cole's fucking face after what he said, he had no fucking right to throw Sky in her face.

I was ready to end that son of bitch until Tristan did it for me, Mera seems more content at Meg's anyway, Kitty of course came with us much to her dismay, she wanted to stay at Creed's because the *view is* better apparently. The little devil burst into tears at the sight of us, she hugged me just as long as she did her dad, and it fucking reduced me to a puddle of goo.

I never thought I would be the type to bend to a child's will, but low and behold, here I am sitting on the back porch of Meg's watching her pick daisies with Kora trailing after her. Kora is just as protective of Mera as any mother wolf, Callie may not have noticed the shift in her wolf, but I have. At the sound of others approaching Kora will block Mera or if someone gets to close, she will growl, Kora has taken on a mother role and Callie doesn't even know it yet.

She is ours; I feel it too. A whoosh of air escapes me and I slouch.

I know.

I've known for weeks now that Atticus has seen Mera as one of our own pups, my own hang up with this revelation is what Tristan will think of it. As if my thoughts alone summoned him, I hear his heavy breaths as he exits the back door and sighs before dropping down beside me on the steps. I peer over at him and see the worry lines that mar his face, we were lucky to escape with our lives back in New York. If Tristan didn't set fire to his own house, we would be dead, we used the house exploding as a distraction and ran. We flew commercial here and used Alias names so they couldn't track us, he told me they will find us eventually, they always do.

"I have to go back." I reel back and stare at him as if he has lost his fucking mind.

"Why? We agreed being here was the safest place for Callie and Mera." He shushes me and darts his gaze to the girls; I reign my anger in and whisper low enough for only him to hear. "Why?"

"One of my hotels in New York just caught on fire miraculously and my club is now flooded," I run a hand through my hair as I shake my head.

"They're doing this to draw you out." He deflates and rests his forearms on his knees as he nods.

"I know, but I won't let them come here, they can't get near Mera and I won't put Callie on their radar."

"If you go there, she will follow you." He turns and looks over at me, the look in his eyes tells me all I need to know. "I won't lie to her Tristan; you will destroy her if you do this." He nods solemnly.

"I know, which is why I need you both look after Mera and Kitty–." I shake my head and cut him off.

"We know nothing about witches, how are we supposed to help Mera and my sister's kid without you?"

"Kitty will be here; she will help you with whatever has to be done."

"You don't get it." I growl. "She let you in, she fucking let you in Tristan. If you do this, she won't come back this time, I thought all hope for her and I was lost until you came into the mix. You forced her out of her pit of despair and made her see there was more to life than her grief. If you run back there, she will follow and so will I, we're a team now and you have to understand that."

"What would you have me do then? If they find us here, they will go after her to get to me, they won't stop at Callie. They'll take Mera to punish not only me, but kitty as well for what she did to Henrick." His words ring true.

"Look, think on it okay, Creed and Ro are throwing a bonfire tonight for everyone, in honor of my pack coming here. Enjoy the night with our girl and reflect on your choices before you go off half-cocked."

After I left Tristan earlier to watch over the girls, I decided to go see my sister at the old cabin her, Ro and Zeke are staying in. This place is just a miniature version of Creed's new house, I guess Jess really did love this place. I don't bother knocking and just left myself in, Belle pokes her head around the corner from the kitchen and smiles wide.

"Cass, what are you doing here?" She wipes her hands on

the dish towel before waddling over to me, I hide the smile that stretches across my face. She pauses in front of me, places her hands on her hips and scowls. "If you make a joke about me being fat–."

"I would never." I deadpan.

"Bullshit." I place my hands on her shoulders and bend, so we are eye level.

"I'm smiling because my baby sister finally got her wish." Her brows furrow in confusion. "Bells, I saw the devastated look on your face every time you would see one of the women in the pack pregnant." Shame colors her features, I pull her to me and wrap my arms around her as I rest my chin atop her head. "You did it Belle, you made all your wishes come true, and I'm so proud of you..." I swallow loudly and take a deep breath before continuing. "I know Blake would be as well, all he ever wanted was for you to be happy." I hold her tighter when I hear her quietly cry against me, we stay like this for a long time until Cairo comes storming around the corner. He looks from me to Belle and growls.

"The fuck did you do to her." I roll my eyes as he stomps over to us, he tries to peel Belle from my hold, but she won't let go.

"Did your dreams have to include a jackass that no one likes aside from you?" Cairo narrows his eyes and Belle chuckles against me. She pulls back and wipes her eyes before gripping my hands in hers, I can see the confusion that mars Cairo's face.

"He isn't so bad, rough around the edges, but I'll straighten him out." Cairo scoffs.

"I take offense to that!" He sneers.

"I know, you were meant to." She jests as she scurries over to him and snuggles into his side, he wraps his arm around her as he places a loving kiss to her head. I smile at the sight;

I'm overjoyed for my sister. My brothers, myself and our dad had been trying to find a *cure* for Belle's visions for years, hoping that one day she would be able to lead a normal life. Little did we know that cure was already hunting her, Cairo and I may not be close, but he will always have my respect because of how he treats my sister. He fucked up after Sky died, but he has spent every day since then trying to prove to Belle that he is worthy of her love, and that goes a long way in my books.

"What's up Cass?" I snap out of my thoughts and look to him.

"I was actually hoping to speak to you about Sky." He tenses at the mention of his former beta, a second ticks by before he nods stiffly.

"Why don't you take Cass to Sky's room, and I'll finish up in here." Cairo nods as he places a kiss to her head again. Belle grips his hand before he can turn to lead the way, she whispers ever so silently. "Remember, he is my brother, and if you hurt him, I'll hurt you." Cairo grips her hips and pulls her to him for a kiss, causing me to swallow a few times or risk gagging.

"Beauty, when you make threats like that, don't show your fangs, you know it makes me hot for you–."

"And that's enough of that, thank you." I grit out causing them both to laugh, I brush past them and head toward Sky's room. I follow her scent until I reach the door on the right, I push it open and freeze when I see Z, Creed, Cole and Jess huddled around her. All their gazes swing to me, a lesser man would cower under the pressure of their stares, but not me.

"Is my sister okay?" I wave off Creed's concerns.

"She's fine, she's with Mera and Tristan." Cole mutters shit under his breath, and it pisses me off. "You got something to say Colton?" His eyes hold so much anger and it confuses me as to why.

"What she is doing isn't right." Jess tries to calm him, but Creed pulls her back, Z shakes his head clearly over his shit.

"Who are you to say that?"

"Her fucking twin! You are both taking advantage of her–." I snap, I close the space between us and wrap my hand around his throat as I slam him against the wall, Z and Creed try to pull me back, but I snap my jaws at them in warning. I hear Cairo enter the room telling Jess to take Belle and go back to their house, I get right in Cole's face so our noses touch.

"If you ever insinuate that I took advantage of her again, I'll rip your fucking throat out. I backed off and gave her time to grieve the loss of her thought-to-be mate, even when my wolf fought me. Tristan didn't even know who she was when they first met, you fucking prick."

"And I'm supposed to just take his word for it?"

"Yeah, because it's the truth." I peer over my shoulder to see Tristan standing in the doorway next to Cairo, I release my hold on Cole and move toward Ro. Creed and Cole glare at him, Z and Ro move to the end of the bed and block Sky from view. "I thought since Callie was distracted this might be the best time to...hash this shit out." Creed narrows his eyes.

"Why the fuck would we hash anything out with you?" T shrugs his shoulders and stuffs his hands in his pockets.

"Because I love your sister and I'm not going anywhere. I originally took Sky back to fulfil her last wish of helping her best friend's kid, I'll be honest. With the trouble it has brought me and my family and not to mention putting my daughter in harm's way, I would have ended the funnel from my sister to the child." Cairo growls, Z grips his arm holding him in place.

"Why didn't you?" Creed's question is barely above a whisper, he knows where T is going with this.

"It's simple, I met a brown-haired, green-eyed girl who I fell for and asked me to do what I could to save the baby she viewed as family."

"You would put your own family at risk for mine?" Cairo queries. I shake my head and roll my eyes, these idiots don't fucking listen!

"No dumbasses, he just told you he is doing all of this because he is in love with Callie, that's why." The four idiots nod like fucking monkeys at a circus, Tristan nods his thanks to me for helping him out.

"I can't support this." Both T and I look to Cole.

"You don't have to–." Tristan cuts me off.

"If my sister came home with two guys, I would feel the same way you do, I certainly wouldn't want two dick heads sleeping with Sky." Cairo and Z chuckle, Tristan turns to them and pulls his upper lip back in a sneer. "I also know you slept with my sister," Cairo clamps his mouth closed like a good idiot. "The images that are running through your head isn't how we work, both Cass and I love her, we will do anything to protect her–." Creed cuts him off.

"So, you will always choose her?" Tristan sighs and shakes his head earning a growl from the Reeves brother. "You fucking–."

"Let me answer!" Creed snarls but allows Tristan to continue. "I made it clear to California that I will always be here for her, but if I was given a choice between her or my little girl..." He drops his gaze to the floor as he finishes. "I would choose, Mera, always." I place a hand on his shoulder in support, I know that was hard for him to admit. Truth is, if I was faced with the same choice...I don't know if my choice would differ from his. That kid has burrowed her way under my skin and into my heart so deep, I love Mera as if she is my own.

TWENTY-TWO

TRISTAN

At the sound of him approaching I slowly lift my gaze to meet Credence Reeve's accusing stare. I get the animosity they both feel toward my situation with Callie, they probably think Cass and I spit roast her nightly–which isn't far from the truth but, she is roasted with love.

I wait for him to lash out when he is a foot away, Cass shifts slightly so he is just in front of me. I appreciate the gesture, but it isn't needed, I could have this asshole thrown against the wall in seconds, I feel my magic coil inside me, ready and waiting for me to unleash it.

Cass growls low in his throat warning Creed, who just nods. I respect Cassius a lot, he doesn't use his rank to get his way, he is trying to earn his place through the respect of others.

"If your daughter wasn't part of the equation, what would your choice."

"It would be California." I cut in, Creed nods his head and surprises the fuck out of me when he sticks his hand out. I eye it warily for moment before I place mine in his and shake.

"I can feel the alpha order of protection Cass has given, but

I want to offer you my mown decree." I stuff my hand back in my pocket and motion for him to continue. "As Callie's oldest brother, I welcome you to the Hasting-Reeves pack. You have my protection whilst you are on my lands, Callie is still classed as rogue, but the pack knows her standing with me and she is treated as an equal."

"Thank you." He smirks.

"Don't thank me yet, I'm not done." I bite my lip to stop myself from smiling when he eyes both Cass and I. "You may be the chief alpha and you may be some powerful wizard thing–."

"I'm not Harry Potter." I deadpan.

"Nah, you're not. Harry was way cooler than you will ever be. But as Callie's brother, I stand before you both with a vow of my own. If either of you two bastards hurt my sister or put her through half the shit Sky did, chief alpha or not, I'll cut your fucking balls off and where them around my neck as a necklace, feel me?" I roll my lips over my teeth to stop myself from smiling.

"Deal." Cass supplies as Creed focuses on me.

"You have my word but–." Cole groans but I ignore him. "You two ever throw Sky in her face like you did earlier, I'll kill the both of you and burn you fucking alive, *feel me*?"

We all stand around the bed that Sky rests on, I glide my hands above her to feel for the magic that Kitty has used to keep her heart beating. As tingles start to prick the tops of my fingers, I know the spell still holds, I wish there was a way for kitty to block us from the elders.

"What happens once the baby is born?" Cairo asks me, I meet Cass's stare and he gives me a look that tells me he has my back.

"Maybe we should have a seat?" Cairo leads us from Sky's room and motions for us all to take a seat in the living room,

Cass and I sit on the three-seater whilst the others drop into the two single seats and two-seater.

"Do you two fuck?" Cass and I both swing our gazes to Cole.

"The fuck did you just say?" Cass grits out through clenched teeth.

"Well, you constantly protect him plus you're always together and defending the other." He says as he shrugs his shoulders, Cass scrubs a hand down his face leaving me to answer the asshole.

"Let me make this simple for you, our cocks only go in your sisters' holes, not each other's." Cole is out of his seat in a second, Cairo jumps up and blocks his path to us as Cole growls and shouts.

"Calm the fuck down, how many times have I told you not to ask dumb shit if you didn't want a dumb answer?"

"That's my sister he is talking about." Cole shouts, I lean back in my seat and cross my legs, I can feel Cass's heated glare in the side of my head but ignore him.

"I know, he will pay for that fucking comment." I scoff, I'd like to see him fucking try.

"Can you all sit the fuck down, we have about two hours before everyone arrives, and just because you fuckers are getting it, doesn't mean the rest of us are, I would personally love to find someone to ride me tonight." Cairo turns to Zeke.

"Really? That's all you're worried about right now?"

"Don't act innocent Cairo, you were just as bad as me not so long ago." Cass growls as Cairo shoves Cole back into his seat and drops down beside Creed.

"Can we get on with this?" Cole snaps. Cass fills them in about everything, yes *everything*. The four guys are in shock that I can wield fire but say nothing, Cole seemed taken back to learn about Callie being bonded to me as well, he thought

Callie was just some fling. Cairo is tense and on edge after learning about my plans for his baby and Mera, I can see the worry in his face, so I decide to reassure him.

"Your child will feel nothing." Cairo Cruz is a warrior and I imagine nothing much scares him, but when his blue eyes look to me and I see fear, I understand it. "I understand your worry–."

"How could you?"

"Because Cairo, I am a father myself, and everything to do with my daughter worries me. If we don't do this, your child will end up like my sister." He flinches at the reminder.

"Why wasn't Mera born with magic like you?" I turn to Creed as I answer.

"I don't know, I for one am glad she wasn't, or Gemma would never have traded her."

"You said you were searching for Sky, why did you trade her power if there was a chance she still lived?" Cole's question is valid, and I can see they are skeptical.

"We had to do what we thought was right, I hadn't found any clues and my P. I's could never find a trail. If kitty agreed to surrender her power, then that was a definite and I couldn't risk that, so we thought we would take a chance on offering my sister. Bear in mind I had no idea she was alive; it wasn't until years later when rumors surfaced from your kind that there was a powerful woman who ran with the rogues. I followed this lead and still couldn't get a trail, I wasn't the only one who heard about her either, the elders learnt of her existence and were tracking her. Whoever outed her to your council is the reason my elders doubled down in their search for her."

"We have to find out who Alex's mole is, if we find them, then we may get our answer about who outed my beta." The conviction and promise in Cairo's voice put some of the tension inside me at ease.

Meeting Cass's dad and brother was...different?

His father is laid back and loving toward his three children, you can still see the hurt that clouds his eyes when he looks to each of his three surviving children. Hunter, he is nothing like Cassius, he's laid back and easy going and nothing seems to bother him much except, whenever they speak about him taking over as alpha. I can understand the loss they feel to some degree, each of them had the chance to know their sibling, I was robbed of that. Many a nights I wished Sky might have found it in herself to find me, and I would have had a piece of my family back, but being in the presence of everyone here, I now see why she never searched for me. My sister built a family of her own, not by blood, but by choice. The affection and love each of these people have for her is astounding, hearing stories about her and what she was like means so much to me. Cairo, Callie and Zeke knew a different side of the infamous Skylar Cage to the others, to them she was funny, loving and just a joy to be around, to the others she was a fearless badass who took no prisoners.

We all sit around the bon fire telling stories, all the packs are here, including the Wilder pack as well. Everyone was in shock when other alphas answered Cassius's call to come to our aide, they all sit around telling war stories. A lot of them are intrigued by kitty, Mera and me, they haven't met a witch or warlock before. The only ones who seem less...intrigued is Alexander and Vincent, which in turn leads me to believe they know about my kind. I have no desire to mingle unlike Cass, I sit back and observe, and so far tonight, I have noticed that

Belle has distanced herself from her biological father and uncle, the bigger shock was when I noticed her pull back from Cole.

I know she has the gift of sight, clearly she has seen something about these three that makes her uncomfortable. None of the others seem to notice her shift, her abilities to forsee the future is held in high esteem and these-fools should learn her ques and adhere to them before it costs them greatly. At the sound of Cass calling my name I'm pulled from my thoughts, Cass waves me over to where he is standing with his brother, Z and a couple of other guys. I stop and place a kiss to the top of Mera's head as her and kitty head back to Megs where she is watching over Harlem and Phoenix, I admit I love the names Jess and Creed chose for their kids. It's definitely a bit odd to name all kids after places, but each to their own, I guess.

"What's up?" I muse as I stand by Cass and eye the other guys, each of them wearing looks of wonder, and it makes me slightly uneasy for reason I don't know.

"These dipshits are wondering how our dynamic works–." Cass is cut off when a young woman pushes her way between us and presses herself against Cass, her tits are literally right against his chest. She is tall, maybe a few inches shorter than Cass, her tits look as fake as her inflated lips and even I can tell there is no way her ass is that round naturally. Cass stiffens as the girl lifts her manicured fingers and trails them down his arm.

"I'm Amber." She purrs, if this is what this girl thinks it takes to garner a man's attention, then she is mistaken.

"And I'm mated." Cass states with zero hesitation. Amber pouts and juts her hip to one side as if the look alone will change the fact he is taken.

"Not by choice though, right?" Cass's gaze cuts to me, the look on his face says it all, he can't believe this girl is still trying to bed him. She lifts her arms and drapes them around Cass's neck, which earns her a growl that she chooses to ignore. "I can rock your world." She tries to sound seductive and enticing but fails, a growl sounds out behind us and a slow smile spreads across Cass's face, I know who that growl belongs to.

"You should back up." Cassius sounds gleeful and the stupid blonde-haired bimbo thinks he's flirting.

"Oh fuck, here comes hurricane California." I bite my lip to stop the laughter that wants to break free at Creed's statement. The girl puckers her lips ready to kiss the chief alpha, but before she can lock lips with Cass she is shoved to the side and stumbles in her ridiculously high stilettoes, who the fuck wears high heels to a bon fire? Callie stands in front of Cass glaring at the bitch who dared to touch her mate, her eyes are her wolf's, I can see from how fast she is breathing she is struggling to stay in control and keeping Kora at bay.

"What the hell, you crazy bitch!" Amber shrieks, we have garnered the attention of everyone now. The bimbo heads straight for Callie who smiles wickedly, Cass wraps his arms around Callie's waist and rests his chin on her shoulder. The girl freezes at the sight in front of her, her lip pulls back in a snarl.

"Amber, I don't believe you've met, my mate?" The bimbo places her hands on her hips and huffs out her annoyance. Callie keeps her glare in place daring the girl to try and touch Cass again, I smile at the sight. She looks so fucking sexy right now staking her claim, I'm going to fuck her so good tonight.

"Everyone knows who that lezbo is." Callie growls and lurches forward but Cass holds her back, before he is able to subdue this bitch she spins and sets her sights on me.

Yippee!

The dirty hooker looking bitch closes the space between us and runs her hand down my chest, I grit my teeth in anger when she fakes a shiver. She reaches up to lock her arms around my neck, but her head is yanked back, and she is thrown to the ground, she screams out. Callie now stands in front of me with growls tumbling out of her, she's ready to shift at a second's notice.

"You fucking bitch! You don't own all the guys here–." Callie's growl cuts her off, I spot Creed and Cole on the other side of us as they push their way through the crowd. They dart their gazes between the three of us, Hunter fills them in on what's happened and both males pale and begin to shake their heads. I spot Jess and Belle next to Creed and both women hide their laughter behind their hand, Creed tries to flee, but Jess holds him in place with a firm look.

"Cassius is mine–." Amber cuts Callie off as she points to me and shouts.

"He isn't Cassius!" Callie straightens and laughs but there is no humor to it, she spins around and grips the back of Cass's neck and pulls him down to her so she can kiss him. This isn't a romantic kiss; this is her way of showing every wolf here who belongs to who. She releases Cass after a second and comes for me, she keeps her eyes on the confused looking idiot who still lays on the ground when she grips my face and pulls me to her, I grip her waist in my hands and squeeze, letting her know that I only see her and no one else. She breaks our kiss and I groan at the loss of her already, Cass and I stand on either side of her.

"They're both mine, touch them again and I'll fucking tear your throat out!" My cock twitches in my pants, hearing her declare her ownership like that has me horny as fuck. Amber pushes to her feet and dusts herself off, two more of her clones come forward and stand either side of their stupid ass leader whilst pinning Callie with a glare.

"Since when did you stop eating pussy and sucking cock?" I feel her stiffen beside me; I interlink my fingers with her offering my silent support. I wish I could defend her, but I

can't, she is the chief alpha's mate and has to assert her dominance over these bitches.

"About the time you started sucking your step-daddy's
cock." Gasps ring out, the crowd to the left parts and I'm in
shock to see Kayla. She stands there with a bored look on her
face, her hair is pinned up in some elaborate updo, she wears
jeans so tight they are like a second skin, her top is taut across
her chest but looks like it's been ripped to show off her midriff.

"Who the fuck allowed your trailer trash ass here?" A growl
so deep and filled with malice sounds out from Cole. Kayla
ignores Cole as she saunters in front of us to stand beside Callie
in show of support.

"Oh, is that all you got?" Kayla steps forward until her and
Amber are nose to nose, the clones' growls but there is no threat
or heat. I can tell from the way they are standing there stiff like
statues that it is taking everything inside them not to cower to
Callie and Kayla. "Amber, when will you learn?"

"This isn't high school anymore; you don't call the shots
you slut." Gasps break out but Kayla just laughs off her insult
as she turns and looks to Callie.

"Did she just call me a slut?" Callie relaxes slightly and
steps forward.

"I believe she did." Amber darts her gaze between both the
girls before settling it on Kayla.

"Babes, if you want to call me a slut, go for it, but at least I
never contracted genital warts from fucking Peter Dawson
under the bleachers." Amber gasps and splutters. "Now, how
about you apologize to California for trying to fuck her mates
and pass on your disease to them and maybe, just *maybe* she
won't kick you out of her pack. Because ya know, she is kind of
fucking mated to the chief alpha *and* bonded to the high
warlock of New York." I preen at the way she speaks my status,

Amber darts her gaze between both girls clearly trying to find her way out of this without having to say sorry.

"Do it, or I'll drag your fucking ass out of here myself!" Cole snaps.

Amber turns to Callie. "I'm so–." I don't let her finish; I flick my wrist and use my magic to collect the tramp from the ground and hurl her through the air. Her screams are deafening, but I relish in it, Callie spins around and pins me with a look, I shrug my shoulders and speak.

"Come on kitten, I saved you from clawing her eyes out." She smirks before spinning back to face Kayla, but she is nowhere to be seen.

"Where did she go?" Callie whispers, Cass slides in beside her wrapping his arm around her shoulders as everyone begins to disappear and go back to the party.

"No idea babe, but that was fucking hot."

"Eww, I don't need to hear that shit!" Jess smacks Creed on the chest and shakes her head.

"I thought it was romantic." Creed throws his head back and groans.

"Of course you do." He mutters.

TWENTY-THREE

CALIFORNIA

The rest of the night is going so swell, no more dramas or any thirsty bitches trying to rub all up on my guys! Jess, Belle and I have been catching up on everything that we have missed in each other's lives. Our guys constantly check on us, mine are never to far as they constantly watch over me. Many of the pack members have come to pledge their alliance, not just to Cass, but me as well. Tristan has become enigmatic to the wolves since they witnessed him throwing that skank with a flick of his wrist. I'm loving being here with everyone but honestly, I'd much rather be snuggled up in bed with the guys and Mera watching a movie.

"Can I talk to you for a sec?" I blow out a frustrated breath and meet my twins gaze, he shuffles from foot to foot and stuffs his hands in his pockets.

"We'll give you two some privacy." I smile at Belle and thank them both as they pat me on the shoulder. Cole drops into the picnic chair in front of me, I hate fighting with him. I cross my arms and lean back in my seat waiting for his lecture, I feel Cass and Tristan staring at me, but I ignore them. Cole runs a hand through his hair and sighs longingly.

"I fucked up and I'm sorry." I narrow my eyes at my brother, he isn't getting off that easy.

"Sorry for what exactly Colton? Throwing my dead girlfriend in my face, or pretty much accusing me of being a slut?" He flinches, he smiles sheepishly at me as he says.

"All of the above?" I growl and ready myself to stand. "What, don't go." I huff and drop back into my chair.

"Get to the point."

"Tough crowd huh?" Fuck it, I stand and so does he. I spin around ready to get the fuck out of here, but he grabs my elbow and yanks me back. A growl comes from my right, and I know it's Cass, within a second he and Tristan are at my sides glaring at my twin.

"Let her go!" Cole bares his teeth at Tristan.

"She's my fucking sister asshole."

"I fucking trump you, now let her go." Cole growls but does as Tristan asks and drops his hold on me. He pulls his stare from Tristan and looks at me, I see it in his eyes, and I get the feeling he is going to hurt me with his words, so I stop him.

"Don't Cole. I don't want to hear any of it, it's my life and you can't tell me what to do." A sad expression overtakes his features and I see tears gathering in his eyes, what the fuck is going on?

"I'm so sorry sister, for everything. When it all comes out, just know I had my reasons, and it kills me that you paid the price."

"What the hell are you talking about?" I'm so confused. Cole grips my face between his hands and places a soft kiss to my forehead.

"I'm so sorry California, please don't hate me." He whispers before letting me go and taking off through the crowd.

"What just happened?" I look up at Cass and shake my head, utterly confused.

"I have no idea." I mutter.

"Something tells me your twin brother is hiding something big, whatever he is hiding clearly won't be hidden for long though." I turn to the other side and stare at Tristan.

"What do you mean?"

"His guilt is eating away at him kitten. He's crumbling, and pretty soon everything he has tried to hide is going to explode around him, at the end of all this, I fear it will affect you the most." Tristan's words make my heart skip a beat.

I wake in the morning and smile when I feel their arms around me, last night they rocked my fucking world. Not wanting to risk waking the others we found...other accommodations. Meaning, we fucked like rabbits in the middle of the woods until I passed out and they carried me home. I feel the dull ache between my thighs and relish in it, having them both inside me at once makes me feel complete, it's as if they are the pieces I needed to be put back together. Cass trails his hand down my stomach as Tristan twirls my nipple between his fingers–.

"Daddy!" Cass and Tristan jump out of the bed and scramble around for their shorts while I watch and laugh, the door bursts open and Mera stands there with a huge ass grin. She runs toward me and leaps onto the bed, I clutch the sheet tighter to hide my nakedness. She curls beside me, and I melt, Cass huffs as Tristan spins around to shield himself.

"Hey sweetheart." She lays her head on my lap when I sit up, she smiles, and my heart starts to flutter.

"We have to talk." Everyone turns to the doorway where Kitty stands with a worried look on her face.

"What's wrong?" She turns to Tristan and the look she gives him has a cold shiver running down my spine.

"Aunt Sky came to see me." I drop my gaze back to Mera and stare at her for a beat before looking to Kitty, the solemn look she gives me tells me whatever Mera has to say isn't good.

"Get dressed, meet me downstairs." Kitty takes Mera from the room, the guy's hustle to get changed while I just sit here. Mera hasn't seen Sky since the night I first met Tristan and now she's back, why?

"Alma?" I shake my head and look to Cass, the concern on his face guts me. I know he must be worried about how I'm going to react to this news, truth be told, I have no idea how to feel. Cass slides on the bed next to me and cups my face as the first tear falls from my eyes. "Whatever it is, T and I will be with you every step of the way." I try to smile reassuringly but fail. "Don't try to hide your pain, let us help you, please." I reach up and place my hands atop of his.

"I'm not going to run from you again, if that's what you're worried about." He sags in relief.

"I wasn't even thinking about that." He jests, causing us both to smile.

"As touching as this moment is, we have to get down there now and sort this out." Tristan has Cass and I both snapping out of this moment and hustling to get ready.

Tristan and Cass sit in the single seaters and Mera chose to sit on my lap as we watch kitty pace the space of my mother's lounge room. The fact she keeps stopping to look at us is making me uneasy. I dart my gaze to Tristan over the top of Mera's head to find him staring directly at his daughter. I look to Cass next and worry he is going to destroy my mom's seats with how tight he is gripping the arm rests. Mera garners my attention when she begins to wriggle on my lap, I wrap my arms around her and hold her close inhaling her scent.

I will not let any harm befall her Callie.

I know Kora, I'm scared.

Don't be, we have two fire wielders on our side.

What if that isn't enough?

That's not what is really bothering you though, is it? I sigh, I can lie to everyone else, but I can't lie to my own wolf. *She won't take her from us.*

She's her mother Kora. What if Mera chooses to go with her?

Kora's reply is cut off when Tristan stands. "Just spit it out Kitty." She pauses her pacing and turns to Tristan with a dreadful look on her face.

"The baby will be here tomorrow night." She states in a matter-of-fact tone.

"And?" She shakes her head and continues to pace while Tristan glares at her. "I'm tired of this, now answer the question!" His voice booms around the room, Mera flinches and huddles in closer to me. I growl, Tristan swings his gaze to me and when he sees the reason for my growl his face drops. He rushes over and kneels down in front of us, he tries to pry her hands from clutching my shirt, but Mera refuses to release me. He drops back onto his hunches and scrubs a hand down his face. "I'm sorry Darling, I didn't mean to scare you." Mera buries her face into my chest as she shakes her head.

"Is papa and momma gonna go away now that aunt Sky is back?" My eyes widen to the point of nearly falling out of my fucking head, I look to Cass who mirrors my facials.

Did she just call me papa? I hold his gaze as I answer through the mate link.

She just called me momma!

Tristan looks to me before focusing back on Mera, I can see he is at a loss for what to say. I decide to take the lead and hope he doesn't get angry that I'm interfering in this moment with her, but I have to say something. I will not allow Mera to think that Cass and I will ever abandon her like that dirty bitch Gemma. I gently push her back until her tearful gaze meets mine, I smile lovingly down at her.

"Nothing in this world will ever take us from you–."

"But aunt Sky said–."

"What did she say?" I hedge.

"She said that you will have to choose."

"Choose what?" I ask slightly confused.

"If you wanted to keep daddy forever." I reel back slightly, shocked at her omission. Before I can ask any further questions, Kitty speaks up drawing all our attention to her.

"You have to mark Tristan as your mate."

"What?" She keeps her eyes on me as she answers Tristan.

"Tomorrow night when that child is born into this world, you will need more strength than you ever have."

"But I'm not strong." A devious smile graces kitty face, she slowly pulls her stare from me to focus on Cass.

"Oh, but he is." Cass reels back.

"I am not sleeping with him to mark him!" Kitty chuckles and shakes her head.

"California is marked by you, so therefore the strength you garner from the packs runs through her. If she marks Tristan, he will be able to pull on the strength of your packs to funnel the power between the child and Mera." My mouth drops open in shock. "You see, the three of you have been paired for a reason, Tristan wouldn't be able to accomplish any of this without you both, and the two of you wouldn't be able to save the child without him. My granddaughter may have loved you first California, but you were always meant to be Tristan's, not hers." Her words stir something inside me, something I think I have known for a long time but didn't want to acknowledge. Weeks ago, I remember feeling the wind wrap around me whilst I was out in the garden with Mera, I knew it was Sky. I remember standing there thinking that this is the place I was always meant to be, then guilt hit me, but before I could give into that feeling, she came to me. She came to tell me that it was okay to fall in love again and be happy.

"What happens to Sky?" Cass's softly spoken question causes the tension in the room to rise.

"She will return to the earth, where she will finally rest." A lump begins to form in my throat.

"If the baby is due tomorrow, then that means the elders will feel the power, they will come to take it." Kitty nods her head at Tristan.

"That is why your sister came to warn us, we have to let the others know to prepare them. I will help them whilst you attend to the child, but I cannot hold them on my own Tristan."

"The packs will fight!" Cass states, kitty shakes her head and blows out and exasperated breath.

"None of you bloody listen, you can make her come faster than amazon prime but not keep up with me." Cass's mouth drops open, I feel the blush coat my cheeks as Tristan tries to mask his laughter. "The packs will be weakened because Tristan will be pulling on their power through you to help him complete the transfer."

Fuck!

"So that means we are all vulnerable to weakness." Kitty nods. "We were already at a disadvantage before but now, we're fucked." Dread pools inside me, there has to be another way.

"How will they know when the baby is born?" I can feel Cass's worry through the mate link, and I know he can feel mine.

"Once the baby is here, a surge of sorts will ripple through the covens, alerting to the fact that old magic is born again."

"Old magic?" I query kitty.

"That child will carry the power combining two generations of witches and warlock inside it, my son's...power will alert all of the elders to being in existence again. Know this, the elders and Gemma will come for that power, it was promised to her and by our own laws she is *owed* that power."

"I will not stand by and let her inherit any part of my family's magic." The conviction in which Tristan speaks has me sitting up straighter. "Kitty is there any way for you to cast a spell to conceal the power of the child long enough for me to do the transfer? If we can mask it long enough, then it should give us time to recover and await their arrival." Kitty nibbles on her bottom lip for a moment pondering his request.

"It could be possible, but in order to conceal that amount of power I will be weakened." Tristan stands and faces off with Kitty.

"For how long?" I feel so out of my depth right now, we have never faced a threat like this before. These elders can strike at us from a distance, our wolves won't be able to get near them if they create a wind force or whatever the hell it is.

"Days." The ominous tone in her voice has whatever hope I had inside me diminishing. Tristan curses and stabs a hand through his hair, I look to Cass who seems lost in his own thoughts when an idea hits me.

"We can take them by surprise." All eyes swing to me.

"How?" Gone is my doting lover, Tristan now stands before me as the leader to his coven.

"Belle, she can give us a heads up–."

"My sister can't bring on visions–." I cut Cass off.

"She can with the help of Alexander, we may be wolves but let's not forget we have two original vampires that can help fight. We also have my brothers and Cairo–."

"Explain what you mean about Belle?" I brush of my annoyance at Tristan cutting me off as I meet his agitated stare.

"If Alex can her bring on a vision, she may be able to tell us where the elders will be, which means we have today to prepare a trap and buy us sometime." Tristan spins to face Kitty.

"Can that work?" She nods eagerly.

"It will give you all extra time to recover, we're going to need all the help we can get." Tristan readies himself to leave the room but Kitty's words stop him. "You will have to take her out, there is no other way." I watch as his back tenses and ripples with unease, he refuses to turn, and I start to question myself if he's still harboring any feelings for the mother of his child.

"I know." Is all he says before he leaves, I don't know where he is going so I look to Kitty for an answer. She smiles sadly at me before coming over and lowering down next to me, Mera snuggles in closer to me. "He has known for a long time that it might come to this; he had hoped she would change her course because of...what they created." I nod in understanding.

"It will destroy him, won't it?" I say barley above a whisper.

"Yes. But, not for the reason you think, he has dreaded this because he is worried, *she* will hate him when she gets older and finds out the truth." Understanding washes over me, Tristan is warring within himself because he doesn't want to take the life of Mera's mother. My heart aches for him and I wish I could offer another solution.

"I'll do it." Both Kitty and I look to Cass, he has a serious look in his eyes. "She can't hate him; it will kill him inside. But I can take her anger should it ever come." My heart races inside my chest at Cass's declaration, he is willing to risk Mera hating him if it means she never hates her father.

"I'll never hate you *papa*." My gaze drops to the sweet bundle of joy in my lap, she slowly sits up and spins to face Cass. He stares at her dumbfounded and confused as to how she knows what we are even talking about.

"You don't understand sweetheart–."

"Yes I do. Aunt Sky told me about it, she said that–" Mera chuckles and shakes her head slightly before continuing. "*Momma's* pet would do it for daddy." Cass growls and mutters under his breath about Sky being an ass which just causes us to laugh at his expense.

TWENTY-FOUR

CALIFORNIA

I stand outside our bedroom and take a steadying breath before opening it, my resolve begins to crumble when I see him standing there staring out the window. I quietly close the door behind myself and pad across to him, I wrap my arms around his waist and rest my cheek against his back. A whoosh of air escapes him and he sags slightly in my hold.

"I don't know how to get us out of this alive." The defeat in his tone tells me I have to be his strength in this moment. I drop my hold and move to stand in front of him, he keeps his gaze focused out the window.

"There is no *you*, it's *us*, we are all in this together Tristan, you, me and Cass. We're a team and the three of us will come up with a way to get rid of your asshole elders, I promise." He blinks a few times before finally looking at me, a slow smile graces his handsome face. He reaches out and cups my cheek, I nuzzle into his hand.

"I never thought I would ever be so lucky to find my bonded, to be honest, I thought it was all a myth until a hurricane came into my life." I bristle at the stupid innuendo from my brothers as he lets out a slight chuckle. "I'll fight till my last breath to make sure you and Mera make it out of this–."

"Tristan–." He places a finger against my lips to shush me.

"Let me finish." I begrudgingly nod. "I need to know that if shit goes south, your first and only priority is to get Mera the hell out of here." The way he is looking at me, imploring me to see things his way has me nodding against my own will. Kora thrashes against my ribs and I try to fight her back, but she won't allow it. My vison shifts and I feel her take over causing a partial shift.

"On my honor, we shall protect our pup." When she relinquishes control, I stumble back and gasp for air, Tristan moves forward but I raise my hand stopping him.

What the fuck Kora?

He needed to hear us vow and I did.

Why?

Because if he is distracted and worrying about Mera, he will be vulnerable.

Oh.

"Are you okay?" I take a breath and straighten.

"Yeah, Kora just took the breath out of me with that." He nods, we stand here in semi awkward silence just staring at each other for a long while. "What now?"

"Now, we tell the others and then you have to mark me." I blow out a long exhale and nod.

I walk in between Cass and Tristan as we head toward Creed's house, nervous energy is thrumming through me. I don't know how my brothers are going to take this news, shit, I don't know how Cairo is going to take knowing his baby is coming tomorrow! He has been an overprotective asshole throughout Belle's pregnancy; I can only imagine what he is going to be like once the baby is here. We climb the stairs of the porch and I pause, Cass and Tristan stop when they notice I'm not with them.

"Please don't hurt them." They both exchange a look before turning back to me.

"Who?"

"My brothers Cass. Creed has two kids to worry about and Cole...well he hasn't been himself lately and I don't know how they are going to react." Tristan comes before me and grips each of my hands in his, squeezing them reassuringly.

"As long as they don't hurt you, then we have no need to hurt them." I nod, knowing that is best I am going to get from either of them. Tristan threads his fingers through mine as we head to the door, I don't bother knocking, they would have heard us coming. I pause in the entry way when I see, Alex, Vince, Jess, Belle, Cairo, Z, Hunter, Gabriel, Cole, Creed and the two kids in the lounge room. They all look to us expectantly and it throws me off kilter slightly.

"I have told them what I have seen, but not all of it, I figured you would want to fill in the blanks." I stare at Belle for a moment stunned, of course she would have seen this coming.

"Care to fill us in?" I nod like an idiot in answer to Creed's question, Tristan's grip on my hand tightens as Cass places his large hand on my lower back and guides me further into the house. The three of us stand as I run my gaze over everyone, a pang of sadness hits me when I notice the one person missing. Cairo's gaze meets mine and I can tell he is thinking the same thing as I am.

"She's here with us in spirit Callie." I smile thankfully at Ro; his words just gave me the courage I needed to fill them all in. By the time I am done explaining everything, they all wear varying looks of anger, worry and intrigue. Ro jumps to his feet and starts pacing the lounge room, Harlem stares up at his uncle for a moment before following after him and imitating his moves. We all chuckle at the sight, that beautiful little boy has no idea that his one small act broke all the tension in the room. Phoenix begins to cry in Jess's arms, Creed takes her from Jess and excuses himself while he puts his daughter down for a nap. Before he can pass by me, I dart forward and gently stroke her soft cheek placing a kiss to her forehead.

"Sweet dreams baby girl." I whisper as Creed smiles at me and carries on his way.

"Before everyone starts shouting and fighting, please remember my son is in the room and none of you will be cussing around him, okay?" Everyone agrees to Jess's terms, I fight the smile that wants to break free. She used to be so shy and unsure of herself, so to see her now, strong and fearless makes me so happy that my bestie has finally realized her worth.

"How do we do this? Is it safe? Oh my god my baby is going to be here!" Ro begins to tear at his hair, his panicked eyes shoot to Belle. "We're gonna have a baby!" His reaction would be comical if the situation we're in wasn't so dire.

"Yeah, that's kind of how being pregnant works." Belle sounds so exasperated and over Cairo's shit, but honestly, I love how he is so caring and overprotective of her and their baby. Ro looks to Tristan and the fear in his eyes has me pitying him, I couldn't image the fear that must be thrumming through him. Having a baby at any time is stressful, but having one under these circumstances most be horrible, his baby will be born on a night where he will have to leave and fight for its freedom.

"You can do this right; you can help my daughter and make sure she doesn't...go through the same thing as Sky?" Tristan releases his hold on my hand and moves toward Cairo, Ro's blue eyes implore him to say he can save his unborn child. Tristan places a hand on Cairo's shoulder trying to offer his reassurance.

"You have my word, I will do whatever needs to be done to ensure the safety of not only your daughter, but mine as well." Cairo's gaze bores into Tristan's.

"Thank you." The weight of those two simple words holds so much more meaning, Ro isn't someone who deals with things out of his control well. For him to put his trust in Tristan is a huge deal.

"Don't thank me yet." Ro narrows his eyes suspiciously. "I have to draw on the power of the packs to harness this power inside me in order to funnel it to the girls." My jaw unhinges at this revelation.

"Say what now?" I utter. Tristan cranes his neck to the side to look at me, an apology shines in the depths of his hazel eyes.

"How did you think this would work kitten?" I flounder for a moment trying to find the right words, I thought it was as simple as clicking his fingers or some shit. I had no fucking idea that he has to pull that much power inside himself. He can already control air and fire, taking in the power from Sky means he will have more power than he can bear. Sky could barely handle three, how the fuck is he going to handle five lots of power?

"Tristan, you can't do this." Cass implores.

"It's the only way for it to be done." I shake my head vigorously denying his claim, he sighs and moves toward me until he stands a foot away. His eyes beg me to understand that he has to do this, but I can't risk losing him the same way I lost Sky.

"Please." I plead; I feel my tears building as I look into the eyes of the man I love. "There has to be another way." He bends slightly so we are eye level.

"There isn't, Kitty and I searched for weeks while we were

in New York. This is the only solution to ensure both girls survive, I won't let this happen to someone else." He wasn't able to help his sister and now he is using this as penance for his guilt.

"Sky wouldn't want you to risk–." He cuts in before I can finish.

"Do I risk the life of an innocent child?" I peer over his shoulder and meet Ro's gaze; I can see he wants to say something but bites his tongue. His pleading gaze is what causes me to cave.

"Swear to me, you can do this and be okay? I won't risk losing you Tristan, I can't." Cass's hold tightens on me, Tristan's fingers flex against my face.

"I won't make a promise I can't keep." I open my mouth to argue but he presses on. "I can do this; I know I can. I just don't know what toll it will take on my wellbeing, which is why I asked your brother for help." I furrow my brow in confusion, Tristan releases his hold on me and steps aside as Creed enters the room again with a manila folder in his grasp. Creed's gaze meets mine and irks me that I can't get a read on what he is thinking.

"They just have to sign." I look between my brother and Tristan utterly confused, Creed hands Tristan the folder reluctantly handing it over. "I misjudged you, what you are doing for my pack and family is something I cannot repay. Just know, that she will be treated as if she is our own and will never go without, you have my word." Tristan nods as Creed releases his hold.

"What the fuck is going on?" Cass demands. T moves to stand in front of both us again but makes sure to keep a foot of space between us. The serious look on his face has a cold shiver running down my spine.

"This is just a precaution."

"For what Tristan?" I can hear the impatience in Cass's tone, being left in the dark is causing Kora to stir inside me.

"I had Creed reach out to his lawyers–."

"Why?" I hedge.

"Because if things go wrong, I have to make sure Mera is taken care of." I stumble back a step, Tristan doesn't move to comfort me or put my worries at ease. "I want you both to sign these." He holds the folder toward Cass, I shake my head in denial.

"What is that?" I ask, he meets my gaze and cocks a brow at me.

"You know what they are–."

"I won't sign them!" I shout, I can feel everyone staring at me.

"If I die, I need to know she will be okay." Cass smacks the folder out of Tristan's grip and pushes up till they are chest-to-chest as he growls right in his face. "Do it Cassius." Tristan grits out.

"You're her fucking father, don't do this to her!"

"It's because of her why I am doing this! Can't you fucking see that, all of this is for Mera." He takes a deep breath and lowers his voice as he speaks again. "I'm her father, but she loves you Cass, she loves the both of you. I am asking you man to man to please care for the most important thing in my life, if something should happen to me tomorrow night. This decision wasn't an easy one, it is the hardest fucking thing I have ever had to do." I can hear the devastation in Tristan's voice, and it breaks the dam, tears flow freely down my face as I stare at the two men I am hopelessly in love with. Cass is fighting so hard, because a part of him loves Tristan as a brother. He will be devastated if anything happened to Tristan, he is finally starting to come to terms with the loss of Blake and losing Tristan will shatter him. "Please Cass." Cass growls and shocks me when he wraps his arms around Tristan in a bro hug, Tristan takes a second to register what is happening before he returns his embrace.

"I swear, I will love her and raise her as my own, *if* something should ever happen to you." They break apart and stare at each other for a moment as if in a silent conversation. "I'll make sure you don't die; you pull every bit of strength I have to make sure you come out of this on top."

"You can draw on me as well." I snap my gaze to Ro in shock.

"And mine." I look to Hunter in shock at his declaration. "If you're important to my brother, then you're important to me. The strength of the Wilder pack is at your disposal." I smile at Hunter; he may not know it, but he just made his first vow as the alpha to the Wilder pack.

"You can draw on me as well, but not my mate. She needs her strength for my kids, my pack is with you *brother*." Tears flow faster at the declaration from Creed, he looks to me and nods. He just gave me his blessing; I hate that it has taken Tristan risking his life for one of my brothers to see he is a good man.

"I'll make you an offer." Everyone turns to face Alex, I startle when a growl sounds from Cole, he glares over at Alex with a look of hatred in his eyes.

"What offer?" Cass enquires on Tristan's behalf.

"I will only offer this once, and it is only because you are dedicating yourselves to save the life of my grandchild." Gabriel growls, Alex rolls his eyes before amending. "*Our* grandchild."

"What is your offer?" I can hear the skepticism in Tristan's tone.

"I will give you my blood if you die, you will be reborn again as one of us." Gasps break out and everyone shouts over the top of each other. The one voice that draws my attention is...my twin. He storms across the room until he is standing directly in front of Alexander, the rage that is wafting off Colton is astounding.

"You fucking destroy everything you touch; you will not go near him." Alex smiles condescendingly at Cole, the noise begins to die down around the room as everyone focuses on the two males.

"Why, afraid he might want the cure as well?"

"Cure for what?" Creed interjects but Cole and Alex ignore him.

"There isn't one, you fucking let her go now." Why do I get the feeling they aren't talking about anyone in this room?

"She is already gone; she knew what she was getting into when she agreed to my offer. It isn't on me that your guilt is eating at you daily." In a blur Cole strikes out and clocks Alexander across the jaw, before he can land another hit Alex lands a blow to his gut. Jess screams and is on her feet within a second grabbing Harlem and running from the room. The two men continue to trade blows until the others step forward and break them apart. More shouting ensues until Belle screams at the top of her lungs blanketing the room in silence. Cairo drops his hold on Cole and rushes over to her, checking her for injury.

"Beauty, what happened?"

"Either I just peed myself or my water just broke." My eyes widen in fright, everyone in the room is deathly quiet as Cairo turns pale. These fucking eight alpha males and two original vampires are literally rendered speechless at the fact Belle is going into labor, I growl as I storm toward them nudging Cairo out of the way. I meet Belle's panicked stare and try to smile reassuringly gripping her hands in mine.

"Just breathe, let's go get you cleaned up and I'll call mom."

Belle shakes her head in fear. "You can do this Belle, you're a badass OG vampire who has visions that save lives."

"Holy fuck!" I cut my gaze to Cairo; he tugs on the strands of his hair as he stares at his mate. "The baby is coming!" He screams so fucking loud I have the urge to cover my damn ears.

"No shit dumbass!" Z snaps at him as he heads toward Belle and I.

"What do you need?" I smile my thanks at Zeke, at least he is able to get himself under control and be productive.

"Call my mom and tell her Belle's water broke, she'll know what to do. I'm gonna take her to shower and prepare the spare room for delivery." I look around the room at all the shocked faces and shake my head in annoyance. "The rest of you, start working out a fucking spell or get the packs ready to fight. As soon as this baby is out, the elders will be coming for it, now move your fucking asses!" I can't believe I just did that; I gave a room full of alpha's an alpha order, I look to Cass who has the sexiest smirk on his face.

"We got you baby." I nod and quickly lead Belle from the room.

TWENTY-FIVE

TRISTAN

Seeing the expression on Cairo's face hits me hard, I never got to experience that with Mera. I missed her first breath and being able to watch her come into this fucked up world, I envy him for being able to have this moment that I was robbed of.

"We have to go back to Meg's." I turn to stare at Cass.

"I can't leave now—."

"Meg and the doctors are in there with Belle, she is only three centimeters dilated."

"What's your point?" I snap angrily at him.

"Callie has to mark your dumbass, unless you want to blow your load in your pants in front of her brothers, take my advice and let's go." Fuck, I forgot about that detail in the midst of the chaos here. Cass grips my arm and leads me toward the front door, without uttering a word he grips Callie's hand and yanks her away from Jess, who has a shit eating grin on her face. Callie follows as Cass drags the pair of us after him.

"What the fuck Cassius?" She shouts still stumbling, I smile at the angry look on her face.

"We have to go." He grits out in frustration.

"Where?"

"You have to mark Tristan and I didn't think you wanted to fuck him in front of your family." Callie shudders and shakes her head.

"Yeah, nah. Lead the way Hercules." Cass growls but there is no heat to it, both Callie and I laugh until our gazes collide. I can see lust and heat in the depths of her gaze, it has my cock hardening in my slacks, getting lost in my girl right now might be the best thing to numb all the doubts in my mind.

Kitty took one look at us before saying she will take Mera to play with Harlem, they both practically ran out of the house as Cass proceeded to drag us up the stairs and into Callie's room—*our* room. He releases his hold on my arm as soon as we cross the threshold, he yanks Callie around to the front of him earning a glare from her. He doesn't give her a chance to protest as he lifts her off the ground, she squeals in surprise as she locks her arms and legs around him. Like he is a man on a mission he still doesn't allow her a chance to speak as he grips the back of her neck and yanks her lips down to his. I stand here and watch as the tension and outrage starts to drain from her body as she loses herself in the kiss, she starts to sag in Cass's hold as she

grips the back of his neck and yanks on his hair, he hums his approval moving them toward the bed. Cass is overcome with his need for her and nothing else in this moment matters, he flops forward onto the bed crushing her beneath his weight. A breathy moan escapes her when Cass rocks his hips, he pulls back and stands between her open legs. He tosses his shirt to the side peering over his shoulder at me, his eyes brim with heat and his pupils are dilated.

"You're the one that needs to be marked, either I'm fucking her while you watch and she marks you after, which will cause you a shit load of pain."

"Why will it cause me pain?" Callie sits up leaning on her elbows peering up at me through her long lashes and speaks.

"If marking is done outside of fucking it can cause immense pain, if it is done during sex it causes a euphoric reaction giving you the best orgasm of your life." I unbutton my jacket and shrug it off as I smirk at the she-wolf sprawled on the bed.

"Give me the best orgasm of my fucking life kitten." Most would think this is the worst moment to think about losing yourself inside someone you love, but for me, this might be my last chance, so I'm taking it, fuck everything else for the time being. Cass begins to unbutton her pants as she peels her top off, I follow suit and undress as fast as possible to keep up with them. I stalk over to the bed and slowly climb on as Cass drops to his knees and widens her legs, her gaze remains fixed on me. I lower myself to my hunches beside her head and grip my hardening cock in my hand, her tongue darts out to moisten her lips before a needy moan escapes her as Cass begins to eat her pussy.

"You're fucking drenched babe." The husky tone of his voice has me gripping my cock tighter and my mouth watering for a taste of her. I reach down with my free hand and grip her hair; I pull until she is high enough to line my cock up with her mouth.

"Open." She ignores my order and bends froward to lick the dollop of pre cum from the head of my cock causing me to jerk, she runs her nose down the length of my dick inhaling my scent before sucking me into her mouth. My grip on her hair tightens as I throw my head back and groan. The vibrations of her moans have me shuddering, I look down at Cass to find his gaze locked on her sucking my cock. I watch as he pushes two fingers inside her, the harder Cass finger fucks her the faster she bobs up and down on my cock. She reaches out with her hand and cups my balls electing a loud groan of pleasure from me. She pulls back and releases my dick with a wet pop, she moans and begins to thrust her hips against Cass's face chasing her high.

"Just like that, don't fucking stop Cassius." Cass grips her hips and holds her in place as he sucks her clit into his mouth, her back bows off the bed as she scrunches her eyes closed and screams out her release. Cassius doesn't bring her down slowly, he stands and lines his cock up with her cunt before slamming inside her, she screams out at the intrusion. He doesn't slow his pace as he fucks her like a crazed man, gripping me she begins to pump.

"Fuck yes baby, stroke his cock while I destroy your fucking pussy." His crass words have her moaning beneath him and her grip on me tightening, I reach over and twirl her nipples between my fingers causing her to cry out.

"Oh fuck, both of you don't fucking stop." Cass growls low in his throat.

"You don't get to come." Cass pulls out of her causing her to growl in frustration, I look over at him.

"Fuck her now." I don't dispute, I shuffle off the bed and assume the position he was in. When I spy him opening the bed side draw, I know what is about to happen. I pick her up from the bed, she wraps her arms and legs around me, I grip her neck and pull her down until her lips crash against mine. This kiss is so primal, we are each staking our claim on the other. I break the kiss as I hear Cass approach, I shift her slightly until I can line myself up with her cunt, not giving her any warning, I slam her down on my aching dick causing her to scream my name. "Reach around and open her ass for me." I shift my grip on her and grab the globes of her ass spreading them so Cass can lube her up, she squirms in my hold causing me to grit my teeth.

"Stop fucking moving." I snarl at her; she smirks down at me and starts to grind on my cock as Cass begins to finger her asshole. She moans at the feeling of having both of us against her, she leans back against Cass's shoulder.

"Put your fucking cock in my ass now and fuck me hard so I can come." Cass rips his fingers out of her and growls, his eyes have changed to his wolf's, and I can tell the beast is more in control than the man. He pushes her against me as he lines himself up, I capture her lips in a kiss as Cass slowly pushes himself inside her. Her pussy clamps down on my cock drawing a heady moan from me. Once Cass is fully sheathed inside her ass does he begin to move, she cries out in pleasure when we find our rhythm, she drops back against Cass, he smashes his lips against hers, I lean forward and suck her nipple into my mouth drawing a moan from her. I pick up my speed and Cass follows suit, Callie leans forward and places her hands on my shoulders for leverage as she begins to ride us both.

"I'm so fucking close." She screams.

"Get there, kitten." I grit out through clenched teeth; I can feel my balls tightening with my impending release just on the horizon.

"Mark him!" Cass snaps, Callie's eyes widen slightly as she meets my gaze.

"Do it." I tell her, she nods and leans forward as I tilt my head to the side giving her better access. She licks the space between my neck and shoulder causing a shudder to roll through me, Cass leans forward and mimics her move on the mate mark that she wears from him. I feel Callie's teeth lengthen against my skin and ready myself for the pain of the bite, I notice Cass's teeth have shifted as well.

"I'm gonna come!" She screams out as she clamps her jaws on my shoulder at the same time Cass clamps his on hers, I scream out. Not from pain, but from the most euphoric form of pleasure I have ever felt in my life as I come inside her. A mirage of colors covers my vision and I blow my load inside her tight wet cunt, I feel like I'm floating. This is a feeling I can't even explain or understand the sensations that are thrumming through my body, it's as if every nerve ending inside me has been awoken for the first time. My vision is sharper, my sense of smell is heightened, my hearing is sharper to the extent of hearing the birds chirping outside. Callie slowly retracts her teeth, a small hiss escapes me at the sting I now feel, she laps at the wound with her tongue, Cass shifts behind us and I hear the moment he pulls out of her. Before I know it, she's on her feet standing in front of me, they anxiously await my recovery, "Are you okay?" The uncertainty in her voice throws me, I cock my head to the side and stare at her. The color of her eyes seems brighter, the shade of her hair seems more vibrant.

"Tristan?" A quizzical expression mars Cass's face, his features seem more pronounced now. "You good?"

"Yeah, I mean, shit seems different." I can't even form a coherent sentence, I'm so over whelmed trying to figure out all these heightened new senses.

Cass, did I do something wrong? My eyes widen and I stumble back a step when I hear her voice inside my head, both looking at me with concern.

Something clearly went wrong. My mouth drops open when I hear Cass inside my head.

What do we do? I point to each of them.

"I can hear you!" They exchange a weird look before turning back to me.

"Tristan, what do you mean?"

"California, I can hear you in my head." To annunciate my point, I jab my temple.

"Wait, you heard her talking to me?" I nod so fast I feel a pinch in my neck.

Can you hear me? I smile wide nodding at Cass. *Try saying something in your mind.*

Hello? Cass scoffs and Callie's eyes widen.

"How the hell can he communicate with us?" The surprise in her voice is evident.

"I have no idea; I mean I've heard of wolves marking humans, but the mark never lasts on them." Cass seems perplexed.

"He isn't human though, he's a warlock, so does that mean the mark will last?" Cass keeps his gaze on me as he shakes his head.

"I honestly have no idea."

"Do you feel–." I cut her off.

"Different? Yes, I can hear, smell and see things so much clearer. I mean, I didn't expect anything like this to happen but hearing you both inside my head is something I never compre-hended would happen." I can see the skepticism on both their faces. "I don't understand how this is possible but I'm not mad about it." My words put them both at ease, the tension drains from their bodies and they smile wide. Callie saunters her naked ass over to me and wraps her arms around my waist. Before I can return her embrace, she pulls back with a contorted look on her face.

"I have to go...clean up." We chuckle as she scurries away and slams the bathroom door whilst mumbling under her breath about us being assholes. I look over at Cass to find his gaze on me. A serious expression clouds his eyes, and it has me straightening to my full height.

"I'll sign the papers." Well, I wasn't expecting that to come out of his mouth.

"Thank you." His eyes narrow.

"I'm not signing them for you, I'm doing it for Merz and because there is no way in hell, I will let anyone take her from us." I nod my head in understanding. "I have a condition though."

"And that is?" He closes the space between us until we are nearly chest-to-chest, his gaze bores into mine.

"You fight with everything you have to stay alive; I'll do whatever I can to help you make it, not just for Callie, but for Mera as well."

"I swear it." I say without hesitation, I don't want to fucking die, but if it is the only way to ensure my daughter is safe, then that is the only option for me. "If things don't go how we plan–." He growls but I push on. "Bury me with my sister, don't let Mera or Callie cry over me. You give them the best fucking life, and you love them enough for the both of us."

"Are you a lover or a fighter?"

"You have to be a fighter to be a lover."

"How so?"

"If you don't fight for your love, then what type of love do you really have?" A sly smirk graces his face as he pats my cheek.

"Remember that tonight when you do the transfer, fight for your fucking love *brother*." My eyes widen slightly as I stare at him, his face scrunches. "You're making fuck me eyes and it's making shit weird." I can't help it, I throw my head back and laugh, a proper belly laugh. I haven't laughed like this in so long, I had no idea how we would work as a trio, but in this moment, I know we'll always find a way to make this work. He has just shown me that he may love Callie, but he sees me as a brother and that, is an honor in itself.

TWENTY-SIX

CASSIUS

Belle's screams can be heard from the living room, I grind my teeth clenching my hands into fists. I hate hearing my sister in pain, and there isn't a fucking thing I can do to help her. We've been sitting here for hours, Mera's head rests in my lap as she sleeps, she has to be close so when the baby is born, the transfer can commence.

My nerves are frayed, I'm worried about my sister and her baby but I'm also fucking scared that Mera won't handle the transformation, Kitty said it is a possibility that she could reject the magic. She didn't elaborate any further, but from her ominous tone I gathered it won't end well for Merz. Tristan has been edgy since we got here, I know he is nervous about what he has to do. On top of all that he also has to deal with all these sensations from the mate mark which is still confusing the fuck out of me.

The feelings he described is what happens to wolves when they partial shift whilst still in human form, I can feel Callie's unease about it through the mate link. I wish there was a way to put her mind at rest but unfortunately we're running out of time, I'm finding it hard to stay in my human form, because all I can scent is every one's feelings.

I need you to stay calm Atticus. I plead with my wolf.

To many emotions and we have to lead them.

How do you suggest we do that?

Calm them down or I won't hold back.

I blow out a frustrated breath and look around the room, Callie is huddled in the kitchen with Jess, Creed, Vince and Cole. Zeke and Hunter are scrolling on their phones opposite me, Kitty is just...knitting? How the fuck can she knit at a time like this? Tristan is pacing the length of the room, and Meg is upstairs with Harlem, she thought it best to put the kids to bed incase Jess is needed down here. Dad, Belle, Cairo, Alex and a couple of the doctors that Creed has on call for his pack. When a ripple of unease thrums through me, I know it's from the packs outside, a couple of the alphas turned up earlier to support us in combat, none of them have any idea what they are up against, but each of them are here because of Sky. They have expressed their fidelity and state that she was one hell of a woman, and had no hesitations in following her to war, as they put it, *'we are here for her last fight'*. Callie burst into tears as they pledge their allegiance, just as we managed to calm her down, Zeke and Ro passed us whilst transferring Sky into Creed's house, causing her to break down again.

"Everyone needs to calm down and relax, Atticus is on edge and ready to shift." My softly spoken words have them turning to me, Creed and Jess look just as tense as I am. Both of them being alpha's and having so many others on their pack lands will be driving their wolves to the brink of engaging in violence.

"Bit hard to do that when our sister is fucking screaming in pain." I grit my teeth and fight the growl that wants to break free, I glare at my little brother in warning. I'm slightly taken back when the little shit holds my stare for longer than he should, a part of me is proud to see him coming into the role of alpha so easily, another part wants to beat his ass and show him who the boss is.

"That's exactly why we need to focus on something else, smart ass."

"What do you suggest Cass?" Relief floods through me at Creed's question.

"We devise a plan on what to do, I wanted to meet with the alpha's earlier, but I had–."

"A pussy to get lost in?" I snarl at Cole; Creed slaps the back of his head and growls in anger.

"That's our fucking sister you're talking about dumbass!" Cole cringes and scrunches his eyes shut, while Jess muffles her laughter behind her hand and Callie's cheeks redden, Tristan wraps his arm around her placing a kiss to her temple.

"Point taken." Cole mutters as he drops into the seat near Zeke avoiding eye contact with anyone, Z just stares at him and shakes his head.

"Will you ever learn?" Cole pins Z with a dirty look.

"No one fucking asked you, you're not even from this pack!"

"Least I got a pack asshole." In the most un-Cole way, he clamps his mouth closed and doesn't retort, his eyes drop to the ground as he remains silent. Either Zeke hit a nerve or there is something more at play here that we don't know about.

"Moving on, what do you suggest we do Cass?" Creed's question has me focusing back on the task at hand.

"We have to prepare the alphas for what is to come, we only have about eight packs here and sadly I don't think that is enough."

"Why not?" Jess's question is a valid one, and I can see the expressions on everyone's faces wanting to know as well.

"Simple, we have power that can attack you at a distance. I don't know who else the elders will have with them and what powers the others can wield, I will be incapacitated for a while."

"How long is a while?" Vince asks Tristan. I can see from the strain on T's face that even he can't answer that for sure.

"I don't know." Chaos ensues at his answer, everyone is shouting and cussing, I cups my hands over Mera's ears as I release a growl loud enough to have everyone in the room shutting their fucking traps and their eyes snapping to me.

"This is a first for all of us, Tristan doesn't have to fucking be here to help us, but he is. Let's not forget that the life of his own child is on the line as well, if you are hesitant about rendering aid, then leave." I run my gaze over each of them honing my point, I will never force anyone to fight against their will. The alphas that have agreed to their patriotism have done so on their own merit, not because I ordered it. "I want all the older pack members and the children moved to the cellar in the woods now." I turn to Creed as I ask. "Can you do that now?" He nods and I watch as his eyes glaze over whilst he links his pack to do as I have asked.

"What's our plan of attack?" Zeke questions, I open my mouth to answer him, but Tristan beats me to it.

"Hold them off long enough for me to do the transfer."

"What's stopping them from taking the power from the kids?" Hunter's question is one I haven't even thought of and has me looking to Tristan for an answer. His arm tightens around Callie as a look of unease crosses his features.

"A child cannot choose to pass their power on." I narrow my eyes at him.

"Why do I get the feeling there is a *but* coming?" A whoosh of air escapes him as he runs his free hand through his hair.

"The elders would capture them and raise them in their

image until the children are old enough to choose one of them as their successor." Gasps sound out around the room; I drop my gaze to my lap and stare at Mera. This tiny innocent child is nothing but a vessel to those power-hungry fucks, they would take her for one reason only. I thought some of the tactics the packs use was corrupt, but they are nothing like these witches. We never use children as a source of leverage, children are sacred in wolf packs, we protect our young at all costs.

"I'll kill all of them before they take my fucking niece from my sister." I grunt in agreement; Hunter and I share a look and I can see we are both in agreement. We will die before we ever let those fuckers take this miracle from her, Belle will never have this opportunity again. This child will be the only one her and Cairo will ever have, I will not lose another family member.

"You can plan all you like but let me give you all some advice." Everyone turns to Kitty who continues to knit as if she has no worries in the world. "Nothing will work, things will go astray, lives will be lost on both sides, all you can do is prepare for the worst and hope for the best." I stare at Kitty open mouthed and at a fucking loss as to what to say to that.

"Well, aren't you full of comforting words today." Tristan snarks, she just shrugs and continues on with her fucking knitting. Belle screams again and this one is different, it's not like the others, something about this scream is worse. Mera startles in my lap and sits up, scaring the ever-loving shit out of me! It was like watching a horror movie where someone is possessed! Tristan and Callie rush over kneeling in front of her asking if she is okay, she ignores them as she turns to face me. Her face is pale, her muddy brown eyes are filled with horror, I reach out and cup her cheeks.

"Merz, what happened?" Her eyes glaze over as if she's in a

daze, I look straight at Tristan hoping he will be able to enlighten me as to what the fuck is going on.

"She's channeling."

"What the hell does that mean?" Cole asks.

"It means she is talking with spirit." Kitty sounds so monotone, and it grates on my already frayed nerves.

"Who the fuck is spirit?" Cole is asking everything I am thinking and for the first time...ever, I'm grateful for his big ass mouth.

"It's what she calls them, she had no idea they were dead when she first started seeing them, so she named them after her favorite cartoon show, *Spirit*." Ironically, the name fits perfectly. Tristan may be able to explain to us what is happening, but I can see in his eyes and the way he looks at Mera that it is killing him and not able to help his own child. Mera's gaze is still locked on me, she hasn't blinked or moved a muscle. "Cass?" I turn to look at Tristan. "Whatever she is seeing has something to do with you, you have to ask her."

"The fuck?" Tristan takes a calming breath, clearly he is getting pissed with my lack of understanding about whatever the fuck is happening right now.

"Just trust me, ask her what she sees!" I look to Callie who seems just as uneasy as I do, her eyes meet mine and she smiles reassuringly.

"You got this, I'm right here with you." Her soft words hit me right in the chest, I nod before turning back to Mera.

"Merz, it's Cass, um...what do you see?" I feel like an idiot for doing this, but I don't really have another choice do I?

"Papa." I growl at the sound of the whimper in her tone, in such a short amount of time I have come to be fiercely protective of Mera and so has Atticus. We view her as our own and no matter what anyone says, we will always be here for her until our dying breath. "The baby's rope is stuck." I dart my gaze to Tristan; he shakes his head unsure of what she means as well.

"Ask her who is telling her this." I do as Tristan asks.

"Tell me who's saying this to you."

"Aunt Sky. The baby's rope is stuck and it's going to aunt Sky every time she...pushes?" Jess gasps and we all turn to her; she takes off running whilst shouting.

"Belle, stop pushing, the umbilical cord is wrapped around the baby's throat." Creed dashes after her with Vince on his heels, my eyes widen as I stare at Mera. This precious girl's extraordinary gift just saved the life of my niece.

"Thank you Merz and thank you...Skylar." I say before I wrap my arms around our little girl and pull her against me.

I can feel your love for her. I look to Tristan who has an unreadable expression on his face.

Is that a problem? I hedge.

Not at all, it means the world to me that I am able to feel this bond, seeing it and hearing it, is beyond more than I could ever hope for. But to be able to feel it... I can't explain what that means to me Cass, thank you.

For what? It is going to take a lot for me to get used to hearing him inside my head, I can see from the tears forming in Callie's eyes that she is listening to every word through our mate link.

For making this whole process easy, for not being a dick and fighting me over Callie, loving Mera as if she is your own, rallying all of these wolves together to help me fight for my family. Thank you isn't enough to show my gratitude, but I don't know what else to say.

Before I can reply, Vince rushes into the room causing us all to stand, Mera wraps herself around me burying her face in the crook of my neck, Callie and Tristan stand either side of me, I feel Hunter at my back.

"They need you now Tristan." Is all that is said before Tristan rushes from the room with Vince tailing him.

TWENTY-SEVEN

TRISTAN

I burst through the door and stumble to a stop, Gabriel, Creed and Vince have Cairo pinned against the wall as he thrashes in their hold trying to get to his mate. He snaps his jaws at them, threatening their lives and promising to kill each of them once he's free.

Vince rushes past me to help his brother as the others hold Ro back, I turn toward the center of the room and that's when I see the reason for his panic. Belle is passed out on the bed with Jess standing to the side holding her hand, the two nurses rush around the room frantically as the doctor positions himself between Belle's open legs. I gnaw on my bottom lip as I dart my gaze to the nurse closest to me, I reach out and grip her arm halting her movements.

"What the hell is going on?" The nurse glares as she yanks her arm free.

"There are complications, and we need to move fast, stay out the way!" I watch as she rushes back to the doctor handing him something, I avert my gaze when he lifts the sheet that covers Belle.

"Joy, we have to prep for a C-Section." The doctor glares at the monitors that are beeping. "Now, the heart rate is dropping and there is meconium in her waters." The nurses move around the room in a blur as the doctor looks to Cairo. "You all can't be in here–."

"Fuck you, I'm not leaving her!"

"I cannot have you behaving like that whilst I am trying to save your mate and child, the placenta looks to have ruptured and your child has an umbilical cord around its neck as well. Calm the hell down or get the hell out, choose!" All the color drains from Cairo's face, he stops struggling and fighting against the others as he cuts a glance to Belle who is passed out.

"Just...save them...please." The brokenness in the sound of Cairo's voice isn't a sound I thought I would ever hear from him. He is always so strong and appears like nothing affects him, except the prospect of losing the woman he loves and the child they share together. The doctor eyes us for a second longer before ushering everyone except for Cairo, Vince and Gabriel. Vince announces that I have to wait outside and be ready for when the baby arrives. I send Creed to get Cass and Mera, she will need to be with me in order for the transfer to start.

"Is she okay?" At the sound of pounding footfalls, I turn to see Cass storming toward me with Mera's hand clasped in his.

"There are some complications–." I cut myself off when Callie, Hunter and Cole followed by Creed appear behind Cass.

"What's going on?" The growl in Hunter's voice alerts me to the fact that his wolf is close to the surface, the last thing we need is for him to shift and cause chaos, so I decide on another approach and just hope that Jess and Creed keep their mouths closed about what is really happening in that room.

"She's nearly ready to give birth, if you have a plan for our defiance, now is the time to put it into action." Cass's green eyes bore into mine, if he detects that I'm lying, he doesn't show it. He drops Mera's hand and steps up to me, I hold his gaze, not in a defiant way but in a way of showing my respect to the man.

"Don't fucking die." Is all he says before he wraps me in a man hug and then spins on his heel barking orders for all the guys to follow him, I glance at Callie and watch as her eyes rim with tears when she looks to Cass. He reaches out to stroke her cheek, she places her tiny hands on his forearms as he leans his forehead against hers. "I love you California." A strangled sob escapes her as Cass places a chaste kiss to her lips.

"I love you too." She whispers as Cass pulls away and leads the others, Jess and Callie both stand there with tears in their eyes. I wish I didn't have to disturb this moment, but I don't have a choice.

"Jess?" She slowly meets my gaze, and I can see the devastation in her eyes. "I want you to take Meg and your children to the bunker, Callie stay with Mera."

"What, where are you going?" I rush forward and wrap my arms around Callie pulling her close.

"I have to go and get Sky; she needs to be here for the transfer." I feel her nod against my chest, and I step back to crouch down in front of my daughter. Her eyes search mine for some form of understanding about what is going to happen. I ignore Jess as she speaks to Callie and leaves the three of us.

"Daddy, I'm scared." My heart shatters inside my chest, I never wanted the darkness of this world to taint my daughters view on the beauty and wonders of life, but I failed. I reach out and grip her small hands in mine and smile lovingly at her.

"Don't be, daddy is going to make sure that all the monsters go away and never come back."

"Will it hurt?" Her question causes me to pause, I know Kitty has filled her in on what is going to happen but knowing about it doesn't prepare you for it to happen. I'm stumped when Callie kneels beside me and answers in my place.

"Your dad and I are going to make this as painless as possible; I promise I will be here with you the whole time." Callie's words have some of the fear draining from Mera's eyes and I am forever grateful for that, I place a kiss to Merz's forehead and leave to fetch my sister. As I near the room that holds her body, regret begins to thrum through me, regret for never having the chance to know her. I know Merz sees her and has been able to communicate with her aunt, but it isn't the same, my daughter was robbed of knowing her aunt because someone snitched to the wolf fucking council. I pause outside the door and blow out an exasperated breath, I can blame their council all I want, but the truth is, it was only a matter of time before Sky's power eventually consumed her.

I open the door and make my way to her bedside, if I didn't know any better, I would think she was sleeping or in a coma. I smile down at my little big sister; she appears so tiny but from the stories I have heard her size didn't matter. She fought men and women double her size and always came out on top, even wolves feared her name alone. My smile widens as I think of the woman she was, she must have been a sight to behold.

"She will be at peace now." I turn to find Kitty standing in the doorway, I nod before turning back to gaze at my sister. "You don't have much time; you need to move Tristan." I nod again, preparing for this moment hasn't been easy, planning and making sure everything was right. But now that I'm here and knowing this is the end of my sister, it's a lot harder to take in than I thought it would be. Kitty makes her way over and stands beside me, she reaches out and clasps Sky's hand in hers, a sigh escapes her causing me to frown. "The life of another is arriving, which is taking essence from her, she is growing cold Tristan." A lump begins to form in my throat. "Your fight is over now granddaughter, live freely with the others and rejoice in the legacy you have left behind. May we meet again my sweet fiercesome Skylar."

I swallow past the lump in my throat and try to focus on anything aside from Kitty's words, I reach down and gather Sky's limp body in my arms. I still when I feel how cold she is, I slam my eyes closed and take a moment. Her life force is leaving her body as the child nears, I shake myself out of my thoughts and exit the room. I pause at the end of the hallway when Callie spots me, her eyes drop to Sky, and I can see from the look in her eyes that she is about to break. If this situation is hard for me and I didn't even get a chance to know my sister, I can't imagine how hard this is for her. A shrill cry pierces the air and I rush forward, Callie snaps out of it and opens the door for me. Alex ushers me over to the single bed that was prepared earlier, as I gently lay my sister upon it.

"I'll get the baby." Alex announces like he's simply grabbing a dish towel, I peer over my shoulder at Callie and motion for her and Mera to come to me. Callie keeps Merz pressed into her side, shielding her from viewing the other bed. I spin around at the sound of a growl; Cairo snaps his jaws at Alexander in warning.

"You're not touching my daughter!" The threat in his voice is clear, Alex raises his hands and takes a step back, Gabriel looks torn as he gazes down at Belle who is just starting to stir. I have no idea why she was unconscious or what happened, at the risk of sounding like a prick, I don't care. Right now, my only focus is to make sure that this transfer is set in motion with no complications. As if my thoughts conjured it into existence, the wind outside begins to howl, and I know without a doubt I felt the power surge the moment the baby came into this world. Cairo meets my gaze; I give him a nod letting him know that it's time. "Stay with

Belle, don't leave that fucker alone with her." Alex sneers at Cairo, Gabriel nods and motions for Ro to bring the baby to me. The tension in his body tells me that I have to tread carefully, he is a new father and I know the feeling. Rather than touch his daughter, I ignore the sounds outside and push aside my worries as I place my hand on his shoulder and meet his skeptical gaze.

"All I have to do is lay a hand on her, she can remain in your arms the whole time, is that okay?" He exhales loudly and I watch as some of the tension in his body begins to drain.

"I just–." I cut him off.

"I understand better than you think, I wouldn't allow anyone to take Mera from me." He nods and relaxes slightly. Mera places her hand in mine, I smile trying my best to comfort her. I can hear the doctor and nurses' rushing about the room trying to do their job at the same time attending to Belle. "Merz, I want you to hold aunt Sky's hand, okay?" My clever little girl nods and reaches out tentatively to grip her aunt's hand.

"This won't hurt her will it?" I turn back to Cairo and see the doubt that coats his features.

"I won't lie to you–." I'm cut off by the sounds of howls and a resounding crack outside, a storm is raging and we're wasting time, I steel myself and give him the harsh truth. "The elders are here; they can track your child anywhere as long as she holds the power inside her. I am the only chance your daughter has at living, either you trust me now to save the life of not only your daughter, but mine as well." His gaze searches mine for a while before he looks to Callie.

"Do you trust him?" I grind my teeth in anger, but Callie doesn't hesitate to answer.

"I wouldn't be here with him if I didn't, he can do this Ro. He loves Sky as much as we do and that *has* to count for something in your book." Ro nods stiffly before dropping his gaze to the swaddled baby in his arms.

"I'll never let anyone harm you or your mother, I swear." He whispers to his child before looking at me. "I don't trust you; I don't even know you!" I open my mouth to argue but he pushes on. "Sky coming to you and knowing about you is the only reason I am allowing you to do this, I may not trust you but I sure as fuck trust your sister with my life, and the life of my daughter." I can hear the chaos raging outside, so rather than argue, I just nod and reach out toward the baby, Cairo growls but I ignore him. I know it's just his wolf telling me to tread lightly, I gently move the blanket, exposing her tiny hand, I wrap mine around hers before looking back to Mera.

"Whatever happens sweetheart, you must not let go of aunt Sky, okay?" Her eyes are filled to the brim with questions, and I wish I had the time to answer each and every one, but the sound of thunder and lightning cracking outside means we have to get a move on.

"Okay daddy." That's all I needed to hear, I close my eyes and block out the sounds of the machines and voices behind me, I focus solely on the magic I feel in the room. I dig inside myself and try to find the tether that will bind the three of them, but it's to far, I push harder to reach it but the closer I get the further away it moves, it's like a fucking rainbow.

"What's happening?" I grit my teeth and ignore Cairo; I need to focus on the tether and pull it toward me, but it keeps moving. I keep my eyes closed as I bark out for Callie to get Kitty, something isn't right here. It's almost as if Sky is holding onto the magic and refusing to release it completely, Kitty's spell won't last much longer, and Sky's heart will give out soon. I have to do this fast before all the power my sister holds slams into this baby, it isn't strong enough to harness that amount of power.

"I'm here!" I sigh in relief at the sound of my grandmother's voice, I keep my eyes closed and focus on the magic inside me as I answer her.

"The tether, I can see it but every time I try to latch onto it, the fucking thing moves." She's silent for a moment and that worries me. A loud gasp sounds out from behind me, I hear Gabe and Alex firing off a million questions and I guess that gasp came from Belle waking up.

"The answer is here."

"What the hell does that mean?" I snap at Kitty.

"She passed out because she was getting the answers from your sister you stupid boy." Grandmothers are supposed to be loving and spoil you, but no, not mine, she hurls insults at you like they are Cupids fucking arrows.

"Where's my daughter?" The anguish in Belle's voice is distracting me.

"She's with me Beauty." I growl in frustration; I drop my hold on the child and eye everyone in the fucking room with an angry look.

"I need you all to be silent–." I clamp my mouth closed when I see the...situation Belle is in, the doctor is stitching her whilst she lay flat on her back with her gaze trained on the baby in Cairo's arms.

"C-can I see her?" Her watery tone has everyone pausing, tears fall from her eyes as Cairo makes his way over to her. She sobs when he bends down and she sees her daughter for the first time.

"She has your nose Beauty; you did amazing baby." The awe in Ro's tone guts me, I missed this moment with Mera and I'll hate Gemma forever for taking that from me.

"She's perfect, we made a perfect little girl."

"Yeah, we really did beauty." Their love for their child is tangible.

"I need Tristan." Cairo's shocked gaze meets mine; I have no idea what Belle wants with me, Ro stands and moves back so I'm able to see Belle. "I have to speak with you privately, can you come here please." I have no idea how she thinks we will get privacy in a room full of supernatural's, but I oblige her none the less and kneel down until my ear is near her mouth. I feel Cairo's gaze boring into me, he has nothing to fucking worry about, there is only one woman I want, and his mate isn't her.

TWENTY-EIGHT

CALIFORNIA

I strain my hearing to catch what she is saying, but it's futile, I see Belle's lips moving but hear no sound, thanks to this fucking storm outside. The house is creaking under the strain of the wind, lighting cracks every second and has me jumping in fright. How this doctor is able to remain calm and steady whilst stitching Belle back together is beyond me, the man is fucking amazing at his job, no wonder Creed pays him a hefty fortune.

Another loud booming noise penetrates the air, Mera screams and it shatters me that I am unable to protect her, I've been trying to feel for Cass through the mate link, but he has blocked me out, I know why he did and I admire him for trying to protect me, but I'm also fucking pissed that I have no idea if he is okay or even...alive.

I watch as Tristan's eyes slowly turn to me, I see a mirage of emotions flicker through his gaze, and it makes me apprehensive. Whatever Belle is telling him isn't good, he curls his hands into fists and nods, Belle shoots him a pitying look. I allow Kora to come forward, she growls in warning, but it turns to anger when Belle eyes us with a look of remorse.

"The fuck did you just say to him?" My voice is hoarse due to the partial shift, Cairo growls at me in warning. I scoff, even though he is the leader to his pack, thanks to being mated to the chief alpha, I now outrank him!

"If you love him, let that be enough to lead him back to you Callie. It is the only way." Her ominous words have my stomach dropping, I turn to the man who broke through my walls and reassured me it was okay to love again. Tristan and Cass put me back together and I cannot, no I will not fucking lose either of them! I close the space between us and grip his button-up in my hands, he won't look at me, he keeps his gaze focused over my head. I crane my neck back to get a better look at him, I reach up to touch his face, but he grips my wrist and pushes my arm away. I stare at him open mouthed as he brushes past me without so much as a second look, tears trail down my cheeks as I watch him grip Sky's hand in his own. Kitty pulls Mera back to the other side of the room while I'm standing here in shock, Tristan just shut me out!

"Call it to you and she will release it, the mark of the child will bring it back when needed." I snap my gaze to Kitty then back to the baby Ro has clutched against his chest, he shifts the blanket to expose the baby's shoulder and that's when I see it. The round birth mark with all the elements displayed inside it.

Earth.

Wind.

Water.

Fire.

Sky only had access to three of those elements, so why does the baby have four? *Oh god*, I rush forward to try and stop Tristan, but arms band around my waist and hold me back. I peer over my shoulder and snap at Alex, how fucking dare he!

"You can kill him if you disturb the transfer!"

"Fuck you, he will die if I let him do this!" I scream right in Alexander-fucking-Maximoff's face.

"He can do this." I slowly turn to peer at Belle, Gabe is helping her to sit up slightly in the bed now that the doc is finished. She's pale and looks so weak, the frail sight of her doesn't curb the rage that is warring inside me.

"You bitch, if anything happens to him because of what you said, I will kill you." Cairo and Gabe both growl, Alex's hold tightens on me in warning.

"It wasn't my vision Callie."

"What?"

"Sky came to me–." Don't get me wrong, I love Sky and always will, but I am getting so fucking sick and tired of everyone saying, *Sky this* or *Sky that*. "Tristan is the only one who can handle the power of the four elements, he isn't just the high warlock to the Cage coven, he is the rightful leader to the elders." I gasp and turn toward Kitty. "Doris knows what I say is true, don't you?" Kitty glares at Belle for using her real name.

"Yes." She grits out, my mouth drops open as I stare at her utterly confused. "The elders work on power, whoever is the strongest will lead, by rights that is Tristan." My mind is reeling, what the fuck is it with people and secrets?

"You could have stopped all of this!" I shout at the old woman.

"Fuck off with your judgment California. I hid my grandson from those power-hungry bastards, they killed my son and daughter-in-law, did you really think I would give up my grandson as well? Tristan has known about this most of his life, he just never had the balls to outright ask me." I growl, my vision shifts to my wolf's.

"If anything happens to him because of you–." Kitty cuts me off.

"Save your threats for someone who will believe you!" I

bare my teeth at her before turning back to Tristan, he's so tense and ridged. I want to reach out and touch him, but I'm petrified of disrupting his concentration.

"Callie?" I turn back to Belle, she's starting to get color back in her cheeks, she cradles her daughter against her chest. A pang of guilt hits me, this is supposed to be a surreal and holy moment for them, instead it is tainted by the threat of their child's life being in danger. Ro balances on the edge of the bed with his arm wrapped around Belle and a wistful look on his face as he stares down at his daughter. A part of me is angry at them, they get this lovey dovey moment *together*, meanwhile the two men I love are fighting for their lives, and the woman I loved with all the fiber of my being is about to die, again. "He can do this." I ignore Belle and hesitantly move toward Tristan; I stand beside him but keep enough space between us, careful not to touch him.

In this one moment I feel like I'm alone again, I feel the pits of despair creeping in, my chest is moving but I feel nothing. I look between Tristan and Sky, and I want to scream, Skylar showed me how to love and I fucking loved her with everything I have, Tristan brought me back from the darkness, he and Cass made me whole again. Now I run the risk of losing them both and I can't live in a world where they don't exist. I ignore all rational thought and reach out to Tristan through the mate link we all share; I can feel his fear and...pain through the bond.

I'm here, I'm not going anywhere. Minutes tick by without a reply from him, I try reaching for Cass again, but to no avail. I startle when the doctor nudges me out of the way to check Sky's pulse, I feel dread creeping it's way inside me. In a short amount of time her heart will stop and the illusion of her being asleep will shatter, she will go back to being...gone. My heart and mind are at war with each other, my heart aches for the loss of her but my mind knows she is doing this so Cairo and Belle's child has a chance at life. I detest that everyone views what she did as a great sacrifice, I will always feel that she chose Cairo over me, and right now in this moment I feel as if Cass and Tristan have chosen where their loyalty to the packs and coven over me.

I love you. I gasp at the sound of his voice inside my head, I move around the doctor and stand at Tristan's other side as I rest my hand on his shoulder.

"Her pulse is slowing." The doctor's words are like a bucket of ice water, I focus on Sky and try to push the anger I feel toward her decision away, but I can't, Kora surges inside me and opens the link she and I share.

She loved us and always will, she did this because she knew our paths were ending.

They would never have ended Kora; she was meant to be our ending.

No, Sky knew we were on borrowed time. Release the anger you feel toward her California, if you don't, you will regret it.

Tears sting my eyes; I can feel it within myself that I can't do as my wolf asks. A hiss that escapes Tristan draws my attention, his face is scrunched in pain and tension radiates off him.

"Once the funnel is complete, he will need to transfer it fast." The panicked tone in Kitty's voice does nothing to reassure me that Tristan will make it out of this okay. I gasp when Sky begins to shake, the doc yanks his hand back and moves away a few steps. Tristan starts to tremble, the grip he has on Sky's hand tightens, he bares his teeth as a groan escapes him. A yellow light starts to spark where their hands are joined causing me to jump back a step.

"What the hell is happening?" I shout over the booming thunder.

"I don't know, but something isn't right, everyone has to get out of here!" The fact that Belle is the one that told Tristan what had to be done and now she is worried about the outcome of this situation pisses me the fuck off! Alex and Gabe help her stand while Cairo grabs baby Sky from her, Kitty grips Mera's hand in hers and shoots me a look of pity, I shake my head vigorously. "Don't you dare pity me, help him!" I scream at the old woman.

"I can't, I can feel the shift of magic in the air, and something has changed, I have to take Mera to safety and help the others hold off the council." My bottom lip trembles as reality slams into me, all Tristan's planning for this means nothing now. They head for the door so they can get to the safety of the cellar, Ro stops in front of me, and I can see he is torn between saving his mate and daughter or stay and help fight.

"I'll come right back as soon as Belle and the baby are safe, wait here." I just stare at him open mouthed; he spins and quickly follows after the others. I scream out and drop to the ground when a branch smashes through the window above the bed Belle was just lying in. Rain droplets pellet inside the room, I turn back to Tristan and stare at him, he's in a trance like state with his eyes glowing golden yellow. I can feel a surge through our link, the power radiating through our bond steals my breath. The temperature in the room drops significantly and it isn't from the rain pelting through the window. I dart forward and try to rip their hands apart, but I'm blasted back and crash against the wall dropping to the wooden floor in a heap. Shockwaves wrack my body; did I just get...electrocuted? I push myself into a sitting position and try to think of something to do other than watch this shit show, my thoughts are muted when a ball of bright light begins to form around their hands. The light glows so bright I have to shield my eyes, it grows big enough to cover them both. A gut curdling scream rents the air and I have to cover my ears, Tristan screams in agony but I can't see a fucking thing thanks to this bright light.

"Callie...run!" The sound of his voice snaps me out of my stupor, I shake my head even though I know he can't see me. "Run...now!" The urgency in his voice has me climbing to my feet using the wall as support, the wind rushes in around us and makes it hard to remain in the same spot. The power of the storm outside is increasing.

"I'm not leaving you." I scream over the whooshing of the wind. I push off the wall fighting against it trying to make my way toward them, pulses of...power come from them and the force of it hits me in the chest the closer I get. The light is blinding me, but I refuse to leave him. I can feel him just in front of me, I reach out but an explosion of light with a force so strong comes from their direction, it sends me sailing through the air and crashing through the wall of the house, I scream out but it's muted when I smack my head against something hard and everything goes black.

TWENTY-NINE

CASSIUS

I race out the back with the others close behind, the force of the wind pushes against me, I scan the area but see only wolves and other pack members. I stumble forward when something slams into the back of me, I glance over my shoulder and growl at my idiot of a brother.

"What the fuck is going on?" Hunter shouts over the roaring wind, thunder begins to boom above us followed by cracks of lightning. There is nothing natural about this storm; the elder fuckers are here somewhere, and we have to get our asses into action. I watch as women and children rush toward the woods near Meg's heading for the cellar. I open the link I share with all the wolves from every pack.

All wolves that are able to fight and willing to stand with us against a force we have never faced, meet us at the front and be ready to move.

A chorus of yes alpha rings out through the link, before I shift, I turn back to face, Zeke, Creed, Cole, Hunter and Vince. Each of these guys has skin in the game, they not only fight for their pack, but they fight for the ones they love. I won't force anyone to fight, I'm not that type of guy. Each of them have looks of fierceness plastered across their faces, growls tumble from them, Vince lets loose a hiss.

"If you have any doubts of committing yourselves to this fight, I understand–." Hunter opens his mouth, but I raise my hand silencing him. "I won't force any of you to be here." I hold my brothers gaze as I say. "You will not be in this fight." Hunter growls and steps into me, I can feel his anger through the alpha link.

"The hell I won't, that is my niece they are trying to get to, you can't sideline me Cassius!" I grip his shoulder and smack my forehead against his, he doesn't understand.

"I won't lose another brother, I can't." I hear the anguish in my own voice, he reaches up and grips the back of my neck.

"I lost Blake too, and he wouldn't let you do this on your own, so please, don't ask me to watch you run off and fight while I stand here like a fucking pussy. I have a pack to lead now Cass, let me lead them brother, please?" Atticus preens at my brothers need to fight alongside me, but the sibling side of me wants to rush him to the cellar and lock him in there with the others. I close my eyes for a moment and as much as I want him to run as fast as he can to safety, a part of me understands where he's coming from, much to my dismay I admire his determination.

"You stay behind me the whole time; we don't know anything about their abilities or what they're capable of." I shout over the thunder; I release Hunter and step back. I give a nod of respect to the others before focusing solely on Creed and Cole. "Don't fucking die, your sister will kill me if anything happens to either of you." Creed rolls his eyes whilst Cole chuckles.

"Dude, these witches have nothing on hurricane California." Cole's jibe at my mate brings a smile to my face.

"Let's go." I bark out and lead them to the front to meet the rest of the packs. Alpha's stand tall in front of their packs, Cairo's will be led by Zeke, while Hunter and Creed lead their own. I will not hide behind my status; I will follow each and every one of them into battle. The wind is picking up, rain begins to pelt down to the point of the droplets almost feeling like a hailstorm. I can feel Callie trying to push through the barrier, if I die out here, she can't know, she will risk her own life to try and save mine. Whatever Tristan is trying to do with this funnel thing, I hope he does it quick, the weather is changing fast. I open the link I share with all wolves and speak to them.

If you are here of your own free will, what we face is a force we have never experienced before. If you want to hide out in the cellar with the others, no one will stop you.

I look around to each man and woman who stands before me, there is well over two hundred of them here, none of them move a muscle. I give them all a nod of thanks, each and every one of them has my gratitude and respect. *We have to find cover, they will attack us from a distance and believe me, they will take us out. Our strength and speed mean nothing against them until they are visible, no one is to attack until I give the signal, we need to hold them off until Tristan is able to finish the transfer. They have come for Skylar's body–.* Growls come from each of the alpha's, Sky is well respected amongst these guys.

What do you need from us? Creed asks.

I need you all to form a barrier around Creed's cabin, stay hidden and anchor down somewhere. This storm will only get worse and until we can see them, we just have to...bear what comes.

Each alpha sends their members out to find a place to hunker down, I'm grasping at straws here. I don't actually know if these fuckers will show themselves or how many of them there actually are, but I do know this, over my dead body will I let them anywhere near my family. I will fight until my last breath making sure they all survive, I know dad isn't happy about sitting this out, but he can't go against my order, his wolf won't let him. Once the alpha's have their packs sorted, I look to each of them, they all wear masks of anger. I can feel their rage, fear and anger thrumming through the link.

Once this threat is neutralized, we will be free of all this loss and bloodshed. I make sure to only speak with the alphas through the link and Zeke, he stands tall and proud. Sky was a loyal as fuck beta, but Z has stepped up in his new role and says he learnt from the best, Cairo is lucky to have him. A boom of lighting sounds out, I turn just in time to see it split through a tree, instantly it's set on fire.

"Fuck!" Creed's roar can be heard over the storm, another bolt of lightning strikes on the opposite side hitting another tree, I watch in horror as three people that were using the trunk as protection are blown into midair. The rain does nothing to subdue the burning forest around us. If we don't find them soon, we'll all be trapped inside this circle of fire with no way out, the wind continues to rage around us helping the fire to spread.

How the fuck is it able to spread with all this rain? I turn to Alaric and shake my head; I can see in his eyes he regrets the choice he made to bring his pack here.

They have magic, this storm isn't by nature, its manmade, they control it. I turn to Vince and quirk a brow in question. In order to end this catastrophe, *we have to locate where they are.*

I don't question him; I bark out an order for all alphas to scatter in search of them. I don't want to put any more distance between Callie and I, but I don't have a choice. I strip bare and call for Atticus, we shift in mere seconds at the back of one of the cabins.

We have to stay hidden and keep to the outskirts so we can come in from behind.

They have to be close Cassius, they are targeting this one area, they know where we are.

Atticus is right, they have to be really close, to know we are protecting Creed's cabin.

Find them!

Atticus growls in agreement, he uses all our strength to fight against the wind which has picked up even more. It feels like a hurricane is coming, I don't know if that is something they are able to conjure but I'm sure it's a fucking possibility. We search the woods to the east but don't catch a scent, being the chief alpha means I know all my wolves' scents and can find theirs with ease but theirs isn't the ones I'm trying to find. I open the link with the alphas only.

The east side is clear, find anything?

North is clear. I growl in response to Zeke.

I got a scent; it's coming from the southern end of the property. Cole and I are following it now!

Hunter, you fucking wait for the rest of us, don't be a hero! Atticus takes the lead and heads to the southern end of Creed's land; I reach for Hunter again, but the little shit has closed the link between us. A growl tears from Atticus, he can feel my worry and pushes himself harder to catch up to our baby brother, I will not fucking lose another sibling, I can't. Thanks to the change of direction the wind finally works in our favor, pushing us faster. The closer we get I begin to catch a strange scent; it somehow seems familiar, but it's overpowered by others.

There is more than a dozen of them.

We have them outnumbered but they can pick us off one by one–. My reply to Atticus is cut off when a force hits me in the side and sends me sailing through the air crashing into a tree.

All I hear is a loud snap, our right leg is broken, Atticus pushes us to stand keeping the weight off our front leg. He darts his gaze around the forest trying to scan for the fucker that just threw us, he scents the air, but comes up with nothing. Our ears perk at the sound of footfalls, whoever is near is on two legs. not four. *Can you track them?*

Yes, I have to reset the bone first or we risk incorrect healing. I agree, Atticus shifts back. I grit my teeth as I clutch my arm against my chest. I assess the damage, its broken just above my wrist. This is gonna hurt like a bitch, I grit my teeth and wrap my left hand around the break and close my eyes, taking a deep breath I snap it back into place causing a small groan to escape me. I slouch back against the tree for a moment as I breathe through the pain and wait for it to heal, when I hear the sound of snarls and growls coming from a distance, I quickly jump to my feet and run.

We need to shift!

Not yet, you can't run on three legs! As soon as we're close we'll shift. Atticus doesn't push, he knows what I'm saying is true. I grind my teeth when I feel the healing process start to take place. Bits of debris pierce the soles of my feet, branches scrape my face and my naked sides, I push all thoughts of pain from my mind as I focus on getting to my brother. I push my legs as fast as humanly possible; I cry out when every bone in my body finally sets. *Now Atticus!* I shout to him, I run leaping through the air as I break through the edge of the forest, Atticus shifts on the fly. We hit the ground on four legs, with a loud howl sounding from us, I dart my gaze around and that's when I see them. There must be at least forty of them standing there in their fucking silk yellow robes, who the fuck wears robes?

None of them look surprised, all their gazes are laser focused on me as if...they've been waiting for this moment. Atticus stands tall and proud, he paws at the ground in warning, stating he is ready to charge if need be. I peer around subtly and snort out my relief when I don't see my brother or Cole, I must have beat them here! The weather begins to change around us, the thunder slows as does the lightning and wind, the fire continues to rage on around us. I feel the heat of the flames creeping closer, I refuse to cower and shy away from the dense brush behind me. One of the hooded assholes steps forward, I scent the air and growl, I know who this fucker is before he even lowers his hood. This is the guy that tried to take Tristan and I out back in New York, his dark brown eyes spare me, his head is shaved to the scalp, his mouth twitches into a condescending smile. He opens his arms and does a swirling motion, then everything stops, no wind, rain or storm, the only sound that can be heard is the crackling of the burning trees around us.

"What a fool you are to come here alone." The gleeful tone of his voice grates on my nerves.

Shift back.

Cassius, we are stronger in my form.

I can't talk to him like this! I have to buy Tristan more time, trust me on this Atticus.

My wolf reluctantly hands over control, I shift back and relish in the burn I feel from the tearing of muscles and breaking of bones. The pain no longer registers to me, I push up from my crouch and stand strong. Henrick trails his gaze over me, I have nothing to hide and I sure as fuck am proud of my dick, so he can stare at it for as long as he likes.

"Hand over Skylar and we will let you have your freedom." Wait a fucking minute.

"Why Sky?"

"Her power was promised to us." I dart my gaze to the others around him, why is he acting like he isn't here for the baby?

"Sky is dead!" His smile widens, two more figures step up beside him, I brace myself for an attack.

"Oh, we know, but that child won't survive more than five minutes with that amount of power inside it. The power will return back to Skylar, now hand her over and we will allow you to live." Holy shit, it was never about the baby!

"You never planned to come for my niece, did you?" Henrick claps his hands and starts to pace whilst laughing. I stare at him in shock, he is out of his fucking mind!

"Of course not, my father would have come for the child, raised it and trained it to be obedient, but I am not him. My daughter went above and beyond for her coven, she did something my father was never able to do, she infiltrated the enemy's layer." I growl and clench my hands into fists.

"Your daughter is an evil bitch!" His eyes narrow as he bares his teeth at me, he snaps his arm out and I'm sent sailing backward with my arms and legs flaying through the air, I land on the ground with a loud oomph. A groan escapes me as I roll to my side and glare back at the bastard, I breathe through the ache in my side and stand. I close the space between us, stopping about ten feet before them, I don't know where the others are, and I am thankful that they aren't here. I can feel deep inside myself that I'm not making it out of here alive.

"Speak about my daughter like that again and I'll tear you limb from limb with the flick of my wrist."

"Fuck you, your daughter abandoned her own fucking kid, your granddaughter!" He waves me off like what I said means nothing.

"The child held no qualities that suited us, Gemma made a sacrifice and was rewarded for her efforts and trouble." I balk at the delusional piece of shit.

"She left her fucking child, a baby for God's sake. Do you even care about her?" He scrunches his face in disgust.

"The child could rot in hell for all I care." That's it, I open my hands and allow my claws to come through, I spread my legs and drop low as I allow a growl to come from deep inside me. My eyes have changed to my wolf's, the gleeful look in his eyes spurs me on, I dart forward and drop to the ground rolling as one of the guys on his left snaps his arm out toward me, I jump back to my feet and quickly dodge the water jet from another fucker. When they are a few feet away, I jump through the air with my arms outstretched and roar so fucking loud as I drop down using my claws to swipe them across their chest and face. The useless fucks fall to the ground withering in pain, I spin back toward Henrick and I'm caught off guard as a tree comes barreling toward me, which has me sailing through the air, again. I curl forward around the tree and grip the branches as it glides through the air, the branches scrap my skin raw but I'm out of options except to hold on. My body collides against the rough bark of another tree, and I bow forward only to howl out in searing pain, my grip on the tree loosens until my arms lay useless atop of the branches, I splutter and cough. I can scent the smell of my own blood renting the air, I look down to see one of the branches is wedged inside my torso, I cough spitting out my blood, the pain that radiates through my body is excruciating. My vision starts to blur, and I know if I pass out, I'll be as good as dead.

"Did you really think you can take my father?" I shake my head and try to focus on anything aside from the pain, I can feel my strength fleeing my body, Atticus howls inside me. I ignore the woman's question I lift my arms trying to push the top of the tree back so I can heal, I cry out in pain when it's pushed further inside me, my vision turns hazy, and I don't have long unless I can get this tree out. The scent of my blood is pungent, my eyes are heavy. "Try that again and I'll push it further into you." I fight with everything I have to lift my heavy head and rest it back against the tree as I stare at the woman through my haze of pain. Her strawberry blonde hair gleams in the moonlight, her brown eyes hold nothing but anger, her teeth are on display and I see her two canine teeth tick out.

"Gemma, I assume?" I wheeze out then begin to cough, more blood splutters out of my mouth. A broad grin stretches across her face, Henrick stands beside her proudly and it's in this moment I see Mera is so much better off without her mother.

"The one and only, now, tell me where that bitch is so I can get what is owed to me?"

"You will never lay a hand on my granddaughter." I lull my head to the side and dread fills me when I see Kitty waltz into the clearing like she owns the fucking show, Henrick and Kitty stare at each other. Kitty looks like she is ready to slit his throat, Henrick looks like he has just won the fucking lottery, Gemma turns toward Kitty and flicks her wrist. Another tree sails toward Kitty but she waves her arm, and the fucking thing catches on fire and burns to ash before it even gets near her. Henrick claps his hands like a fucking clown and throws his head back and laughs.

"Oh, my love, you still amaze me, just think of the fun we could have had together." Kitty snarls at the bastard.

"I would rather burn to death than ever allow your disgusting hands to touch me you sack of dog shit!" The venom that coats her tone is awe inspiring, Kitty is a badass. I cough again and this time it takes me a good minute before I can get myself under control, my vison is turning black at the edges and I no longer have control over my limbs, my legs give out and I scream out in pain as I drop my full weight onto the branch, I feel it. I'm about to die, I swore I wouldn't do it, but I can't say it to her one more time, I open the link with Callie.

I love you Alma. Her relief can be felt, and I hate myself for allowing her to know I'm about to die, she will be able to feel my pain.

You're not dying today Cassius! I'm coming, hold on.

Everything goes black before I can tell her not to come, I'm just glad it's me here and not my brother or Callie.

THIRTY

TRISTAN

Holy shit!

The fire burns in my veins, I feel it pulsating through my blood stream filling with a source of power I never knew existed. My grip on Sky tightens as I feel a surge, my knees begin to tremble from the influx of power inside me. I grit my teeth as the fire spreads from the tips of my fingers all through my body until I feel like I'm ablaze, I scream out as the magic overcomes me.

I have to dispel this power or I run the risk of it taking over. I throw my head back and roar as the power disperses from me, I feel the waves of magic flee my body, the longer I keep this up the less tense I feel. A stabbing pain in my head begins to take over the blissful feeling, I scream out when the pain becomes too much, I try to release my hold on my sister, but I can't get free. The pressure builds and my skull feels like it is about to shatter into a million pieces, the pain is blinding and has white spots dancing behind my eyelids.

The fuck is happening?

Tristan, let go! At first, I thought the woman's voice I hear inside my head was Callie, but it's not her.

I'm losing my fucking mind; I should never have done this transfer!

You're not losing your mind brother. I try to open my eyes when I realize who it is, my eyes refuse to open, the pain has become nothing but a dull ache, and my mind is reeling at the what the fuck is going on.

Sky?

It's me.

I can't see anything, why can't I see anything?

Because your mind has taken you to a place where you won't register the pain, the power coursing inside you is too much.

I had to do this, if I don't, they will all die!

You have all the elements coursing through your veins, each are warring inside you to become the victor of your body. You have to dispel them now, or you will be lying beside my body.

How are you even here?

I have a niece who is more powerful than you think, if you do this Tristan, there will be a price to pay.

There always is, can you help me?

No, once the final transfer is complete and you let go, I will be gone. I can try and guide you now though?

How long do we have?

At most, three minutes, listen carefully to everything I say, and you may just make it out of here tonight.

THIRTY-ONE

CALIFORNIA

I groan and roll to the side, I cringe when I see the massive hole in the side of my brother's house, he's going to fucking flip when he sees it. White light is still pulsing inside the room, I reach up and touch the back of my head but flinch, I pull my hand back and see the tips of my fingers are coated in blood. I push to my feet and wobble slightly as dizziness takes a hold of me for moment, I sway slightly and reach out to grip the tree beside me. I take a moment to gather myself and wait for my healing to kick in.

Kora?

Yes.

Can you feel for Cass? I can't explain it, but I have this feeling of dread inside me, something is telling me Cassius is in danger.

He's still sealed off from us.

I can feel it, something is wrong. It's times like this that I wish I wasn't such a stubborn asshole and pledged myself to Cass so I would be able to communicate with my brothers, I'm technically still pack less since Creed released his hold on me and Cole. I feel for Tristan again hoping that I am able to get through, but it's like a wall is in place and I can't break through it! I'm going to fucking skin each of these assholes when this fucking nightmare is over. I push off the tree once the wound is healed and prepare myself to brave the power Tristan is pushing out but cease mid step when the wind stops and the storm just disappears. I look around utterly lost at what the hell is going, I spot members of my brothers and Hunter's pack come out from behind cabins in the distance and they seem just as perplexed as I do. Before I can ponder it too much I'm shrouded in darkness, I gasp and turn back toward the room, the light from Tristan has stopped.

"Tristan?" I call out hoping that he is okay, I push aside the feeling of guilt knowing that I will be overjoyed to know he is safe. But, in order for him to be safe and have been successful in the transfer, it also means Sky's heart has stopped beating for the final time. I cautiously hedge closer toward the house, my stomach is in my throat, I pray to whoever the hell is listening that he and Cass are both okay.

As I get closer, I strain my hearing trying to hear for any signs of life inside the room, I close my eyes and focus, I block out the sounds around me. I feel a gust of wind blow around me, its warmth encompasses my entire body like a warm embrace. A startled gasp escapes me when I feel it brush over my lips as if placing a tender kiss like a lover would, quiet tears leak from the corners of my eyes, I scrunch them closed and breathe through my nose as the realization hits me full force.

"Goodbye my love." I whisper, my words carry around me and I feel the warmth slowly start to dissipate, I want to reach out and hold onto her, but I know not even my love can keep her here. "I'll always love you." I say barely above a whisper before the breeze is gone as quick as it came. A feeling of peace washes over me, now that I know she is finally free and not fighting every day to remain in control of her own body. I may love both Cass and Tristan with everything I have, but Sky will always hold a special part of my heart for as long as I shall live. My eyes fly open when I feel two hands cupping my cheeks, tears leak faster as I stare into his hazel eyes, I wrap my arms around his neck and pull him to me, I smash my lips against his and melt into his embrace, he pulls back and smiles down at me, but I can see in his eyes he's in pain. "What's wrong?"

"We need to get to Cass now." Is all he says before he grips my hand in his and pulls me after him, I would have no trouble keeping up with his pace if I shifted, but as it is I'm sprinting just to keep up with his long strides. My relief of knowing he is okay is overshadowed by his need to get to Cass, I can feel through the link now that Tristan hasn't blocked that he is worried, but also...afraid. I grip his hand tighter and push my legs faster, something inside me knows that Cass is in danger. I stifle my gasp when I feel the link between Cass and I open.

I love you Alma. Oh, fuck no! I can hear the pain in his voice, he is not dying on me today, not now, not ever.

You're not dying today, Cassius! I'm coming, hold on.

Tristan's grip tightens around my hand, and I know he just heard what Cass said, at the sound of footfalls behind us I chance peeking over my shoulder and spot Zeke in wolf form with his pack following behind us, I look to my side and see Cairo, Vince, Alex and Creed with his pack running behind them. I don't waste my energy on asking how they know where to go, I just trust in the fact that they know their alpha needs them. Tristan breaks through the forest and we dodge branches and fallen trees, the storm they created has caused so much damage to Creed's land. We navigate our way through the forest for what feels like hours, I can see a break in the tree line up ahead but at the sound of Kitty's voice I gasp and look up at Tristan, his jaw is ridged and stiff from grinding his teeth in both anger and pain.

He hasn't said it, but I can feel the power pulsating from him, for some reason he hasn't transferred the power to Mera and Ro's baby. If I had time, I would ask him why, he must have a fucking good reason as to why he is risking what he is by keeping the power inside himself. We break through the brush and Tristan slows his pace; my breathing is ragged as I dart my eyes around. I spot Kitty as she faces off with a man and a girl around my age from the look of it, yellow hooded figures stand behind them stoically. I try to search amongst them for Cass but can't see him, Tristan stops when he reaches Kitty, before I can even focus on the two in front of us the scent of blood hits me, oh god.

I turn to the left and scream, I drop my hold on Tristan as I race across the clearing to Cass, he's pinned against a giant oak tree with a massive branch in his torso. Panic fills me as I near him seeing his head flopped forward, I'm mere inches away when I'm blasted backward by a strong gust of wind, I crash into someone who breaks my fall. I roll off them when I hear a grunt and see it was Creed who caught me, a manic laugh catches my attention. I spring to my feet and growl at the plain looking bitch who stands in front of Tristan. Her strawberry blonde hair looks oily and in need of a trim, her soulless shit-brown colored eyes bore into me as I bare my teeth at her. The bitch stands there and pushes out her bottom lip mocking me.

"Your lover will die." I snap, I launch at the bitch only to be thrown backward when she simply waves her hand, this time Cairo catches me. I push off but he wraps his arms around my waist and anchors me to him.

"Let me go!" I scream.

"You can't win." He whispers low enough for only me to hear. "Scent the air Callie, his blood has stopped flowing, his heart still beats slowly." I sob at the pathetic rhythm of Cass's heart, if I don't get that fucking branch out of him, he is going to die!

"Ro..."

"Shhh, I swear to you I won't let him die." Call me stupid but I believe Cairo, I push my worry for Cass's life out of my mind and focus on the battle that is sure to ensue. The woman eyes Tristan with a lustful gaze that has Kora wanting to rip her throat out, the man beside her stares at Tristan for a moment before his gaze widens and an angry look overtakes his features.

"That doesn't belong to you boy." Tristan lazily slides his gaze from the woman to stare at the man with a broad expression.

"Henrick, always a displeasure to see you alive." Oh my god, he was the guy that was supposed to marry Kitty! If that's Henrick then that mutt must be... I look at the woman again and that's when I know, she's Tristan's first love, the mother to his child, she's the bitch that broke his fucking heart.

"That power belongs to my daughter, and by coven law it will be passed to her!" Tristan's upper lip pulls back in a snarl, he turns his hands palm up at his sides and within a second two balls of flames dance in each of his hands. Henrick pales slightly, Gemma looks like she's just seen a ghost.

"She had the power of a fire elemental." The awe in Gemma's voice is tangible, the robed figures behind them creep forward for a better look, some of them even lower their hoods as they stare at Tristan in wonder. Tristan chuckles but there is no humor to it, Creed moves so he is standing beside Ro and I.

"No, you daft power-hungry leech, I always had the power of a fire elemental, I just never told you about it." To the bitch's credit, if what he just said affects her, she doesn't let it show.

"You hid it from me on purpose, I told you when I came back–." Tristan growls, he may not be a shifter but even I can feel the heat behind it, he launches a ball of fire at the bitches' feet making her jump back a step or risk being burnt.

"You assumed I was weak because I allowed you to believe it." Tristan conjures up some type of swirling motion with his hands and punches the air, a stream of fire spews from his left hand, he does the same momentum with the right, and in that moment the robed figures are surrounded by a circle of fire. I watch in fascination as the people in the middle dart forward and streams of water pour from their hands extinguishing the fire. Tristan stands tall and wears a proud smirk on his face, he has a glint in his eye that equally terrifies me and thrills me at what he might do next.

"Don't make us kill you, I would hate to leave Mera father-less." A growl so feral and wild tears from me, everyone is staring in my direction. I allow Kora forward so that bitch can see the wolf inside me that wants to tear her flesh from her bones.

"Keep *my* daughters fucking name out of your filthy mouth." My voice doesn't waiver, the strength of my words is laced with an alpha tone that surprises me, but I make sure to keep that expression from my face. Tristan eyes me for a moment before darting his gaze toward Cass, it appears as if this is the first time, he has noticed Cass. His eyes narrow as he lifts his arm and with his fingers outstretched, he slowly curls them into a fist, Cass screams out in pain as Tristan uses his magic to pull the tree free. I watch as Cass drops to the ground on all fours, I want to run to him and make sure he's okay, but the robed figures quickly move to form a line and block him from our sight. The sound of laughter pulls my attention back to Gemma, her manic laughter is like nails on a chalk board.

"She will never be yours; she is half him and half me. I will always be the one who gave him his heir, you will simply be a constellation prize. His betrothed will come along one day and you will be thrown out like the dog you are," Tristan's laughter stumps me, I peer over at him and gasp, his eyes are yellow! Gemma steps back when she sees the change, she looks to her father and instead of fear, I see a hunger. Henrick waves his hand and two of his followers move through the mass of people and I furrow my brow as I peer over at my brother, he shakes his head in confusion as we wait. When the two return, growls sound from me and Creed, I thrash in Cairo's hold, Alex and Vince rush forward to hold Creed back as we fight to get free.

"I'll fucking tear your head off, let him go!" The anger in Creed's tone is potent, Henrick smiles like a gleeful idiot, Gemma closes the space between her and Tristan and runs her index finger down his front. Normally I would be focused on her and wanting to tear the bitch apart, but my sole focus is on Hunter and Cole, both have their hands tied behind their backs, a cloth is stuffed in each of their mouths, and I can see gashes on their chests, arms and faces. The wounds are deep but not fatal, I don't understand why they aren't healing. A pained growl sounds out and I turn back to Cass to see he is trying to climb to his feet, Zeke and Asher help him stand but I can see from how pale he is that he is in no shape to fight. His wound is still open and healing slowly, each step he takes toward us has a pained expression crossing his face.

"Give me what I want and your brother lives." Tristan grips a handful of Cole's hair and yanks his head back as he speaks. I look to Tristan ready to beg if I have to, but his gaze is focused only on Gemma, Kitty stares at the pair of them with an unreadable expression.

"I want the power, and if you do this we'll let them live." I wait for Tristan to refuse her and tell her that I am his bonded, but he just stands there silently. The silence in this forest is eerie as we wait for Tristan's reply, I try to reach him through the link, but he's walled me off again!

"Tristan please, he's my brother!" I shout. Still, Tristan stands there and does nothing, I begin to worry that the power inside him has taken over like it did with Sky.

THIRTY-TWO

TRISTAN

Her touch repulses me, her scent angers me, the sight of her makes me sick!

I allow her to think that her charms have me in a trance like state, hearing the defeat in Callie's tone as she begs me to help, almost has me crumbling. I cannot show Gemma what she means to me, if she catches even a hint of the love, I feel for California, she will make her pay just to get at me. It's taking everything I have to keep this power inside me from not exploding, if what Belle said is true, then I just have to focus. Sky told me I would have one shot at this and if I blow it, that means it could cost us all our lives.

"Did you miss me?" The sickening tone of her voice feels like glass shards grating against my skin. I keep the link between Callie and I closed, and pray I don't fuck it up when I reach for only Cass, I feel the moment he allows me into his mind.

What are you doing Tristan? I can hear the pain even as he thinks the words.

Trying to save us all

They have my brother, what is there to think about?

I need you to get everyone out of here.

Why? I can feel his unease through the bond.

I'm going to save both your brothers and burn these fuckers to the ground. His surprise filters into me.

They won't leave, you have earn't their respect–.

Make sure she doesn't hate me.

What are you going to–.

His reply is cut off when I reach out and grip the back of her neck yanking her to me, I slam my lips against hers. The strangled gasp coming from my left guts me, but I don't focus on Callie's hurt as I use my tongue to push inside Gemma's mouth. Her being the vindictive bitch that she is opens for me and she lets out a breathy moan, even I can tell it's fake, she's putting on a show just for Callie. I pray Sky is right and this works, I focus on the fire inside me and push it outward. Heat coats every part of my body, I feel it creep from the tips of my toes to the top of my head, as the heat intensifies, Gemma tries to pull away, but I tighten my hold on her. She pushes against my chest, but her struggle is futile, when I feel the magic inside her pickup, I force all the fire inside her, she screams into my mouth and its only when I release her and shove her back a step. She clutches at her throat; fear shrouds her eyes as she looks to Henrick in a panic. I feel the rise of power from behind me and know she is near; I need to do this now. I respect the wolves for trying to fight this battle, but they are no match for my kind.

Get them out of here now! I scream at Cass. I step forward and call on all the elements inside me, I pull on my earth magic, each of the elder's followers rush forward and surround Henrick and Gemma, he can try to save his daughter, but it won't work, Gemma is as good as dead now. I strike out and use every bit of strength I have to cause a crater, as the ground begins to rumble and shift beneath their feet, a dozen earth elementals step forward and fight against me, I may have the power of all the elements, but I am still just one man. I block the noise coming from the wolves, I feel kitty slide up beside me as she begins to chant a spell. The strength they have is greater than mine, I feel my grasp on the earth around them weakening. Just as the grip I have starts to slip through my clutch, I feel them, I meet the gaze of Colby, one of the other elders and watch as he frantically searches behind me. His eyes widen at the sight, and my sense of strength is bolstered by the notion I have more than surprised them. My coven has come to my aide and so have other outcasts Kayla managed to find, I don't know how or why she did this, but I am grateful to her. I look side to side and see each of them fan out around me, the elders and their followers shift to form a line, Gemma lets loose a painful cry from behind them.

"What have you done?" Henrick roars, I ignore the son of a bitch as more of his followers start to call on their elements and join in on the fight, I turn to Kitty.

"Get them to hold the earth and create a crater, I want water users ready to sink them once they drop." She nods her head and begins to bark out orders, I watch Zara and Eli begin to chant in front of me, they are Henricks pets, he has groomed these siblings to be nothing more than his killing machines. Zara's white eyes meet mine and I brace myself for her spell to hit me full force, she pushes out her arms and a burst of light flies toward me, just before it makes contact a blur of brown hair jumps in front of me. I drop the hold I have on the ground and catch her before she falls, her body lays limp in my arms. Fear and panic like I have never felt before surges through me, I gaze down at her to see her chest is charred, Zara did a fucking fire spell! I bare my teeth and turn my head to snarl up at the bitch who is still throwing out spells. Creed drops down beside me and tries to gather her in his arms, but I tighten my hold and glare at him.

"I need to get her to safety, she's my sister Tristan!" I want to fight him on this. "Let me take her, just...save my brother please. Colton is an ass, but he is everything to Callie, I can't get near him, those witches keep taking us out every time we get close." I grit my teeth before gazing down at Callie, I'll do whatever I have to and make sure no harm befalls her, I place a gentle kiss to her lips before handing her over to Creed.

"You keep her fucking safe." He nods before adding.

"Don't die, not a lot scares me in this world, but my sisters temper is at the top of the list." He pats me on the shoulder before standing with my heart in his arms, I watch him race off with her and pray that won't be the last time I get to kiss her. Screams of anguish draw my attention, I smirk triumphantly as I watch Gemma drop to her knees clawing at her throat, her skin has turned orange from the fire coursing through her veins.

"What the fuck have you done?" I smile at Henrick as he drops down next to his daughter.

"I gave her what she wanted." I shout over the chaos. "She wanted me inside her again and I gave it to her, my fire now courses through her veins burning her from the inside out." His eyes widen in shock before it quickly bleeds way to anger. He rises to his feet and readies himself to attack me, I spy Cole and Hunter still on their knees in the middle of their circle, I have to get them out of there. I form a barrier of wind around myself as Henrick throws his magic at me, I keep the shield up as I link Cass.

I need you to get your brother and Cole.

I can't get to them!

My coven and I will distract everyone, retreat to the forest and come in from behind.

There is to many, your outnumbered.

My army is bigger, I just need to take Henrick out and then the rest will fall. Hurry Cass, I don't have long before this power overrides me!

I close the link and focus back on Henrick, I need to keep him focused on me and give the wolves a chance to retreat and attack from behind. I push the barrier outward and make sure it surrounds all my coven, blow after blow hits the barrier and I grit my teeth against the strain. The wind I have called on is loud and will cause damage, but I need this moment to speak with my coven.

"All of you need to keep them distracted, I'm going for Henrick–,"

"The power will consume you Tristan!" I turn to my grandmother and smile; her face is scrunched. "Your eyes have changed." I nod my head; I know they have but I can't focus on that now.

"Trust me Kitty, I have to do this."

"We will follow you master." Callum, one of the young warlocks Kitty and I took in when he was fifteen says as he steps forward bowing his head as a sign of respect. I don't have time to thank them for coming to our aide, I spy movement behind them and that's when I see Kayla at the edge of the tree line. I nod my head in thanks to her, if she didn't bring them here, we would never have lasted this long. I owe Kayla Michaelson a great debt, I have no doubt she will collect on that debt.

THIRTY-THREE

CASSIUS

I ignore the pain in my abdomen and shift, I grit my teeth and allow Atticus to take over completely. He whines but doesn't protest as we hit the ground running, the pain is excruciating but he and I will never stay dormant and allow our packs to fight whilst we sit back and cower like a pussy. We stick to the tree line and hide amongst the shadows, I don't like the idea of leaving Tristan there with...whoever the fuck those others are that came with Kayla, but they do seem more equip to handle those elders than we do.

I slow my pace as we round the back part of the woods, there is fallen trees, debris and trash that litter the ground from their windstorm earlier. I'm not at full strength and if I don't pull myself together, I am going to wind up being a liability for my pack. The thought of my baby brother being out there with no way to defend himself, scared and in two minds if I'm going to save him, or thinking he might join mom and Blake fucking kills me. I push the pain from my mind and creep through the trees silently, I feel the others close behind, their anger at this situation can be felt through the link, each of them is ready to take down these bastards for entering their lands. Wolves are territorial and having someone come here uninvited is not something we take lightly; these elder scums will pay for that mistake with their lives!

I Pause at the edge of the woods and stare at the pure carnage that is unfolding in front of me, Tristan fights with fire coming from one hand and air from the other, using the wind to push the fire further he resembles the grace of a dragon, his yellow eyes shine bright against the moonlight. Kitty covers his back and fights with fire herself, the elders congregate around the two of them whilst leaving the others fight against few of the alpha's followers. Clearly Kitty and Tristan are viewed as the greater threat here and not their coven. I link the pack to stay put and wait as I try to fight my way inside Hunter and Cole's mind, I whine low in my throat when a stabbing pain pierces my skull, I try again, and the pain escalates each time.

I can't reach them!

Those witches must have done something, we have to move, they are putting distance between them and the guys.

I turn back to the clearing and see Cairo is right, Tristan and the others are drawing them further away from Hunter and Cole, only two remain behind to watch over their captives. Under other circumstances I would attack now and take out the two, being that they are witches I hold back, I watched one say a few words and then boom, they knocked Callie down! That bitch will pay for that, I have her face burned into my memory and will make sure she gets what is coming to her.

We need a distraction. Atticus eyes Zeke's wolf, he may have a point.

What do you suggest? We ask.

Wait for my signal, Asher and Chris with me. The two wolves follow after Zeke, I look to Bexley who doesn't even seem fazed, his beta just commanded his pack and gave an alpha call.

I feel your gaze burning into me Atticus. The sound of Cairo's wolf's gruff voice inside my head tells me Ro has stepped back and allowed Bex control over what happens next.

You allowed your beta to command your pack, why? Atticus sounds truly perplexed about this, I decide to do the same as Ro and allow him control while we wait for Zeke.

Because he's proven time and time again that he can lead, Ezekiel Cross is a great beta, but he will be an even better alpha one day.

His words hold weight, Cairo and Bex don't seem distraught over the idea that Z will one day leave them and form his own pack. Ro truly is an amazing alpha; I can't say I would be as calm as him if I knew my beta would someday leave and start a pack of his own. The sound of Z's voice pulls me from my inner thoughts.

When they attack us, you go for Cole and Hunter and get them out of here! Atticus releases a growl of pure alpha power through the link which has some of the wolves behind us whining.

You don't order me around pup. Another growl comes from Atticus as Z ignores him and races into the clearing toward the two witches. Asher is thrown back when one of them shoots a jet of water at him, Chris zigzags making it harder for them to hit him with their magic, Zeke does the same, I can see the fear on the witches faces as they start to get closer. Chris and Z move as one, like a well-oiled machine, no words are needed they just know how the other fights. I break out of my daze and push Atticus to move into the clearing, the others stay beside me as we race to recuse my brother and Cole. Screams and cries of pain can be heard throughout, but I tune it all out as I focus on Hunter, his eyes widen when he sees us coming for them. I don't shift back, Atticus uses his teeth to bite the ropes that bind Hunt's hands and legs, Cairo frees Cole in the same way.

"We can't shift!" The uncertainty in Cole's voice is haunting, if they can't shift, they won't be able to get out of here! I nudge Hunter's leg and motion with my snout for him to run into the woods, he shakes his head which earns him a growl from me. I ignore my wolf's protests as I force him to shift back, the pain is present but not as bad, I grip Hunter's shoulders and cringe when I hear the screams of pain coming from Tristan's side of the clearing.

"Get out of here now, that's an order." Hunter's eyes widen as he stumbles back a step out of my grip.

"I didn't feel it!" I bare my teeth in frustration.

"I didn't either." I turn to Cole utterly pissed that I don't know what the fuck they are talking about.

"Cass, I didn't feel it!"

"Feel what Hunter?" I grit out. He throws his hands in the air and glares at me.

"The alpha command, I didn't feel it." I look to Cole and see the same amount of fear in his eyes. "Whatever they did to us, it took away out abilities to shift, I can't even feel my wolf anymore Cassius." I open my mouth but snap it closed when I hear Tristan scream out in pain, I peer around Hunter to see him drop to his knees.

"You and Cole get the fuck out of here, now!" I shout as I take off toward Tristan, Atticus surges forward and I allow the shift to wash over me with ease. My paws pound against the earth, I dodge the bodies of fallen witches and a few wolves, I block out the shouts for me to comeback as I head straight for the asshole standing above Tristan with his arm raised in the air, ready to unleash whatever magic he has. I leap through the air and tackle the bastard to the ground, the momentum sends us both tumbling, I dig my claws in skidding to a holt and launching back onto my feet. Henrick stands there with his hands splayed out at his sides, I ready myself to attack when suddenly the air around me shifts, I find it hard to breathe. A cruel smirk ghosts across his hideous face.

"He took my daughter from me, now I will take all those he holds dear from him." Realization sinks in, he's sucking all the air out of me and causing me to slowly suffocate. I sway on my feet and try to stay up right as panic begins to filter through me, I dart my gaze around the clearing and that's when everything slows down. The coven members that came to T's aide are surrounded and subdued by the elders; my wolves fight to free them but are unable to get close enough thanks to the magic they hit them with. I look back to Tristan and find him on his hands and knees panting, my eyes begin to lose focus, I open the link with Tristan.

We're gonna die here if you don't do something. I begin to gasp for air as I drop to the ground, my head feels like it is going to explode from the lack of oxygen. My last thought before I black out is that I pray Callie is able to get her and Mera out of here and to safety.

THIRTY-FOUR

TRISTAN

I war within myself to try and gain control of this power, it's taking over every part of my being and making it so hard that I no longer exist, almost as if I'm just a passenger to my own body. The sound of Cass's faint whispered words inside my mind have me latching on to them to try and help me find my way to myself.

I fight with everything I have to gain the control I need; I grit my teeth as I fight with every fiber of my being to regain control of my own body. I gasp for air as soon as I am able to see again, I look side to side and see the mass of bodies that litter the ground and the ones that continue to fight for their lives and the lives of their loved ones. My coven is cornered and incapacitated, they are inexperienced and nowhere near as powerful as the elders who train daily to be the deadly force they are.

At the sound of a whimper, I lift my head and see Atticus on the ground gasping for air, my eyes widen in shock as I push to my feet. I sway slightly but right my footing, Atticus's eyes are bulging out of his head, I see Henrick standing there and snarl. The fucker is suffocating him to death! I don't even question what I am about to do next, with great sacrifice comes great reward. I push all my fears aside, I block out thoughts of Callie and her safety, I push thoughts of my daughter from my mind and shut off the panic inside me at wondering if Kitty is okay. I open my arms wide and lull my head back, I focus on the matter at hand but the sounds around me and the magic inside my veins.

Help me, help them, please.

I don't know who I'm begging for help, but I just hope that the magic inside me registers that I am kin, I need my parents and sisters magic to help me save the lives of everyone here that I care about. I can't let Cass die, I never had a sibling growing up, but if the bond I feel toward him is an example of having a brother, then I can't lose that. I won't risk these bastards taking us out and going after Callie and Mera, the dreadful things they would do to them just to get at me has a shudder tearing through me. At the thought of them I feel the magic spark to life, but this time I'm in control. I feel all the elements come together inside me, intertwining with each other to create a force so powerful I can taste it on the tip of my tongue. Just as the power hits the cusp of my fingertips, I look right at Henrick as I speak.

"Your reign is over." The look of pure malice in his eyes cements my decision to eradicate him and his followers, I throw my head back once again and roar like a crazed mad man, power expels out of every part of my body. I picture in my mind's eye who to target and aim directly for them, screams and cries of help are muted by the whooshing sound in my ears. I pray that I don't hurt my friends and only take out the ones that wished to harm us, I feel my consciousness slipping and the magic taking hold of me again. I have to keep my focus on the task at hand or I risk killing everyone within reach of me, I want to fight for control, but it requires effort and concentration. A pained thought filters through my mind as I feel the claws of this darkness inside me weave its way through my veins vying for control of my body to use as it's vessel.

THIRTY-FIVE

CALIFORNIA

As soon as I regain consciousness, I fight against Creed's hold to allow me to get back to my guys. I can feel it with every fiber of my being that they need me, if they go down, I'm going with them. The pain from that bitches hit doesn't even register, I'm good with compartmentalizing shit, always have been, I'll deal with the pain later.

"You'll just be a distraction!" I bare my teeth at my brother.

"They need me–." He scowls down at me earning himself a growl from Kora.

"They need you to stay alive, not kill yourself trying to save them." He doesn't understand, how could he? He got the girl; he has the white picket fence and perfect family.

"I wasn't living for months until I let them in, they make my heartbeat, without them I have nothing, I'll be nothing but a shell. Losing Sky nearly killed me Creed, If I lose them both I won't survive. You and Cole may not agree with it, but those two put air back into my lungs, they gave me a reason to live again, I don't just love them, I'm unconditionally and irrevocably in love with them both." His eyes gleam with understanding as mine fill with tears of dread and worry for my guys. I can feel deep in my bones they aren't okay; Cass had a fucking branch through his torso and a wound like that will take days to fully heal internally. Tristan has magic inside himself that he shouldn't, the same magic that killed Sky. "I need you to let me go, I have to get to them Credence, please!" My brother stares down at me for a beat, I see the reluctance in his gaze, I ready myself to fight my own brother if I have to, but then he nods.

"You stay beside me; do you hear me California?" I nod and quickly chase after him when he breaks into a run, we stay in our skin rather than shifting. I feel Kora right below the surface, ready to take over if she has to, having her so close and ready to defend our guys is beyond comforting.

We will save them.

Can you feel them Kora?

No, they each have us blocked. I can sense they are in danger though, run faster Callie.

I push my legs as fast as I can, Creed's longer strides eat up the dirt as he moves, we are close and I hear screams of agony and cries for help but that isn't what has me skidding to a halt. It's the sense of Déjà vu, I can taste the potent magic on my tongue, I feel it wash over my body and I know he's on the verge of losing it. I shove past Creed and ignore his shouts for me to come back, I break into the clearing and that's when I spot him. He's emersed in a cloud like light, it swirls around him with lightning bolts shooting out at each member of the elders, I spot Atticus launching through the air and latching onto the side of Henrick's throat.

I shake myself out of my stupor and take off toward Tristan and hope like I never before that I'm not to fucking late to save him. I will not lose him the same way I lost Sky. I spot Z and Cairo rushing toward me, I manage to sidestep Z only to be caught by Ro wrapping his arms around my waist and hoisting me off the ground.

"Let me go!" I scream as I thrash in his hold.

"I can't do that."

"He needs me Cairo, I have to save him."

"You can't, you couldn't..." He cuts himself off but it's too late, I know what he was about to say.

"It's different, I can do it this time Ro." He places me on my feet and turns me to face him, he searches my gaze for what, I'm not sure. We stand for a few seconds just staring at each other, the sound of Creed screaming my name pulls Ro from his thoughts.

"Run, if your brother gets here, you're never getting to Tristan." I turn to flee but then remember something.

"Get Mera and baby Sky, he'll need them here to transfer the power!" Ro doesn't argue, he just nods and starts barking orders to Z as I head for my guys, if I was still part of Creed's pack, his growls and shouts for me to come back would work, fortunately I'm not in his pack. I unintentionally formed my own with my guys and Mera. Right now, they need me to be the alpha, I need to be strong enough for them to end this and save Tristan's life. The force of the magic hits me square in the chest the closer I get to him, I brace my arms in front of my face to shield it from the light and the winds around him, my feet skid back along the ground, and I stumble but right myself before I can fall. I keep pushing trying to get to him, more rods of lighting emerges from his body, from what I can see he is only taking out the enemy.

I hear Atticus growl and turn to see him struggling against Tristan's force to get to me, blood drips from his jaws and I know he ended the life of the man who wanted to take our own. I don't bother to look for the body, I don't need Henrick's lifeless body staring in my nightmares. I push forward and this time, I make sure to dig my heels in so he can't push me back, I won't let history repeat itself. I'm only a couple of feet away, his head is lulled back, arms out wide, I stop in my tracks when I see the black lines crawling up his neck, the same black lines that his sister had. A rush of wind hits me, and I'm blown backward, strong arms wrap around me and save me from falling. I look over my shoulder and melt, Cass stares down at me without judgment, he doesn't try to sway my decision about proceeding to Tristan, instead he helps me. He uses his weight and stature to our advantage and ushes against my back shoving me forward, before I can be blown backward, I wrap my arms around Tristan's waists and hold on.

I turn back to Cass just in time to see him smile and wink before the wind sends him sailing, fuck! I have to stop this now; I focus back on Tristan and gasp when I find his yellow eyes staring directly at me. I search his gaze for any sign of my Tristan still being alive inside, my bravado begins to falter when I see no recognition in his gaze. A lump forms in my throat and tears threaten to spill, I reach up and cup his face between my hands. His skin is cold to touch, he stiffens but I ignore it as I stare into his eyes.

"Come back to me, our story isn't finished yet, it's just beginning." Tears begin to fall down my cheeks, I fight past the lump in my throat to say what I need to. "I love you, if you have to go now, then I'm coming with you, because where one of you go, I'll always follow, *always*." The look on his face never changes, an emotional mask still remains in place as he stares down at me blankly.

He's gone. A sob tears from me as I stretch up on my tip toes and touch my lips to his, I pull back and wrap my arms around his waist as I rest my cheek against his chest and cry. I failed to save Sky and now I've just lost Tristan in the exact same way, everything becomes white noise around me as I get lost in my inner turmoil. I'm so angry at myself and him, I pull back and grip his shirt in my hands barely managing to look up. Still his gaze is locked onto me, the black lines have traveled to his face now, I begin to wail, slapping his face repeatedly and then pound against his chest as I scream out in excruciating pain. It's a pain I know well, it's so encompassing that it steals the very breath from your lungs, you lose your sense of smell, and everything appears so dim, almost lifeless.

"I fucking hate you for doing this." I scream as I hit him. "You bastard, I fucking hate you for making me love you, I hate you for fixing me only to break me again." My arms feel like they weigh a tone, they drop uselessly to my sides; I drop to my knees in front of him and sob. "Most of all, I hate you for making me need you." I whisper as I resign myself to the pain inside, my chest feels like it is being ripped open. What use is a fucking heart when it's constantly being broken? What a fucking useless artery, you can't live without one and yet, I can't seem to live with one because it's constantly being ripped apart. The feeling of someone's hands on me doesn't register for a moment until my face is lifted and I stare into hazel eyes mixed with flecks of gold, he's crouched down in front of me.

"Hate me all you want baby but hate me while I'm holding you." A strangled sob escapes me as I launch at him taking us both to the ground, he pulls me to him and captures my lips in a searing kiss. I cling to him like my life depends on it, he attempts to sit up, but I refuse to break the kiss as I wrap my arms and legs around him. He grips my shoulders and pushes me back, I growl at the small amount of distance he has put between us, he smirks but its dosed in pain. "Believe me, I want to keep kissing you but whilst I have control, I need to transfer this power otherwise I can't come back next time." I scramble off his lap so fast I trip and nearly fall until Cass catches me, I look up at him and smile my thanks as he offers Tristan a hand, which he accepts. They both stand here and stare at each other for a moment, I can feel the respect and love they have for each other radiating off them.

"It's good to have you back." Tristan beams at Cass.

"It's good to be back *brother*." Cass grabs Tristan and pulls him in for a bro hug, my chest constricts at the sight. They pull apart and give each other a weird guy nod, Tristan darts his gaze over my head and when I see relief in his gaze, I spin around to see Kitty standing beside Cairo, she looks battered and bruised but she's alive. A faint cry can be heard from behind Kitty, she steps aside so Belle can come forward with baby Sky in her arms, Merz pushes her way between Belle and Kitty. Her little nose scrunches up as she takes in the carnage around her, Tristan rushes forward, I feel his panic through the bond and quickly take off after him.

Gemma.

Is all Cass says through the link and then it all makes sense; Tristan doesn't want Mera to see the...remains of her mother. Once we reach them, he drops to his knees and engulfs her in a bone crushing hug.

"Daddy." She squeals in delight at the sight of her father, she clings to him and my heart swells. She may not have had her mother throughout her life, but she sure as shit has an amazing father who adores the very ground she walks on; it makes me so thankful for my own mother. We may not share blood but Meg Reeves loves us like we are her own, we never felt the void of not having Davina because of her. When dad was away it was always her with us, she never treated us like we were a burden, she still tells us to this day that we are the reason her life has purpose.

"I'm here baby girl." Mera looks to me and a broad smile stretches across her beautiful face, she pushes Tristan back and runs to me, I scoop her up into my arms and bury my face in the crook of her neck.

"I missed you."

"I missed you too, Merz." I say, she struggles in my hold and reaches out for Cass who doesn't hesitate to reach back out and pluck her from my hold. She cups his cheeks and smiles brightly at the big guy.

"Hi papa." Cass melts, she has him wrapped around her tiny little finger and she doesn't even know it.

"I need...to do...the transfer." The sound of Tristan's voice pulls me back to the present, he stands on shaky legs, his gaze bores into me as I see the color of his eyes flicking between his normal hazel color and yellow. Belle comes forward and smiles up at him warmly, Ro wraps his arm around her waist and pulls her into his side protectively before nodding to Tristan. My brothers come forward to stand either side of me, Z is at Ro's side ready to pull him back if he has to. Cass moves closer to Tristan, so he is able to hold Mera's hand as well as baby Sky's.

"This won't...hurt her, will it?" The concern in Belle's voice is understandable, the fact she is even out here and walking around is a testament to her character, she is a badass woman.

"I don't think so." Cairo growls at Tristan's reply.

"You don't *think*, what the fuck does that mean?" A shudder rolls through Tristan, I'm about to go ham on Cairo but Cass growls.

"Shut the fuck up and allow him to do this, it's not like there is a fucking manual is there?" Before Ro can contest Cass, Tristan cuts in.

"I don't believe there will be pain, I'll do my best, but I have to do this now."

THIRTY-SIX

TRISTAN

The magic wars inside me, trying to dig it's hooks in and doesn't want to let go, I push against the force trying to expel it from my body. My grip on the girls tightens as I start to feel it shift inside me, it feels like sandpaper grating on my insides as it flows through my veins. I push with everything I have to transfer it between the girls, I just hope I don't fuck it up, I push the earth and water magic to Skylar-Blake and the fire to Mera.

A heat starts to work its way through my body the harder I push; I grit my teeth through the onslaught of pain and make sure not to make a sound or I risk alerting Mera to me being in pain. She won't take it well if she knows this is hurting me, warmth travels down my arms and I feel it flow from my finger-tips to the girls. I start feeling dizzy and weightless like I haven't eaten in days as more flows out of me, I feel unsteady on my feet and I take it this means that I must be at the end of the transfer, well I hope I am.

"She's glowing!" I slowly open my eyes and peer side to side to see both girls are in fact alight, almost like a glow bug.

When I feel the last of the magic filter its way out of me, I release my hold on the girls and step back panting, I bend over and rest my hands on my knees as I catch my breath. I feel her beside me, the touch of her hand on my back cooling inside my body, my breathing begins to even out as I slowly calm down and settle the war inside myself.

"Are you okay?" The sound of her voice is like a balm to my battered soul, like the call of a siren luring me back. I whirl on her, and she stumbles backward but I reach out and catch her before she can fall, gripping the back of her neck I lift her until her lips meet mine, her shocked gasp allows me entry, no sooner does my tongue touch hers she's melting in my hold. She reaches up and wraps her arms around my neck deepening the kiss—.

"Yeah, that's enough of that shit!" Cole snickers and he pries us apart shooting Callie a disapproving glare which she matches with one of her own.

"The fuck Colton?" Cole places his hands on his hips like a parent would when they are about to lecture their child.

"Kissing a girl in front of me, I can stomach that. But I cannot and will not stand here and watch you make fuck me eyes and pash each of these assholes in front of me." Callie bites down on her lips to stop her smile from breaking free.

"You know you sound like a sexist pig, right?" Everyone erupts into fits of laughter at Cass's remark, Cole huffs out his annoyance but dousing us in a bucket of ice water with his next words.

"Yeah well at least I'm not making out while everyone else is mourning their dead." I grab Mera from Cass and hold her tight; Kitty slides up next to me and I wrap my arm around her and place a kiss to the top of her head. Bodies litter the ground, some of them are from the packs, some from my coven, but most of them belong to the elders and their followers. That's when a thought hits me, I turn to Kitty and ask.

"How did Kayla get our coven here?" Her brow furrows as she shakes her head.

"I didn't, I thought you did?" I shake my head in answer.

"If neither of you two got them here, who the fuck did?" That is the million-dollar question Cole, I eye everyone out here but when my gaze lands on Vince, I see it in his eyes. He gives me a subtle shake of his head; I can feel from the tension radiating off him that he and his brother had something to do with Kayla locating my coven and bringing them here.

The surviving elders and what is left of their followers are sent to another side of Creed's pack, apparently the old alpha there has cells or cages as Cass called them to hold them in until we figure out what to do next. The dead elders are piled into trunks of cars and sent off to be cremated, my dead coven members are being sent to a mortuary so they can be prepped to return home to New York where they will be buried in the cemetery near Kitty's home—which will need to be rebuilt. The wolves are either buried here or sent home with their packs, apparently, they are just as protective of their dead as we are. I place a kiss to Mera's head and sit back and stare at her sleeping form, worry gnaws at my insides. I'm scared that she will face the same troubles I did when it comes to controlling the fire magic inside her, aside from me and Kitty, there is no one else able to teach her control.

I agreed that I would help Cairo's daughter when she

comes of age to channel her power, I still don't know if she is just a witch, I know Cairo is hoping for her to be a shifter as well. I sigh and climb to my feet at the sounds of shouts coming downstairs. I stop on the last stair and watching Callie and Cairo argue over who stole Sky's body–again. When they hear the bottom step creak, they both turn to me.

"You promised you would give her back!" The anguish in her voice has me wanting to wrap my arms around her, but she needs to do this on her own, she has to fight past her grief and stand on her own two feet.

"Where the fuck is she?" Cairo growls, his eyes have turned to the onyx of his wolf, I detest the threat in his tone.

"One, don't fucking speak to me in that tone. Two, I never took my sister's body."

"Then where the fuck is she?" I keep my gaze on Callie as I answer Cairo.

"The moment the funnel of power was complete, Sky... disappeared. I told you from the start I couldn't give her back to you." Callie's eyes widen.

"You knew this would happen?" I shake my head.

"I didn't kitten, I knew there was a chance, but I wasn't a hundred percent sure. The spell Kitty cast kept her whole per se, without the spell and the magic, there was nothing left of her." Cairo curses and growls, he moves toward me and stops short when Callie jumps in front of him and growls, I've never heard her growl like this before. It's pure dominance and full of power.

"Touch him and I'll break your fucking neck." Cairo's eyes widen, not from fright or fear, but with...respect. A slow smile spreads across his face as he nods.

"She would be proud of you." Callie reels back. "You have come into your own, you finally see yourself as Cass's equal. It pains me to say this, but you never had the balls to stand up to me before, now because you have Tristan and Cass who will back you through anything, you've found your strength. Sky will be smiling down on you California." Cairo places a hand on her shoulder before turning to leave, Callie calls out to him halting his getaway. She races over to her purse near the entryway and pulls out an envelope, realization dawns on me when she hands it to him. "What's this?" She reaches out and places her hand on his forearm, an irrational sense of jealousy flows through me at seeing her willingly touch another man. Huh, I'm good with Cass fucking her and touching her but not anyone else, the thought of fucking her has my cock hardening in my pants.

"She wrote letters, one for you, four for me, and one each for Cass and Tristan." Ro shoots his gaze to me, and I can see the confusion in his gaze, I make my way toward them and wrap my arm around Callie pulling her into my side, affectively making her drop her hold on Cairo.

"Apparently your mate told my sister about me, she also knew about Cass as well." Ro's eyes widen as he looks between us, the sound of the back door slamming sounds out, I don't have to look to know it's Cass, the guy sounds like an elephant when he walks. He slides in on the other side of Callie and wraps his arm around her just below mine.

"She knew...she...knew about the three of you?" Callie smiles sadly and nods.

"She wrote to each of them and gave me her blessing, I guess you could call it." Ro smiles at her and then at each of us.

"I knew Belle was hiding something from me, she also told me I would find out soon enough." He chuckles lightly. "Look, Sky was my best friend and if she knew about this and was content with it, then let her go Callie. Your love for them will not dimmish the love you felt for her, she knew the day would come when you will eventually find your true mate. I mean, she did vow to kill him or her." The four of us chuckle, my sister sounds like she was a badass. "I know you have your brothers, but I'm always here if you ever want to kick it and reminisce about her, she's gone but she will never be forgotten." His gaze bores into mine. "Thank you, you saved my daughter's life tonight and I can't repay–." I cut him off.

"You already repaid me tenfold, by being the brother to my sister I could never have been, we're even Cairo."

THIRTY-SEVEN

CASSIUS

Exhaustion settles in as I lay back and tuck my arm behind my head, Tristan settles in on his side as we wait for Callie to finish in the shower. I feel like a new person after that, my wound is fully healed on the outside, but I can feel that the inside of me is still mending, its tender but I'm grateful as fuck to be alive, which reminds me.

"You know you could have left me for dead out there?" I say as I lull my head to the side, Tristan meets my gaze with a bored expression.

"Maybe I should have, at least then I wouldn't have to share her." I narrow my eyes and growl but there is no heat to it, he laughs. "That will never happen Cassius, not because losing you would destroy Callie, but because I view you as a brother." His words have a sense of loyalty escalating inside me.

"And I you T, I got your back always." The sound of the shower shutting off has us both turning toward the ensuite, my cock swells inside my sweats, I can scent Tristan's need as well. The door swings open and Callie prances out with a towel around her body and one on her head, she heads toward her bag on the other side of the room but pauses when she feels our gazes on her. She turns her head slowly and looks from me to Tristan and back again, I watch as she clenches her thighs together and I smirk knowingly. "Baby, I can smell how fucking wet your pussy is, stop playing hard to get and let me fucking feast on your cunt."

Like the fucking tease she is, she unwraps her hair and drops the towel as she shakes out her long waves. She has us both eating out of the palm of her hand as she slowly reaches up and tugs at the knot of her towel, as if in slow motion the fucking thing takes it time falling away from her. I palm my cock over my sweats as I watch her slowly glide her hands down her throat as her head lulls back slightly, she caresses her tits and tweaks her nipples and breaths out a moan that has Tristan and I both shifting to a sitting position. I wrestle out of my sweats gripping my aching cock in my palm and stroke it as she glides her hands across her taut stomach and cups her pussy. She sashay's forward and lifts her leg resting it on the ottoman at the foot of the bed, I shift toward the middle at the same time Tristan does, we're shoulder to shoulder and both have our cocks in the palms of our hands. She runs a finger through her slick folds and cups her breast with her free hand rolling her nipple between her fingers,

"Fuck!" Her lustful gaze swings to Tristan at his outburst, she pushes her finger inside her wet cunt and moans. "Fuck this." Tristan snaps as he leaps up, grips her waist and then hauls her on the bed with him, she doesn't play around, she straddles his lap and grinds down on his cock rubbing her pussy along his hard length. I hiss as soon as her dainty fingers wrap around my length. I grip the back of her neck and pull her to me so I can kiss the shit out of her, Tristan lines his cock up with her opening and slams down, she cries out breaking our kiss.

"Cass, I want you both inside me, I need to feel you both." She need not say anymore, I jump off the bed and snag the lube from the bedside draw and slide up behind her. I lather my dick with it then spread her cheeks and squeeze the lubricant watching as it trails down her crack to her puckered hole. She squirms on T's cock as I run my fingers over her asshole, her breathy moan causes my dick to pulse. I move forward on my knees and line myself up, I push forward slowly and relish in the sounds that tumble from her sinful lips, Tristan sits forward and captures her nipple in his mouth, she bows back and rests her head against my shoulder. I smash my lips against hers as I push inside her tight ass, Tristan moans once I'm fully sheathed inside her causing her pussy to strangle his cock.

I grip her throat and hold her against me as I rock my hips, her eyes roll back when Tristan meets my thrusts, she pushes back against us both wanting more.

"You like that baby?" I coo.

"Fuck yes, now fuck me harder."

"Such a greedy girl." Tristan taunts.

"We're gonna fuck you hard and then we're going to come down your fucking throat and you're going to swallow every drop, got it?" She moans in answer, but I have to hear the words. "Say it!"

"Yes, I suck both your cocks and enjoy every minute of it, now fuck me so I can come!" We do as she asks, Tristan slams into her pussy, I grip her hips and grind into her at a ruthless pace that T matches.

"Fuck, lift her off me!" I do as he asks and then push her down onto all fours, I pull out of her and slam into her cunt as Tristan shoves his cock in her mouth causing her to gag. "Fucking suck it!" Her head bobs up and down on his cock as I grip her hips hard enough to leave bruises, her pussy flutters around my cock and I know she's close, I reach around and pinch her clit between my fingers, Tristan moans in ecstasy, she releases his cock with a pop and screams out my name like a fucking prayer. I pull out of her and then grab a handful of hair yanking her around until her mouth is on my cock. She tries to pull back due to her swallowing me so deep, When she hollows her cheeks, I'm done for, she sucks dick like a pro and has me coming down her throat within seconds, her name tears from lips like a prayer. She swallows every drop of me, I watch in amazement as she sits back on her hunches running her index finger across her lips and sucks the digit into her mouth.

"Hmmm, you both taste finger-fucking-licking good."

Jesus Christ, I'm hard as fucking rock again!

THIRTY-EIGHT

CALIFORNIA

Three months later...

I smile up at the beaming sun, its warmth soothing as if it's wrapping me in a cocoon of its protectiveness. I haven't felt this weightless in a long time, since leaving my family and friends in Rosewood I finally feel complete. We didn't leave them in the lurch, Tristan gave each of the imprisoned witches a chance at redemption, pledge allegiance to him as the new high elder.

Needless to say, they chose to follow Tristan now, he didn't want to lead the new elders, but he knows it's the only way to ensure Mera's safety. She is a fire elemental and others will come for her power; we returned to New York so Tristan can have his coven around for Mera's training. When Skylar-Blake is ready she will come out here as well and train with Tristan.

Things have been great between me and the guys, I offer my help to each of them, and that consists of running the packs, covens, hotels and clubs. We eat dinner together every night, even if one of the guys is away on business, thanks to facetime we still manage to indulge in a meal together. They have plans for a new adventure, they want to open a hotel and club in California, yeah, I know, they are fucking cute, but it's so cliché. Hunter has been staying out here *a lot*, Cass has to push him out the door when he and Tristan flew out four days ago and made him return to his pack!

"Momma!" I sit up and smile as I watch Mera blow bubbles. "Look how big it is momma!" It still has my heart skipping a beat hearing her call me that, I never asked, and T never forced her, she just started saying it two days after the fight with the Elders. Tristan took the time to explain to her about her bio mother going to heaven, Merz just smiled and said *okay*, we were all taken back by her easy going nature at the news of her mother's death.

"They are so big!" I clap my hands cheering on my little girl, my love for her grows stronger every day.

"It's nearly bigger than Pappa!" She shouts, Cass is Pappa and Tristan is daddy, it may seem unconventional from the outside, but for us it works. "Daddy is small, so these are to big for him." I snort trying not to laugh.

"Still got a bigger dick than Pappa." I gasp and jump to my feet, both Mera and I squeal in delight at the sight of Cass and Tristan stalking toward us, my mouth waters at the sight. Cass's attire as of late involves wearing three-piece suits, and fuck me, does he look good in them with those thick thighs, Tristan has gained a lot of muscle since he's been working out with Cass, his suit jacket is very fitting around his biceps. God, these two are like a wet dream, the pair of them ravish me nightly and worship me like I am their queen. Tristan crouches down ready to catch Mera as she races toward them, Cass imitates the same move. Tristan's smile quickly vanishes when Merz veers left and leaps into Cass's arms, the look of utter disbelief on Tristan's face is priceless, his mouth hangs open in shock. "The fuck is this shit?"

"Come here." I coo, he looks absolutely adorable as he stands there pouting, he closes the space between us and scoops me up kissing me breathless. He pulls back and rests his head against mine, I wrap my arms around his neck and inhale his intoxicating scent.

"I planned that."

"Planned what?"

"For Merz to go to him so I can have you all to myself." Laughter bubbles out of me. "Come on, let's make a run for it." His playfulness is infectious especially when a growl sounds out beside us.

"I can hear every word you're saying dick." Tristan holds my gaze before linking his hand with mine and winking.

"Now!" He shouts, we take off laughing whilst Cass stands there fuming, the tearing of fabric tells me he has shifted. I can't help peering back and my heart soars when I see Mera climb atop Atticus. She loves Cass, but every time he shifts, I swear she loves Atticus more.

Run all you want baby, I'll catch you. Tristan snorts through the link.

You have to catch her first asshole. He mocks Cass.

You forget, I can track her scent around the world. Keep running, I'm a predator and I live for the chase, but when I catch you, I'm knocking Tristan out and fucking you raw all by myself.

His crass words have butterflies taking flight inside me, don't get me wrong, I love this, but I also missed him to much to keep running. I slow to a stop and Tristan groans beside me, he takes one look at me and rolls his eyes.

"Why couldn't you have just met me first and never found

him?" I shake my head, they poke fun at each other all the time, but I know they would lay their life down for the other.

"If she hadn't of met me, she would never have experienced what a real orgasm is, your pin dick, couldn't make anyone come." My mouth begins to water at the sight of Cass's nakedness, he cups his dick behind his hands, to prevent Mera from getting an eye full. Tristan opens his mouth to respond, but Mera cuts him off.

"What's an orgasm pappa?" We stand here eyes wide and Gob smacked, Cass looks to me for help, but I shake my head and smirk. Tristan will love watching him try and squirm his way out of this one–.

"Momma will explain what that means while me and Pappa go help Kitty with supper." I splutter as I stare up him, that fucking traitor! He mouths *I love you*; I growl low in my throat as he backs away with his hands up surrendering. He places a kiss to Mera's head before patting Cass on the shoulder and leading him inside.

I hope you both like your fucking hands, because my pussy is shut to you assholes. I can hear their laughter and it pisses me off.

Baby, you'll give that pussy up–. I cut Cass off.

Roger is fully charged and ready to make me scream his name! They both come to a halt, shoulders tense as they slowly turn to look over their shoulders at me, I smirk and mouth *Roger*. Just then, a warmth spreads over me as a gust of wind starts to surround me. I look straight to Tristan thinking its him using his magic, but both him and Cass are baffled by the sight, as the wind continues to wrap around me, I feel its warmth like a lover's touch, I smile trying to reach out and stroke it, I close my eyes and breathe in, allowing it to surround me in it's magic.

"Thank you for giving them to me." I whisper to the wind knowing this gust is Sky, she comes to me randomly and I live for those moments, she'll always hold a special place in my heart, but my place is with my guys and my baby girl now. Loving Sky and then losing her broke me, these two men put me back together and made me whole again, Tristan and Cassius are my ever after, I am one lucky bitch to have them both!

EPILOGUE

KAYLA

"You lying son of a bitch!" I snap, he crowds me, and I tense. I fucking hate my body's reaction for being this close to a male, I'm not that weak girl anymore, I can fight now, I can defend myself against unwanted touches.

"How the fuck did I lie?" I glare at the fucker.

"You promised me you will end this bond, not take away his fucking wolf!" Alexander shrugs his shoulders and steps back.

"You wanted an out, I gave you one." I hate this feeling of guilt, I shouldn't feel a shred of anything for him. I fucking hate that this has all been about him and me trying to find a way to break this bond between us.

"You didn't give me shit; I have done everything you have ever asked of me—."

"I got you out, I gave you the freedom you craved so badly." I growl and step right into him.

"I clawed my fucking way out from under his rule and became who I am because I'm not a quitter. I owe you nothing, you and I are done, and you can do your own fucking dirty work from now on!" I spit the words at him and storm away from the lying sack of dog shit, I'll stake that bastard through the heart soon. I grind to a halt as I round the edge of a cabin and see Creed standing there with a pissed off look on his face.

"Care to explain?" He can try and use his alpha tone all he likes, but it won't work on me, I have no pack and I don't want one. My wolf and I have a deal, as long as I keep up my end, she won't bother me.

"I'd really rather not." I tartly reply as I try to step around him, he snags me by my elbow and slams me against the cabin, my head knocks against it and I bare my teeth at him.

"Start fucking talking now, Kayla!"

"Or what, Creed? You gonna reject me? Kick me out of your pack?" I laugh but there is no humor to it. "I'll be gone within the hour, and you can go back to your happy fucking family and turn a blind to everything like you always have!" He cocks his head to the side in confusion.

"What the hell are you talking about?" I scoff and roll my eyes heavenward.

"Don't play coy with me, you knew what was happening, you just chose to ignore it, so it didn't disrupt your plans of claiming your mate." He snarls at the mention of his wife.

"If you hate her, why did you save her?" I decide to be honest for the first time in a long while, I drop my mask of anger and let him see the real me, he startles when he sees the vulnerability in my eyes.

"I never hated her, I envied her, there is a difference, Credence. I would never wish what I had to go through on another person. Now, I need to go." He blocks my path as I try to move around him.

"What happened to my brother's wolf?" I fight to keep my look of indifference in place.

"No idea, nothing to do with me." His upper lip pulls back.

"I fucking know you had something to do with it, tell me!

Why the fuck did you want him to lose his wolf, not only him, but Hunter as well? Hunter is an alpha and can't lead his pack without a wolf, Cole is...Cole and–."

"I can't help you." I say and move around him, I slam to a halt for the second time when Cole rounds the corner. The devastated look in his eyes nearly has me crumbling, but I hold firm, we have done this dance for years and we know how to mask it. He darts his gaze from me to stare over my shoulder at his brother.

"She thinks cutting a deal with the witches and Alex to have my wolf removed will remove the bond." I tense.

"What bond?" I can hear the confusion in Creed's tone, I implore Cole with a look to shut his fucking mouth. His cold eyes meet mine and I can see from the anger swirling in the depths of his gaze that he is going to open Pandora's box, I'll never be able to hide from him or his family again after this moment.

"Oh brother, did I forget to mention that the reason Kayla wasn't a virgin when you two first hooked up, is because I broke her in? Oh, did I also forget to mention that you were fucking my mate?" His cruel words cut through me, they flay me open and suddenly I'm back to being the weak bitch that my father created, the one each pack member he'd use and throw away like a piece of trash. I fight back the tears that want to spill over, I make sure he can see the hatred in my eyes as I speak the next words.

"If losing your wolf means the mate link between us is severed, then I will make sure you never get your wolf back. Mark my words Colton, fucking you and letting you mark me was the worst mistake of my life!"

THANK YOU!

What a bad bitch right?

Callie is one badass that I am in awe of.

I hope you enjoyed Cass, Callie and Tristan's story as much as I did.

I never planned for this to be a MFM but Tristan was adamant that he was going to be a part of this book and I'm not even mad about it.

At this stage Cole doesn't have a book written, I'm not sure if there is enough love for him to warrant one.

Are you dying to know what Sky's letter to Cairo says? Click here to find out!

If you loved Brutal Beauty, please leave a review on Amazon, Bookbub, or Goodreads.

ACKNOWLEDGMENTS

First up, I have to say thank you to my mum. Without her Savage Lies wouldn't have made it to be published, she edited each of these books and I think she did a fucking epic job. From the bottom of my heart mummy, thank you.

My baby daddy, I may not have a Roger but I sure as fuck have you to ride. Love ya!

My kids, my daughter you were this inspiration behind this series, each of the FMC has a trait of my girl in them. My son, you sulked because you didn't have a book dedicated to you but I love you enough to create a series based on you, watch this space.

My dad, I love you pups.

My Dream team, thank you all so much for pushing me to write Callie's book, I didn't know if she would make the cut but I'm so glad she did.

My readers!

Without you all none of this would be possible so from the bottom of my heart I thank you.

I hope I did Callie justice and you love her as much as I do.

Sam xx

ALSO BY SAMANTHA BARRETT

Mafia Romance

Murdoch Mafia Series

Played By The Bishop

Tormented By The King

Tortured By The Knight

Tempted By The Queen

Turned By The Pawn

Ruined By The Rook

Murdoch Mafia Novella

Stalemate

Memento Mori Series

Reign Of Royal

Broken By Sin

In Havoc Lays Chaos

Godfathers of the night

London has Fallen

Damned By His Angel

Re Della Strada

Shattered Soul

Fractured Heart

Tainted Essence

Fairytales With A Twist

Condemned Beast

Secret Society/ Bully

Filthy Few

Forever Filthy

Filthiest Of Them All

Masked Men Novella (Pure Smut)

Dirty Priest

Dirty Daddy

Sports Romance

Playing For Keeps

Offside

Touchdown

End Game

Hail Mary

Blindside

RH Sports

Hate Us Like You Mean It

MM

Love Me Like You Mean It

Paranormal Romance

The Veil Of Obsidian

Of Time And Carnage

Curse Of Fate

Dream

Fate

Nightmare

Redemption

Anarchy

Brutal Savages

Savage Lies

Brutal Truth

Savage Beast

Brutal Beauty

ABOUT THE AUTHOR

Samantha Barrett is originally from Auckland, New Zealand but living in Brisbane, Australia.

Sam writes all things dirty dark and delicious with a side of twisted mind fuck.

She is a lover of all things red flags and an anti-hero is a must.

www.ingramcontent.com/pod-product-compliance
Lightning Source LLC
Chambersburg PA
CBHW062006190726
48283CB00002BA/438